CUNNING ATTRACTIONS

SQUEAKY CLEAN MYSTERIES, BOOK 12

CHRISTY BARRITT

COPYRIGHT:

CUNNING ATTRACTIONS: A Novel
Copyright 2016 by Christy Barritt

Published by River Heights Press

Cover design by The Killion Group

COMPLETE BOOK LIST

Squeaky Clean Mysteries:
#1 Hazardous Duty
Half Witted (Squeaky Clean In Between Mysteries Book 1, novella)
#2 Suspicious Minds
#2.5 It Came Upon a Midnight Crime (novella)
#3 Organized Grime
#4 Dirty Deeds
#5 The Scum of All Fears
#6 To Love, Honor and Perish
#7 Mucky Streak
#8 Foul Play
#9 Broom & Gloom
#10 Dust and Obey
#11 Thrill Squeaker
#11.5 Swept Away (novella)
#12 Cunning Attractions
#13 Cold Case: Clean Getaway
#14 Cold Case: Clean Sweep
#15 Cold Case: Clean Break

#2.5 Random Acts of Scrooge
#3 Random Acts of Malice
#4 Random Acts of Greed
#5 Random Acts of Fraud
#6 Random Acts of Outrage
#7 Random Acts of Iniquity

Lantern Beach Mysteries
#1 Hidden Currents
#2 Flood Watch
#3 Storm Surge
#4 Dangerous Waters
#5 Perilous Riptide
#6 Deadly Undertow

Lantern Beach Romantic Suspense
#1 Tides of Deception
#2 Shadow of Intrigue
#3 Storm of Doubt
#4 Winds of Danger
#5 Rains of Remorse
#6 Torrents of Fear

Lantern Beach P.D.
#1 On the Lookout
#2 Attempt to Locate
#3 First Degree Murder
#4 Dead on Arrival
#5 Plan of Action

Lantern Beach Escape
Afterglow (a novelette)

Lantern Beach Blackout

#1 Dark Water

#2 Safe Harbor

#3 Ripple Effect

#4 Rising Tide

Lantern Beach Guardians

#1 Hide and Seek

#2 Shock and Awe

#3 Safe and Sound

Lantern Beach Blackout: The New Recruits

#1 Rocco

#2 Axel

#3 Beckett

#4 Gabe

Lantern Beach Mayday

#1 Run Aground

#2 Dead Reckoning

#3 Tipping Point

Lantern Beach Blackout: Danger Rising

#1 Brandon

#2 Dylan

#3 Maddox

#4 Titus

Lantern Beach Christmas

Silent Night

Crime á la Mode

#1 Dead Man's Float

#2 Milkshake Up
#3 Bomb Pop Threat
#4 Banana Split Personalities

Beach Bound Books and Beans Mysteries
#1 Bound by Murder
#2 Bound by Disaster
#3 Bound by Mystery
#4 Bound by Trouble
#5 Bound by Mayhem

Vanishing Ranch
#1 Forgotten Secrets
#2 Necessary Risk
#3 Risky Ambition
#4 Deadly Intent
#5 Lethal Betrayal
#6 High Stakes Deception
#7 Fatal Vendetta
#8 Troubled Tidings
#9 Narrow Escape
#10 Desperate Rescue

The Sidekick's Survival Guide
#1 The Art of Eavesdropping
#2 The Perks of Meddling
#3 The Exercise of Interfering
#4 The Practice of Prying
#5 The Skill of Snooping
#6 The Craft of Being Covert

Saltwater Cowboys
#1 Saltwater Cowboy

#2 Breakwater Protector
#3 Cape Corral Keeper
#4 Seagrass Secrets
#5 Driftwood Danger
#6 Unwavering Security

Beach House Mysteries
#1 The Cottage on Ghost Lane
#2 The Inn on Hanging Hill
#3 The House on Dagger Point

School of Hard Rocks Mysteries
#1 The Treble with Murder
#2 Crime Strikes a Chord
#3 Tone Death

Carolina Moon Series
#1 Home Before Dark
#2 Gone By Dark
#3 Wait Until Dark
#4 Light the Dark
#5 Taken By Dark

Suburban Sleuth Mysteries:
Death of the Couch Potato's Wife

Fog Lake Suspense:
#1 Edge of Peril
#2 Margin of Error
#3 Brink of Danger
#4 Line of Duty
#5 Legacy of Lies
#6 Secrets of Shame

#7 Refuge of Redemption

Cape Thomas Series:
#1 Dubiosity
#2 Disillusioned
#3 Distorted

Standalone Romantic Mystery:
The Good Girl

Suspense:
Imperfect
The Wrecking

Sweet Christmas Novella:
Home to Chestnut Grove

Standalone Romantic-Suspense:
Keeping Guard
The Last Target
Race Against Time
Ricochet
Key Witness
Lifeline
High-Stakes Holiday Reunion
Desperate Measures
Hidden Agenda
Mountain Hideaway
Dark Harbor
Shadow of Suspicion
The Baby Assignment
The Cradle Conspiracy
Trained to Defend

Mountain Survival
Dangerous Mountain Rescue

Nonfiction:
Characters in the Kitchen
Changed: True Stories of Finding God through Christian Music (out of print)
The Novel in Me: The Beginner's Guide to Writing and Publishing a Novel (out of print)

CHAPTER
ONE

"WHAT DO YOU THINK, Gabby? Does she speak English?" Sierra swirled the tea in her mug as we stared out the window of The Grounds, our favorite coffeehouse and hangout spot.

My best friend and I had a perfect view of our apartment complex from our table and, right now, our neighbor's new girlfriend was arriving. We'd been anxious to see what she looked like after Bill McCormick, our neighbor, had made her sound too good to be true. You'd think he was dating a supermodel from the way he described her. Then again, he also described his ex-wife like the devil, so Bill obviously had a proclivity for exaggerating.

Gripping my ancho-chili latte—not my best choice for a drink—I watched as the woman slipped one long leg from her car. She then slipped out another shapely leg before standing at full height—full height that looked close to six feet. Long, brown hair flowed down her back. Her outfit hugged her body in all the right curvy places.

I blinked, certain my eyes were deceiving me. Maybe

Bill hadn't been exaggerating. Did that mean his ex really was the devil also?

"So?" Sierra asked, still staring out the window.

I looked back at my friend, wondering what she was talking about. "So what?"

She turned away from Bill's new girlfriend long enough to give me a "what for?" look. "Do you think she speaks English?"

"You can't be serious." It was my turn to give Sierra the look now. "You're not really asking me that."

Sierra pushed her plastic-framed glasses up higher on her cute, little Asian nose, looking halfway offended as she narrowed her eyes. "It's a legitimate question."

I couldn't stop myself. I burst into laughter. "Sierra, she's of Russian heritage, not a mail-order bride."

Her eyes widened, and her bottom lip dropped. "Bill is getting married?"

On an ordinary day, I might attribute Sierra's loopy train of thought to losing too much sleep lately because of her sweet, teething baby, Reef. My friend, who'd graduated at the top of her class from Yale, was usually sharper than a shark's tooth during a feeding frenzy.

However, I'd just brought her home from the doctor. She'd injured her knee while doing a stunt during an animal rights protest two weeks ago. Against all good sense, Sierra and her employees had decided to pose like lambs at the slaughterhouse. I'll spare you the details of exactly how they'd enacted it.

Needless to say, the stunt hadn't closed down the new meat-processing plant, but it had torn her ACL.

Chad—her husband—and I finally convinced her to go to the doctor. Now she was on pain medication, which I wasn't sure she'd ever taken before, not even after childbirth.

I looked back at Katarina and tried to clarify what I'd said earlier about the woman. "Okay, okay. Maybe I should have said: She's not a mail-order *girlfriend*."

"Let me get this straight: she is mail-order?" Sierra didn't crack a smile. She was dead serious.

"No, she's not a mail-order anything. She's just Russian." Somewhere in the back of my mind, I realized this conversation was anything but politically correct, but I couldn't seem to steer it in a different direction.

Sierra propped her leg up on an extra chair and took a long, slow sip of her drink. "They did meet online—supposedly. It's not out of the question that he paid money to bring her over. I suppose it wouldn't be called mail-order anymore, but maybe it's the modern-day equivalent."

"They met online on a *dating* website." I needed to clear all of this up before any dirty, nasty rumors were started.

Sierra shrugged, obviously still not convinced. "Or so he says."

I apparently had a little more faith in Bill than she did. "Maybe we should be a little nicer to our dear, loud neighbor."

"Nicer? He's the crankiest man I've ever met—and that means a lot coming from me because I can be pretty cranky. Besides that, the man's far from being handsome or debonair—"

"That sounds so harsh—and that means a lot coming from me because I can be pretty harsh."

We both laughed. We were a pair. No one could deny that.

I nodded toward the woman standing in front of our

apartment complex looking a little lost and bewildered. "A woman who looks like that does not look like she belongs beside Bill McCormick. I suppose his newfound fame has made him a little more desirable." I did air quotes around the last word, feeling so very adult in doing so. Probably because that's what my sixth-grade math teacher had always done. However, she'd been annoying.

With election season in full swing, Bill, radio talk show host of *America Live!*, had just released a book that had done surprisingly well. He was now a guest on talk shows and morning news programs instead of vice versa. His show had been picked for additional syndication. Sponsors were pouring in like rats out of the woodwork.

He truly did seem on top of the world.

Add his new girlfriend to the mix, and he should feel like a king. Based on the way he was walking around lately with his chest puffed out and his shoulders back, he did. He didn't care if anyone knew it either.

"Bill's not home." Sierra continued to stare across the street, a knot forming between her eyes.

I stared also. His girlfriend—he'd told us her name was Katarina Sokolov —seemed to notice that Bill's car wasn't there, and she stood on the sidewalk out front, checking her phone and tapping her foot impatiently. Thankfully, the day was unseasonably warm for October, so at least she should be comfortable.

"Maybe we should go meet her," I suggested.

"You think?" Sierra's eyes lit with enough excitement that she jostled her tea right out of her paper cup.

"Oh, I think. I totally think."

We grabbed our drinks and sauntered—well, I saun-tered; Sierra limped—outside, trying not to look overly eager. I found it hard to keep a pleasant smile on my face as the scent of trash wafted around me. Today was garbage day in the neighborhood, and disposal bins lined the street. That, mixed with the unusually humid air, made for one big, bad smell of rot.

I comforted myself by thinking about snooping. It had been a long time since I'd meddled in anyone's love life, and it seemed just as good a pastime as any.

As we got closer, I observed Katarina more closely. With every new detail, my doubts about her relationship with Bill grew deeper. Her skin appeared to be olive-toned and flawless. She wore a short skirt—short enough that I knew those legs were all hers, a chest-hugging short-sleeve sweater, and high heels that just begged for male attention.

She basically looked like a supermodel, which contrasted sharply with Bill's pudgy, I-couldn't-care-less-how-I-looked persona. He often had stains on his clothes, wore outfits that didn't properly fit, and his hair was unkempt.

The two just didn't fit together, no matter how I looked at it.

Not that it was my business. But going through life minding my own business had never been my M.O. Just ask . . . oh, any one of the dozens of people whose lives I'd meddled in over the past few years. Most of them loved me for it.

Except the ones I'd put in jail. But those were stories for other days.

"Good afternoon," I called. "You must be Katarina Sokolov."

She turned her head and studied Sierra and me. Her eyebrows flickered upward, as if she didn't approve of us, and she pursed her lips.

In my mind, she would sound like Natasha from *The Rocky and Bullwinkle Show.*

I held my breath, waiting to see if I was right.

"Who you are?" Her Russian accent was strong and lent a mysterious, exotic air about her. And she did kind of sound like Natasha Fatale.

Score one for Gabby.

"We live here." Sierra pushed her glasses up higher again. "We're friends of Bill. I'm Sierra. This is Gabby."

Her lips twisted into a half-frown. "He supposed thirty minutes ago to meet me."

"He must be running late," I said.

Her eyes flickered. "He never late. Not for me."

Her statement made it loud and clear that Bill was her puppy dog.

"I'm sure he'll be here any time now," I assured her. I kind of hoped he was late, though, just to get her off her high horse.

As if to show her annoyance, she glanced at her watch one more time. "I suppose I wait here in heat."

Sierra's eyebrows shot up, and that dopey look filled her eyes. "You're in heat—?"

I had to stop my loopy friend before she said something that would deeply embarrass her.

"She means she thinks it's hot out here," I quickly corrected.

If 75 degrees was considered heat then, yes, that was what she could do.

Then I heard the gentle voice inside me. *Whatever you did for the least of these brothers and sisters of mine, you did for me.*

My gut twisted. I didn't want to do this. But I knew

better than to ignore The Voice—and I wasn't talking about the television show.

"You can wait up in my place, if you'd like," I finally said. The words felt like acid reflux as they came out.

Katarina offered me that cold stare again before nodding. "Very well, then."

Before I could say anything else, she charged toward the door.

Well, she was going to be fun.

Sierra and I exchanged a look.

I couldn't picture Bill with someone this high mainte-nance. But I supposed he would put up with it if it meant dating someone who looked like Katarina. In his mind, it probably upped his social status. I could mentally hear Tal Bachman singing "She's So High."

Thankfully, I heard a car pulling into the parking lot at just that moment. I turned and spotted Bill in the brand new Mercedes he'd just purchased after receiving a hefty book advance.

Thank You, Lord.

Now I wouldn't have to entertain his girlfriend. I didn't need any more opportunities to put my foot in my mouth.

When Bill stepped out of the car, I immediately noticed the sweat across his forehead and his unusually tousled hair. He wiped his forehead with a handkerchief and started our way.

Katarina stood at the front door of the building with a hip popped out, waiting for him to approach her.

Diva.

Something was wrong, I realized. Something bigger than him running late and facing the wrath of his new mail-order—I mean cyber-arranged—girlfriend.

He stopped short of Katarina and turned toward me. I

immediately felt Katarina's eyes boring into me, but I had other more pressing concerns. Like my curiosity, which beckoned for answers.

"Gabby, you'll never believe this," Bill started.

"What happened?" It must be serious if he was addressing me before his girlfriend.

"It's my ex-wife. She's dead."

CHAPTER TWO

"WHAT DO you mean your ex-wife is dead?" I asked. Certainly, I hadn't heard him correctly.

Bill squeezed the skin between his eyes. "I'm still trying to process everything. I just got the phone call."

Katarina clacked toward him and wrapped her long, skinny arms around his neck. "Oh, you poor thing. You are okay?"

She made duck lips at him and stroked his cheek.

I wanted to look away, but, like watching a car crash, I couldn't. It was too horrifying to miss a single minute.

"I'm okay. Thanks, darling." Bill leaned forward and planted a too-long-for-my-comfort kiss on her lips.

I cleared my throat, having no choice but to break them from this moment. "How did she die?"

He tugged at his collar. "She was . . . murdered."

Sierra, Katarina, and I all let out a collective gasp.

"Do the police know who did it?" I asked.

Bill shook his head.

"How . . . ?" I asked.

"Bludgeoned to death."

My stomach turned at the thought. That wasn't one I heard every day. I'd expected a gunshot wound or stabbing, even strangulation. I'd encountered very few bludgeonings.

"The police don't think you're a suspect, do they?" I asked.

He sighed and turned away from Katarina, but—have no fear—she kept her lanky arms around his neck.

"Emma Jean and I had an argument the other night," Bill said, aging before my eyes. "You know we had a tumultuous relationship. It's not going to look good."

Bludgeoning usually showed some kind of personal connection and deep-seated anger. But that fact alone wouldn't point to Bill as being the guilty party. It certainly wouldn't help, either.

"Did the police say when she died?" My brain went into detective mode.

He shook his head. "No, I didn't ask. My impression is that they don't know yet."

"What do you know?"

"I just know that her other ex-husband reported her missing."

"Her other ex-husband?" That was the first I'd heard of that development.

Bill nodded. "That's right. They got divorced right before the baby was born."

The baby! That was right. Emma Jean hadn't wanted kids when she was married to Bill, but then she'd remarried and had gotten pregnant right away. Bill had lamented many times about the fact.

"Where's the baby?" I asked.

"Her other ex had him. He's safe."

Well, at least that was good news. "Is there anything else you know?"

He shook his head. "No, not really. It's not like the police are going to share anything with me."

I let the facts settle in my mind. "Bludgeoned to death, huh?"

That was the one thing I couldn't get past.

He nodded. "That's what they said. If I were going to kill someone, I would have used one of my guns. It's a lot less work."

"Do me a favor, and don't tell the police that." I cringed as another thought crossed my mind. "She wasn't killed with a microphone or something of that sort, was she?"

Bill narrowed his eyes and dropped his head to the side. "Really?"

"I'm just checking. You never know about these things."

He quickly sobered. And an instant of fear flashed through his gaze. "What should I do, Gabby?"

"Just hang tight. There are no guarantees that you'll be charged. The police will need a lot of evidence before they're able to get an arrest warrant."

He rubbed his forehead. "Of course."

"Would you like for me to look into this for you?"

He was silent a moment, so I waited. Katarina squeezed his arm and seemed to snap him into action. His chest puffed out again, and his shoulders went back.

"No, I'll be fine," he said. "The police will figure this out."

I didn't want to be offended. I really didn't. But I was frequently sought after for investigations like this. The fact that Bill had rejected my offer stung like a friend accidentally tasering you.

But I didn't want him to see that, so I nodded. "Okay, then. I'll be praying in the meantime."

"Thanks, Gabby."

With that, he and Katarina walked toward his car with their arms around each other, murmuring things undistinguishable to me. I could only imagine. I didn't *want* to imagine.

Sierra and I remained where we were until they drove away.

"There's only one logical conclusion to this," Sierra said.

"What's that?"

"Katarina hired her mafia relatives to do away with the competition. Oh, and she's secretly a spy planted here in the US to steal political secrets. Who better to get them from than Bill McCormick?"

My hand flew over my mouth. "Oh, no, you didn't."

She snorted, and that was when I realized she was joking. I doubled over laughing.

"You've been hanging out with me too long," I finally said. "For that, I apologize."

"I must admit that thinking like you think makes life a little more interesting. Especially when I'm on pain meds."

My thoughts quickly sobered as I remembered Bill's dead wife. Bludgeoned to death. No one deserved to die that way. I should be ashamed of laughing so hard at a time like this. But when you worked around death, you learned not to take every case personally or take it to heart. You'd be miserable all the time if you did. It was compartmentalizing at its finest.

"Do you know how often he's talked on his radio show about his evil ex-wife? That can't look good," I said.

"You're right. It doesn't. He doesn't seem incredibly worried about it, though."

"He's on an endorphin rush right now. He's on top of the world, and nothing is going to bring him down." Katarina. Best-selling book. Inflated paycheck. He probably felt untouchable.

"Obviously. I think I'd be more concerned."

"Must be nice to be that carefree." I glanced at my watch. "Anyway, I'm going to go make dinner before Riley gets home, and then I've got to get ready for my workshop tomorrow."

"Keep me updated if you hear anything else."

I nodded. "I will."

I hated to admit it, but the next morning I was still slightly miffed that Bill hadn't asked me to help him. Maybe it wasn't so much that I was miffed as that I was anxious to jump into another investigation.

It had been a good . . . oh, I don't know . . . two weeks since a mystery had popped into my life. That felt like an eternity.

Riley, my husband—it was still weird to call him that—had left earlier this morning for work at his office. He was an attorney, and his caseload had been especially heavy lately. When he wasn't working, he was training for some kind of American Ninja Warrior-like event that was coming up in a couple of weeks. I couldn't wait to see him in action.

I still had three hours before I had to be at my presentation. It might seem odd, but I'd crept over to my old apartment across the hall. There was just something about the space that still felt like home, even though I'd officially moved into Riley's place after we married last month.

I settled back on my ratty couch with a cup of coffee and flipped on the news. For years, when I'd worked primarily as a crime scene cleaner, I'd watched the news for business opportunities. When I heard about a crime committed in someone's home, I swung by and dropped off one of my cards there. You never knew when someone might need help getting blood out of the carpet.

Looking back, maybe it had seemed a little desperate and slightly insensitive, but I supposed I was desperate to make ends meet and to feel like I was doing something with my life. I'd dropped out of college to help care for my mother, who had cancer. Then my father had spiraled into alcoholism and had almost become homeless. My history was built on struggle.

I sighed, grateful for the place I was in right now. Married to the man of my dreams. Working a job I enjoyed. Surrounded by some of the best friends a girl could have.

I took another sip of my coffee. Most of the stories on the news this morning were about an upcoming presidential election between newcomer Philip Munich and establishment candidate Ed Stead. The election had been contentious, at best; downright violent at other times as protesters on both sides threw temper tantrums. I personally couldn't wait until November, not only so I could vote but so this whole fiasco could be over.

Another news story caught my attention, however. I grabbed the remote and cranked up the volume.

It was about the murder of Bill's ex-wife, Emma Jean. My heart pounded in my ears as I waited to hear an update.

Emma Jean's picture flashed on the screen. She had

short, dark hair that was curly, but it had been cut in a style popular two decades ago. There were too many layers, which made her features look even more rounded, and not necessarily in a flattering way. Her smile didn't look sincere—or maybe I'd been tainted by all of Bill's many, many stories about her.

The news anchor continued, "Radio talk show host Bill McCormick is being questioned in her death. Lewis, his ex-wife, was often fodder on his show. A source who didn't wish to be named told us that Lewis thought she deserved more money than she received from the divorce settlement since McCormick's income has seen a substantial surge in light of his newfound popularity. She was threatening to take him to court."

Screen footage flashed to Bill leaving the radio station with Katarina at his side. Lights flashed around him as he covered his face, trying to shield himself and Katarina from the media surrounding the building.

This wasn't looking good for Bill. Even if the police didn't think he was guilty, apparently the media had already tried and convicted him.

At just that moment, a knock sounded at my door.

I hopped from the couch and answered it. Bill stood on the other side. Sweat droplets sprinkled across his forehead, and he wiped his cheeks and the back of his neck with a yellowing handkerchief. Without invitation, he stepped inside.

"I need your help, Gabby."

Music to my ears.

"How'd you know I was here?"

He pulled his head back and two extra chins appeared at his neck. "Everyone knows you come to your old place during your free time."

"Really?"

I paused for only a moment before closing the door and following behind him as he charged into my living room. "What's up?"

He rubbed his forehead. "My manager is all over me. He said everything we've worked for is on the line, all because of some false accusations. It's like a witch hunt out there—only I'm no witch, despite what the pundits might say."

"What's going on?" I pretty much knew what he meant, but I wanted to hear it in his own words. There was no need to draw on false assumptions. I stood close, watching his body language as he paced and shook his head.

I could interpret that. He was frustrated. People didn't call me astute for no reason.

"If people think I killed Emma Jean, then everything will be ruined!" His hands flew in the air, shaking like an angry cheerleader waving her pom-poms.

"Yesterday you said the police didn't consider you a suspect."

He wiped his forehead again and jerked his gaze toward me. "You don't know the things I do."

Now he had my attention. I sat on the edge of the chair, desperate to know what things he referred to. "Like what?"

He crossed his arms, wearing my rug thin with his pacing. It was a good thing I'd gotten it at a thrift store.

"We've been fighting. Emma Jean wanted more money. She couldn't stand it that I was suddenly 'doing well.'"

He did the air quote thing, followed by an exaggerated smile.

If things didn't work out with Katarina, maybe I'd introduce him to my sixth-grade math teacher.

"Honestly, I don't think she liked it that I was dating Katarina, either."

I hadn't considered that angle. "What gave you that impression?"

He paused. "She told me: I don't like that Katarina girl you're dating."

Well, that settled that.

I twisted my head in a contemplative nod. "Okay, then. But why would she care? Didn't Emma Jean leave you and file for divorce?"

He sat down hard in the accent chair across from me. "Maybe it was one of those if I can't have you, no one else can either."

I really had trouble visualizing two women fighting over Bill. Like *really*, really had trouble. But stranger things had happened in the world.

Like the fact that *Avatar* was one of the best-selling movies of all time.

"In other words, you and Emma Jean loved to hate each other? Is that correct?"

"Maybe. She'd actually talked to me about getting back together. That was right before I met Katarina, though. Once I met Kat . . ." He let out a low whistle. "It was all over for me. I've been smitten ever since."

I pictured the stunning but stone cold Katarina. "She's quite the woman."

He nodded, all signs of panic gone and replaced with a dreamy look. I could practically see a mischievous Cupid flying around his head, shooting him with lovelorn arrows.

"I know. She's totally out of my league, right?"

"I didn't say that." But, yes, she was certainly out of his league. Anyone could see that.

"You don't have to. I've never had such an attractive woman interested in me before." He paused and ran a hand over his pasty skin. "But none of this addresses the real problem right now. Emma Jean's death."

I nodded, reminding myself to focus on the mystery with the most at stake: the murder, not Bill's love life. "Yes, let's get back on track. Do you have an alibi for the time of her murder? If you do, that could make things very simple and clear this up right away."

He locked gazes with me. "I'm not sure exactly when she was murdered, so I can't say. I assume as soon as the police know the time of death, they'll ask me for an alibi."

"Probably. But they'll also be talking to her other ex-husband—Jerry, I think you said his name was—as well. Where did Emma Jean work?"

"She was a bookkeeper for The Crispy Biscuit."

I'd heard of the restaurant before. I was pretty sure the menu focused on organic, always-fresh and never-frozen ingredients in a trendy, expensive package. I seemed to recall people raving over their harvest bisque soup. "Did she have any problems there?"

"If she did, she didn't tell me about them. It wasn't like we chitchatted."

"I see." I waited to find out why Bill had really come here. Just to share this? I doubted it. I was just waiting for him to officially ask me the question. I looked down and realized I was literally on the edge of my seat.

"I need to find out what happened to Emma Jean before everything I've worked for is destroyed. The media loves to see the mighty fall. They'll delight in every piece of evidence that makes me look bad."

I couldn't deny it.

He stared at me. "So, what do you say? Gabby St. Claire—I mean, Thomas—will you help me find the person who murdered my ex?"

Yes, yes, a million times yes! I controlled myself.

Excitement spiked in my blood. Those were the words I'd been waiting for.

After a moment of fake contemplation, I nodded. Yes, I was downplaying it. I didn't want to seem desperate.

"I suppose I could see what I can do. But I'll have to ask some uncomfortable questions. You understand that, right?"

"Of course. Ask anything you want. Whatever it takes to clear me." He sliced his hand through the air to emphasize his words.

"Tell me about Katarina."

His eyebrows shot up. "Katarina? She has nothing to do with this."

"You said, 'Ask anything you want.'"

He sighed. "What do you need to know? She's from the Ukraine. She's thirty-eight years old. She models on the side, but she's taking a break right now."

"Where does she live?"

"She was up in New York, but she's staying at a hotel in downtown Norfolk while she's here."

"Not with you?" Not that I thought they should live together. It was just that most people did unless they had a good reason not to.

His eyebrows shot up. "Have you seen my place? She'd be running for the hills. No, she's better off staying at a classy joint."

"Is she paying for it?"

Bill turned his head to the side, giving me a sideways glance. "What are you getting at?"

"I just want the facts."

"I'm paying for her hotel room. There. Are you happy?"

"Not happy. Not sad. Just inquisitive. Why are you getting defensive?"

"Look, I know she's out of my league. But she has nothing to do with this. Just like Philip Munich doesn't have anything to do with this. I have no idea who would have killed my ex, but it's not connected with me. I promise."

I glanced at the time on my phone. "I've got to get to a workshop soon, but I'll get started when I get back. Sound good?"

"Sounds good. Besides, Katarina wants to take me for a massage at some fancy spa down at the beach. She thinks it will help me relax."

"Maybe it will." Or maybe she just wanted to be pampered on his dime. That seemed more like it.

Of course, Katarina could be a perfectly nice girl. I needed to keep that in mind. However, I was doubtful after our chilly encounter yesterday. Very doubtful.

What if Sierra's outlandish theory was right: What if Katarina had something to do with this?

Russian mafia?

I planned on finding out.

CHAPTER THREE

I LINGERED in the police station after I finished my workshop, my eyes glued on a single desk across the room. There was one person in particular I was waiting to see. I hoped he would be back soon.

As I waited, I mingled with several of the officers, many of whom I knew by name. We talked about donuts, of all things. Whatever it took to develop a good rapport with them, that's what I had to do. That was important in my line of work.

In fact, I'd taken it on myself to start bringing a baker's dozen with me whenever I came to these events. The participants loved it. Maybe they even loved me a little more for it. I wasn't above bribing anyone with sweets, as long as I didn't have to bake them myself.

When I saw movement across the room, I excused myself and made my way over to Detective Adams as he arrived back in the office. He was one of the first detectives I'd encountered when I decided to make a living out of being nosy. He'd held a special place in my heart ever since.

He was short, bald, and rumpled. And he offered a tired smile as I approached him.

"If it isn't Gabby St. Claire." He put his holstered gun on his desk and tugged his jacket off. "I knew when I met you that you'd be around for a while. I was right."

"It's actually Gabby Thomas now." I dangled my fingers in front of him, displaying my new wedding ring.

He raised his wiry eyebrows. "You and Riley?"

I nodded. "Me and Riley. Finally."

A grin stretched across his face. "Well, congratulations. I always knew the two of you were meant to be. Anyone could see that."

"Thank you. We're very happy. And when you said 'be around for a while' you really meant I'd be a thorn in your side. Am I correct?"

He chuckled. "I would never say that."

He didn't have to. I knew my persistence could be irritating.

"What brings you by?" He pointed to an out-of-date chair across from him.

I happily sat down, my heels killing my feet. I was a flip-flop girl, but my boss didn't exactly approve of them, as was clearly spelled out in the company's dress code. "The murder of Emma Jean Lewis."

He ran a hand over his face. "I should have known."

"Bill McCormick is my neighbor."

"I remember."

I leaned closer. "I don't suppose there's anything you can tell me about the case? After all, I did just teach half of the officers here about advanced fingerprinting techniques. That should count for something, right? And I brought donuts."

I pushed a sprinkle-covered glazed pastry—on a

napkin, of course—across the desk. I'd saved it just for him.

That cracked another smile. I was on a roll today.

He clucked his tongue. "You know I can't share very many details, Gabby. This is an ongoing investigation. And no matter how charming and friendly you are, there are still protocols in place."

I'd expected that, but I had to try. "Could you at least tell me . . . oh, I don't know . . . time of death?"

He raised an eyebrow and stared at me. "We should know in a few hours. The nature of the crime has made it a little hard to ascertain."

"The nature of the crime?" What an interesting way to word it. She'd been bludgeoned to death.

His eyes narrowed, but then he looked at the donut. After a moment of silence, he picked it up and stared at the sprinkles on top.

I'd heard through the grapevine that sprinkles were his favorite.

"Mr. McCormick didn't tell you?" he finally said.

"Tell me what?" I could hardly stand the suspense.

"She was found at The Crispy Biscuit in a commercial freezer, which has made pinpointing the exact time of death challenging, to say the least. You know the role temperature can play in determining the time of death."

"That's going to make rigor and lividity hard to figure out."

"What?"

"Of course. When a body's frozen you can't use the core body temperature to estimate the time of death. Not accurately, at least. The body will lose about three degrees per hour in a freezer that's kept at -18 degrees Celsius.

You'd have to subtract the measured temperature of the body from—"

"Gabby?"

I realized I was rambling. "Yes?"

"You were saying . . . ?"

I snapped myself out of CSI mode. "You'd really have to check her schedule and then the contents of her stomach. That will give you the most practical idea on time of death."

He nodded slowly. "I'll let the medical examiner know."

But that wasn't even the most interesting thing to me. What really struck me was that just last week, Bill had called Emma Jean the Ice Queen on his show. Said her heart was frozen and that her blood was so frigid it made the Bering Strait seem tropical.

A chill spread through me. But not as big of a chill as the one that had spread through Emma Jean when she died.

I chewed on Detective Adams's words as I left.

My mind continued to review that diatribe from Bill on his show. I hadn't thought a lot about it at the time because I was used to Bill bad-mouthing his ex. It was part of his banter. But . . . were his icy references a coincidence?

Maybe.

His word choice couldn't have been more unfortunate.

What was the name of that restaurant where Emma Jean worked again?

The Crispy Biscuit.

I knew where I needed to head next.

Thankfully, the eatery was only about ten minutes away, located in downtown Norfolk. As I drove, I turned on the radio, tuning into Bill's show to see if I'd missed any important updates.

"Philip Munich is the devil," Bill said, his voice deep and gravely. It was his radio voice because he didn't always sound like that. He did, however, always sound this convicted. "If you elect him this November, you will be devil followers and worshippers. Is that what you want to be?"

Ouch. That was a little harsh. And inciting.

"Besides that, I'm telling you, the Philip Munich you've been seeing on TV isn't the real Philip Munich. He's a robot for his political party, manufactured by people who want something from him in order to help secure his win.

A political robot? Bill's conspiracy theories were more and more interesting in this volatile election season.

"The real Philip Munich's background is obscure, at best. He has an amazing lack of personal history. I'm telling you—the control he has over the information that he's had released is unprecedented. And it means he's hiding something."

I turned it off. That was about all I could listen to. Politics really weren't my thing, especially as of late. This whole election had become so volatile.

I parked in a nearby garage and made my way toward The Crispy Biscuit. It was only 4:30, so I should beat the dinner rush. That was the good news—if the place was even open again, which I highly doubted.

Since there was no crime scene tape outside, I moved ahead with my plan and pushed the front door open. The place used to be a bank, from what I'd heard. I paused in the entryway and marveled at how much of the original building had been preserved.

Where the teller counter used to be was now a bar. There were actually two tables in the former safe area. The old partitioned offices to the left now formed interesting alcoves for intimate dinners.

I also marveled because everything looked like it was continuing on as scheduled.

Which I found odd.

This place was a crime scene. It should be shut down still.

"How many?" a perky blonde asked me.

"Just one. But I'm not here to eat. I was hoping to talk to someone about Emma Jean Lewis."

Her gaze suddenly lost its spark. She glanced around, as if to make sure no one had heard me. "What about her?"

"Is there someone I can speak with?"

She lowered her voice, which came out in a quiet bark. "We're not supposed to talk about it."

"Why?"

"Because it's bad PR!"

"I can really give you some bad PR if you'd like." I lowered my voice to make my point. "I'm talking quietly right now."

She let out a steamy sigh and then turned around to look at the other patrons, who were nestled at quaint tables eating their food. "Wait there."

A moment later, she returned with a man in tow. He looked just as uncomfortable as the hostess seemed to feel. He had an artsy look with his well-gelled hair, tight jeans, and bow tie. He was probably in his early thirties, and his scowl made him look agitated.

"Let's go back to my office," he snarled.

He didn't wait for me to follow him—luckily one of my talents was not letting people get away. I could stick to people like glue. Or flypaper.

I followed him out the backdoor, across an alley, and into another building.

My senses went on alert. What was going on here?

He paused just inside the door, as if sensing my first question. "There was no room in the old bank building for the kitchen or offices, so this is where the food is prepared."

"That's why it didn't come out that the murder had occurred here. This building is actually at a different address so no one in the media picked up on it." I looked beyond him and saw the industrial kitchen.

He scowled. "Not yet. Give it time."

I extended my hand. "Gabby St. Cla—Thomas. Gabby Thomas."

He hesitated before accepting my handshake. "Greg Borski."

Something in the distance caught my eye. Yellow crime scene tape over the walk-in freezer. Bingo!

Then another thought hit me. "You say your food is fresh, never frozen, but you have a . . ." I used my best game show hostess hands, "a freezer."

Hypocrite!

He narrowed his eyes. "I ask for your discretion. No restaurant can operate without a freezer."

I made sure my gaze clearly showed my challenge of his assertion. "Are you sure?"

"Yes, I'm sure!" His words came out fast and loud. He seemed to notice how he sounded and relaxed his shoulders.

As another blonde walked past—this one appeared to be a cook—Borski actually smiled and nodded.

His expression went sour again as he looked back at me. "Listen, it's complicated. There are certain fruits and vegetables that are seasonal. There are some things it's easier to make a day before . . ."

That was interesting and all. I was sure a firing squad of food critics and foodies might demand his head on a platter—fresh, never frozen, of course. But I had bigger, sushi-grade fish to fry.

"That's not what I'm here about."

He leaned toward me, his nostrils flaring. "How'd you find out we're connected with the incident?"

"I'm an investigator. Finding out things is what I do. It's just a matter of time before other people learn the truth also."

He muttered something not-so-nice sounding beneath his breath. "I've worked too hard to have this ruin me."

A lot of people were saying that lately. Wasn't anyone thinking about poor Emma Jean and how this had ruined her life? Or the life of her son?

I wasn't above saying insensitive things, but people needed to keep the main thing the main thing.

"Who found Emma Jean?" I started.

"My sous chef, Julian. We don't use the freezer often. Best I can tell, Sunday was the last time we went in there—until Emma Jean was found."

I glanced back at the freezer. There appeared to be a lock on the front of it. I wasn't sure if that was normal or not, but I needed to do some research. "Is your sous chef here today?"

He shook his head. "No, his car is in the shop, so I told him to take the day off. We're not that busy anyway."

I leaned against the stainless steel counter behind me and made a mental note to try and talk to this Julian guy sometime. For now, I had to take this a little deeper. "Can you tell me what Emma Jean was like here at work?"

"She made things as difficult as humanly possible for everyone she encountered. Is that what you want to hear?" His hands flew in the air before landing on his hips.

How do you really feel? I kept my sarcasm silent . . . for now.

"Only if it's the truth," I finally said.

"Oh, it's the truth all right."

"How so?" I asked instead.

"She was our bookkeeper, but she acted like she ran the place. She was always telling me how I should spend my money, where I should cut back, what I was doing wrong. Like she knew anything about running a restaurant. You'd think that working for three years at McDonald's in high school made her an expert."

"I see. That had to be frustrating." Frustrating enough to kill over? "Was there anyone here that she didn't see eye to eye with?"

"Everyone. She didn't see eye to eye with anyone here."

Well, that narrowed it down.

Before I could ask more questions, he stopped another employee—also a blonde—and spouted something about reminding all of the wait staff to stay quiet about what had happened.

As he talked to her, I glanced down at his desk. I spotted a hotel key card for Motel Luxury as well as several pink notes on his desk calendar. Messages for Borski to return a call. The name Patton Patrick was there, along with a phone number. I quickly memorized it before Borski turned back to me.

"You were saying?" he said.

"Was there anyone in particular Emma Jean didn't see eye to eye with?"

He let out a sigh. "Well, the sous chef threatened to chop off her fingers if she told him how to do his job. The hostess told her on more than one occasion that there were no seats available for her here. She even threatened to give Emma Jean's desk to a customer just to keep her away. One of the waitresses was caught spitting in her food."

"Wow. You weren't kidding. Why'd you even keep her here?"

He let out another sigh and leaned closer. "Between you and me?"

"Between you and me."

"I didn't have time to hire anyone else. I was putting up with her until I could replace her."

"This place keeps you busy, huh?"

"Ever worked in a restaurant?"

"Nope."

"It's exhausting. Tiring. Relentless. You don't do it unless you love it. I've poured my life savings into this. I go in the hole more months than not. I pay my employees before I pay myself."

"It almost sounds like there's more stress than there is joy here."

"You can say that again! But when you've put everything into something, you can't afford for it to fail. That's where I'm at." He seemed to realize what he said and froze. "Don't read too much into that."

I tilted my head. "What do you mean?"

I knew exactly what he meant.

"Emma Jean wasn't standing in the way of this place succeeding or failing."

"I see."

"You don't believe me?" His cheeks reddened.

"I didn't say that."

"I know how it sounds."

"Who do you think did it, then?"

"I have no idea. But I hope the police figure it out and soon!"

I did too. But until then, I had my first potential suspect, someone with motive . . . and most likely opportunity and means.

CHAPTER
FOUR

I HEADED BACK HOME after my visit to The Crispy Biscuit. Since I was running late, I grabbed some Chinese food from My Dung. Yes, that was really the name of the restaurant. Someone should have really checked with an American on the cultural images those words provoked before finalizing that doozy of a name.

As I climbed out of my car at our apartment complex, I paused. The hairs on my neck rose.

That was never a good sign.

Slowly, I swiveled my head, looking for a glimpse of what had caused the reaction. The sun had just set, which meant twilight surrounded me. Darkness could mask too much. Could make people become shadows. Could play tricks on your eyes.

I was well aware of that fact.

I didn't see anyone suspicious. I didn't see anyone at all, for that matter.

I glanced across the street to the coffeehouse. Could someone be sitting inside, staring at me from one of the windows there? Or maybe a neighboring apartment building? In one of the parking lots?

I couldn't be sure. But I didn't like how my spine clenched.

Instead of standing out here like a lame duck during open season, I scrambled inside the apartment building. I ran up the stairs, immediately headed to the apartment on the right. Then I remembered that was no longer my apartment. I mean, it was officially still in my name. But now Riley's place was my place.

Carefully balancing the food in my arms and one of the rice containers in my mouth, I unlocked the door and shoved it open with my hip.

"Hey there!" Riley rushed over. "Let me help you."

I drank in the sight of him. He was tall, lean, and all muscle. He had dark hair and incredible blue eyes. He was the most beautiful man I knew—both inside and out.

"Thank you." I wasn't going to complain if he wanted to assist.

As he grabbed one of the bags, he leaned over the food and kissed my forehead. "Glad you're home."

"That's crazy because I'm glad you're home too."

I couldn't wait to fill him in.

I began pulling out the food from the paper bags. "I've got a pu-pu platter from My Dung with your name on it!"

"If you never say that again, it will be too soon." He let out a rumbling chuckle as he pulled out some plates and sat across from me. His warm eyes crinkled as he smiled at me. The look filled my heart with warmth and my stomach with butterflies. "How are you?"

"Wait until you hear about my day." I sat at the mission-style dining room table, anxious to divulge what I'd learned.

As we ate, I rehashed everything that happened. Riley was my sounding board. He approached problems from a different perspective than I did—when he wasn't fighting with me about investigating things that could put me in danger. I had to say that in the brief twenty-seven days we'd been married, he'd been surprisingly willing to help me out. I suppose he figured, "If you can't beat 'em, join 'em."

"So maybe all of these years Bill hasn't been exaggerating." Riley paused with his chopsticks in midair.

"I know. Who would have thought? His ex-wife truly might have been the awful person he always talked about."

He leaned back in the sturdy wood chair. "So what are you going to do next?"

I slowly chewed a piece of broccoli. "I'm not 100 percent sure. I'd like to talk to her other ex-husband and see what he says, but the fact that this murder happened at the restaurant makes me think there's some connection there."

Borski had said they didn't use the freezer every day, and I thought he was telling the truth. But I could be wrong. Because, after all, I had been wrong that an always-fresh, never-frozen restaurant had a freezer at all. Who could say what else I was incorrect about?

"I'm sure you'll figure it out."

I leaned forward and kissed him again. His support meant the world to me. "Thanks for believing in me."

"Always."

Riley was right, I mused the next morning. I was going to figure things out. I just needed a plan.

But first I needed coffee to start my day off.

Which was exactly what I was drinking at the moment.

With Riley.

My husband.

I let out a mental sigh.

It was just an ordinary day in the Thomas household. Riley and I were seated at the table, sipping our java. Outside, someone was having a very loud conversation with someone else. A car gunned it down the street. A neighbor's dog barked.

It was funny how I'd never noticed just how noisy it was here before. But the past couple of weeks, I had observed that the neighborhood appeared to be getting louder and louder. Maybe even more crowded. Or maybe it had always been this way, but I hadn't paid attention until Riley pointed it out.

"You know, I make enough that we could move," Riley said. "We could get our own place. Nothing big or fancy or overwhelming to our paychecks."

"Could it have a picket fence?" I took another sip of my coffee.

He grinned. "If that's what you want."

"And a cute tree with a little swing tied to the branches?"

"Absolutely."

"White shingles, blue shutters, a fireplace, and an open floor plan?"

"If you can find it, it's yours."

As my tongue-in-cheek suggestions faded, my smile slipped. Riley knew my feelings on the matter. He knew how hard it was for me to let go and accept change.

In truth, it boiled down to the fact that I couldn't stomach the idea of moving away from Sierra and Reef. Even Bill downstairs had become a fixture in my life. And Mrs. Mystery upstairs always added some comic relief. Besides, having my own place seemed so adult. Was I really ready to go adult all the way? Maybe I should ease into it. I now had a steady job. I was married. The house could come later.

"We should stay here a while longer," I finally said.

He shrugged. "It's up to you."

I was glad he wasn't pressuring me because I'd over-heard his mom—she talked very loudly on the phone—asking him why he wasn't getting a nicer place. His folks were well-to-do and wanted only the best for their son.

Riley stood and glanced at his watch. "I've got to run. Remember—I'm going to the gym after work. Stop by if you get bored."

Because I got bored so easily. But I did like to watch Riley in all of his physical prowess. Since he was my husband now, there was no shame in that thought. None. At. All.

"I'll see what I can do."

He kissed me goodbye, and I wanted to pinch myself. I still couldn't believe we were married. I felt like the luck-iest girl alive.

I took three more sips of coffee before standing. I had to prepare for another training session I had at the beginning of next week. But, before I did that, I called my friend Chad. Chad was Sierra's husband and my former business partner.

"What's going on?" he said.

I heard hammering in the background and figured he was already on a job site. "I need a favor."

"What's that?"

"If you get a call about cleaning Emma Jean Lewis's crime scene at The Crispy Biscuit, I want to help."

"Gabby . . ."

I feigned innocence. "What? I need to see it."

"You want me to pay you to snoop?"

I frowned, realizing the dichotomy. "If you don't need my help, then I'll volunteer. Does that make you feel better?"

"Actually, it does. Just a little. However, I am a little shorthanded this week. So if I get called about it, then I'll let you know."

"That sounds great." I put my coffee mug in the sink—then changed my mind and put it in the dishwasher. Riley was a bit more of a neat freak than I was, and I didn't want to start the marriage off by being a total slob. "If you think about it, you should drop off your card at the restaurant."

"For real, Gabby?"

I hardly heard him as another idea clicked into place in my mind. "Better yet, send Clarice to drop off your card."

Clarice also worked for Chad. She was a pretty blonde, who turned many heads. She seemed like just the type that Borski might want to see again. He seemed to like hiring pretty blondes.

However, Emma Jean hadn't been pretty nor a blonde. So why had he hired her? It still didn't quite fit for me.

"You're serious?" Chad's voice rose higher in pitch. "You want Clarice to do this? Clarice who mistook paint thinner for wood stain and ruined a table at one of our client's houses?"

"The one and only. Just trust me on this."

"If you say so."

I leaned against the kitchen counter, liking my idea more and more as I thought about it.

"I'll see what I can do," Chad said.

"Thanks, Chad. You're the best." Before he hung up the phone, I rushed, "How's Sierra?"

"She's gone off the deep end since she started taking these pain meds. She's been singing and dancing around the house. Singing and dancing, Gabby. I'm not sure what's wrong with her. I feel like I married . . . you."

He made it sound like that would have been a terrible thing. I chose to let it slide rather than taking it as the insult it was. "It's kind of funny."

"Well, she can't have this surgery soon enough. She's not in her right mind." Just then, I heard my friend down-stairs—her voice traveled up through the vents sometimes. She was singing *Bohemian Rhapsody* at the top of her lungs.

I repressed a giggle.

As I ended the call, I dropped my phone on the table. At least there was that. I could tap back into my old days as a crime scene cleaner and use that as a means to snoop. I did help Chad on occasion, as long as my schedule permitted it.

But, until Clarice dropped the card by, I had to make the most of my time. The mystery wasn't going to solve itself. I needed to talk to more people who knew Emma Jean. I needed to collect information. And I needed to start my suspect list.

CHAPTER FIVE

TWO HOURS later—two hours of attempting to put together Emma Jean's timeline, but stopping because I didn't have enough information—I finally stepped out of my apartment. I'd left a message for Patton Patrick, the man whose name I'd seen on Greg Borski's desk. I hoped he might call me back.

Yes, I was fishing for any answers I could catch. You never knew when you just might hook something.

As I started down the stairs, I spotted Bill pacing by the front door, sweat again pouring down his skin. He really might need to have that looked into.

As I clunked down the stairs, another noise caught my ears. It almost sounded like a . . . crowd? A riot? I couldn't be sure.

"There you are! I was hoping to catch you." Bill paused for long enough to stare at me.

"What's going on?"

The sound outside was louder, and, as facts collided in my head, my muscles cinched tighter. Something was going on. Something bad.

"There are protesters outside."

"Protesters?" I tried to peak out the window atop the door, but Bill pulled me back as if my life was in imminent danger. I'd noticed the outside noises this morning, so I'd turned up the TV to drown them out. I supposed that was why I couldn't hear any of this from inside my apartment.

He shook his head as perspiration dripped down his temple. "I guess these are people who hated me anyway. But now that they think I could be a murderer, they really hate me."

"How'd they find out where you lived?"

"I have no idea. You know what it's like. You can find anything on the web today if you look hard enough."

"So are you going to stay in here all day?"

"No, of course not. That would make me look spineless and weak." He spit a little as he said the words. "But what if I hit someone as I'm backing up? I doubt these people are going to move. In fact, they possibly want me to hit them—they'd sacrifice themselves—to make me look bad."

"I can help direct traffic, if you'd like."

His eyes widened with gratitude. "Would you, Gabby?"

"Of course. But let me check what it looks like out there first." I peered through that little window. My eyes widened this time. There were probably thirty people in our little parking lot. Most of them held signs reading . . . Kill Bill?

Certainly they were talking about his talk show, not his actual person.

Most of them wore shirts supporting Philip Munich, the pundit Bill constantly dissed on his show. Apparently, the other side now had ammunition against Bill, and they intended to use it.

"They look relatively peaceful. That's the good news," I told him, coming back down on my heels.

"Their signs say Kill Bill!"

I backed away. "Well, that's true. I'm sure they don't mean it."

"Are you?"

Was I? That was a good question. "We can do this."

He froze for a moment, and I thought he might change his mind. Finally, he nodded. "Okay. Let's go."

I couldn't afford to freak him out by hesitating. Instead, I took his arm, drew in a deep breath, and then opened the front door.

Outside, the sound of the protesters rose to double the decibels and the sun blinded me—not a great combination. This was insane. Absolutely insane. And all of this over an allegation? There was no sense in it.

The rioters crowded closer when Bill emerged. I felt a bit like a Secret Service agent as I pushed past everyone, leading Bill to safety. If only I'd brought my aviator sunglasses.

Next time, Gabby. Next time.

Thankfully, Bill was parked close by. He clicked his car unlocked, I opened the door, and he slipped inside. I quickly slammed it shut.

As I did, the crowd's chant assaulted my ears. "Kill Bill. Kill Bill."

"Are you people insane?" I muttered.

The Secret Service would never say that. But I wasn't Secret Service. Scratch that idea. I was nowhere near politically correct for that job.

"He killed his wife, and he thinks he can get away with it!" a man in the crowd yelled, his eyeballs nearly coming out of their sockets.

"Justice for everyone—the rich and the poor!" Another woman yelled.

What are you people? Freaks?

I mean, really. Did the woman see the apartment complex? It wasn't exactly fancy. In fact, I was pretty sure people on welfare might have nicer places than this one. Not that I was complaining. Or putting down people on welfare. It was just a fact.

"Everyone, back up! Otherwise Bill and his car really might kill someone." I probably shouldn't have said that one. But I couldn't resist.

I pushed forward, actually moving people out of the way without ever touching them. All I had to do was stretch my arm out and people seemed to fear me making contact with them, almost like I had leprosy. Or the Force.

The Force. I was going to stick with that.

The crowd backed up.

I motioned for Bill to pull his car out. As soon as it was in drive, the crowd tried to close in again.

These people were insane.

"All right. He's gone. You can leave. Adios, amigos. Go find another Bill to torture."

A few people scowled at me. A few actually left. Until one guy yelled, "Let's follow him to the station!"

Great. I couldn't follow Bill there. I had too many other things to do.

I remained on the front stoop, standing my ground, as a few stragglers remained. I even crossed my arms, just daring someone to question my authority.

I mentally giggled at the thought. This was so not me. But I was going to make the most of it.

At least, I was until I felt my blood freeze.

There was that feeling again. I should be familiar with it.

That feeling of being watched.

I glanced around, looking for the source of the feeling.

I saw no one. Again.

There were a lot of places people could be hiding to watch me. There were shrubs, trees, businesses, cars. I suppose that was the tricky part about living in the city—all the nooks and crannies surrounding you on a daily basis.

I surveyed the area once more for any watching eyes. No one registered with me, though.

Wasting no more time, I climbed into my car.

<hr />

After my bodyguarding experience, I stopped by the home of Jerry Lewis, Emma Jean's second ex-husband. I couldn't help but wonder if he supported the Muscular Dystrophy Association. Especially on Labor Day. But that was neither here nor there.

The tangents my mind went on could astound the most ADD of personalities.

Jerry Lewis lived in a brick ranch house in Portsmouth, the city right across the river from Norfolk. He looked older than I had expected; his head was nearly bald; his red beard looked grizzly; and he smelled like motor oil. Not only that, but he wore a motorcycle jacket, complete with all kinds of patches, and a chain dangled from his belt.

He seemed slightly scary, to be honest. It didn't get any better when he looked at me and sneered, making it clear I wasn't welcome on his porch. In fact, his front door mat read, "Go Away."

"What do you want?"

What was it lately with people with unfriendly greetings? Was there something about me that put people on guard? I thought I looked perfectly approachable.

"Hi, Jerry. I realize you don't know me, but I'm hoping to ask a few questions about Emma Jean."

His eyes narrowed. "Who are you?"

"I'm Gabby St.–Gabby Thomas, I mean. A private investigator." It never failed to thrill me when I said those words—both my new name and my title. I got to wear a lot of hats lately: forensic workshop leader, occasional crime scene cleaner, and all around busybody. I was practically a quick-change artist, as of late.

"I already told the police everything I know." He started to shut the door.

I raised my hand, ready to stop the door. I didn't have to. He paused and stared at me with smoldering eyes, just daring me to challenge him.

"Please, Jerry. Answer some questions. Not for me. Not for you. Not even for Emma Jean. Answer them for your son. He'll want to know one day."

I waited to see what he would decide. His chest heaved with every second of contemplation that passed. This could go either way.

"Besides, the only reason I can see that you wouldn't want to talk would be because you're . . . guilty." Yes, it was a power play. I hoped the risk paid off.

Finally, he shoved the door open. "Come on."

I fully expected him to only give me five begrudging minutes. Instead, without asking, he poured me a glass of lemonade, set it down a little too hard on the breakfast bar, and motioned for me to sit.

I did.

I looked around his cluttered home, expecting to see his son somewhere.

I didn't.

Instead, I saw posters with cars and tools. Even the bookcase displayed toolboxes and racing photos.

"AJ is with my mom," Jerry explained. "Since Emma Jean and I were still in the process of settling things, I'm having to deal with a lot of paperwork and legalities. Even in death she's making my life miserable."

"I'm . . . sorry?" I wasn't sure how to respond to that.

"And I'm a mechanic, but I also sell tools for Williamson Tools. I was a race car mechanic when I was younger, and Williamson sponsored my driver."

"Sounds like fun."

"What do you want to know?" He took a sip of his own lemonade but remained both standing and staring at me.

"When was the last time you saw Emma Jean? Alive, that is." I mentally kicked myself for fumbling my words.

"I saw her on Sunday evening when I picked up AJ at her place. He spent the weekends with her. That was our arrangement."

"Do you have custody?"

"Primary custody."

"How'd you manage that? Usually the mom gets it." And Emma Jean seemed manipulative enough to figure out a way to make it happen, whether she was stable or not.

His lip pulled up in a sneer. "She took me to court. But on our first trial date, she went ballistic in front of the judge. Anyone could clearly see she was unstable. She was ranting and not speaking in coherent sentences."

"Was that unusual?"

"No, it wasn't. She flew off the handle all the time."

Maybe Bill had been telling the truth. "I'm sorry to hear that."

"I'm not. I only wish I'd realized that earlier. Like, before we got married." He shook his head. "I love AJ, but sometimes I regret the mess I brought him into. Of course, that doesn't matter anymore."

His head dipped.

The man didn't appear to be a heartless killer. And, even though he recognized the issues he had with Emma Jean, that didn't mean he thought murdering her would make things better.

But I had to remind myself not to always take things at face value. I'd been surprised before. I'd be surprised again.

"Did she have any enemies?" My fingers slipped around the dewy glass in front of me, but I didn't drink it.

He laughed, his grief instantly disappearing. "Any enemies? There's a line so long, you can't see the end."

CHAPTER
SIX

I DECIDED I should rephrase my question. "Maybe I should ask: is there anyone in particular who disliked her?"

Jerry ran a hand over his smooth head. "I honestly can't narrow it down."

"It's really that bad?" Again, all these years of thinking that Bill was exaggerating . . . and now I was finding out that he wasn't. What would be next? Discovering that James Cameron really was the king of the world?

Jerry nodded and sat down with a hard thud. "It was that bad. She had a way of turning people against her."

"You obviously didn't always think that. You did marry her."

His cheeks actually turned a deep red. "Well, she could be very charming when she wanted to be. But she could turn it off just as fast. Of course, I didn't see that side of her until after we married. Talk about buyer's remorse."

"If you don't mind me asking, how did you meet?"

"I took out a classified ad." He stared at me, as if silently daring me to make fun of him.

I was smarter than that.

"Unconventional," I said instead.

He shrugged again. "I didn't think anything would come of it. But Emma Jean responded, and she was in good form when we met. We got married quickly. That was my first mistake. I didn't have time to see how difficult she really was."

"Why'd you divorce?" I felt like I knew the answer, but I had to ask anyway. I sipped the syrupy sweet lemonade as I waited for him to respond.

"Right or wrong, I realized that life was too short to be so miserable. For AJ's sake more than mine." The man's gaze locked on mine. "I wasn't much help, was I?"

"No, you were. Thank you."

"I want to know what happened to her. I didn't love her anymore, but I didn't wish this on her. Bludgeoned to death? Left in a freezer?" He shook his head. "That's no way for anyone to go."

"I agree."

He tapped his finger on the counter, as if thinking about something. I let him have his moment. Finally, he looked up.

"There was one person who bothered me," he said. "Greg."

"Greg Borski from The Crispy Biscuit?"

He nodded. "Yeah, the man was abrasive and demanding, and nothing was ever his fault. It was always someone else who was sabotaging him. I'm not saying he's a killer. But I am saying he's worth looking into."

I thought the same thing. As of right now, he was at the top of my suspect list.

I took out a sheet of paper and pushed it toward him. "Can you fill in any of these blanks on this timeline?"

He looked at it and pointed to Tuesday. "This is when she was supposed to show up and take AJ so I could work late."

"Where do you work?"

"Carter's Auto Corner. Anyway, I was going to hire a sitter, but Emma Jean insisted that she would watch him."

"Her body was discovered on Wednesday. Did you talk to her between Sunday and Wednesday?"

"Only on Sunday evening when I picked up AJ."

"How did she seem?"

He shrugged. "Agitated. I figured it was because she found out I was dating someone new. She didn't like it. I think she was fighting some kind of virus too, which never made things anymore pleasant. And she was muttering something about half lord of the fishes."

"Half lord of the fishes?" *What?*

He shrugged. "Your guess is as good as mine. I figured it was some type of buried insult, and it was better if I didn't know."

I paused and leaned closer. "Do you think I could get into her house, Jerry?"

He nodded, like the request wasn't a big deal. "I can get you in. The house is still in my name. I moved out on my own free will. It was just easier that way."

"That would be great. I want to see if there's any evidence there." I was sure the police had taken most of it, but it couldn't hurt to look.

He nodded. "As soon as the police say it's okay, I'll meet you there."

"Thanks, Jerry. That sounds perfect."

I decided to stop by the radio station and update Bill in person. Unfortunately, a crowd was gathered outside. I recognized several of the faces from this morning.

Bill really did know how to stir things up, didn't he?

These people had obviously been looking for a reason to vilify Bill, and they'd found one in Emma Jean's murder. With any luck, they could ruin his radio show, ruin his personal life, and get a few extra votes for the candidate of their choice.

The security guard at the front recognized me—I'd been in before. I slipped past the "Kill Bill" protesters, waved to the receptionist, and stepped toward the studio in the back.

I waited on the other side of the glass for Bill to take a commercial break. In the meantime, I listened to his show being piped through the overhead system.

"The political operatives are going crazy this election season, stooping to new all-time lows. Protesting outside of my home and my studio? Signs that read 'Kill Bill'? Is this what politics has boiled down to? Trying to silence those who oppose you?"

Sometimes I didn't see eye to eye with Bill, but he was spot on with that. As much as I didn't agree with some people, they still had the right to their opinions. Slander and hatred had no place in my life.

Seven minutes after I arrived, Bill was able to step out. He looked paler than usual. The brazen talk show host usually didn't let anything rattle him.

"Anything new?" he asked, with what was becoming his trademark handkerchief in hand.

I shook my head. "Not really. I'm still in the information gathering phase. I've heard a lot of bad things about

Emma Jean. Apparently, it will take me a year to go through her enemy list."

He frowned. "I don't have a year. I just had three sponsors pull out."

Surprise shot through me. "Because of this?"

"People are talking about me being a killer. That gossip columnist Godfrey Arnold is the one who started this whole campaign against me. Word is that Philip Munich's folks have him in their pocket, and he helps them do their dirty work."

"The guy with the blog?" *Godfrey Gossips*, if I remembered correctly. Not that it was really my thing to read entertainment blogs. No, I'd rather watch *48 Hours Mystery*.

He nodded. "That's right. That guy is determined to ruin me because he doesn't agree with my political views. He spews venom—all for ratings."

Funny, because a lot of people would say the same about Bill. I supposed it just depended on what perspective you were coming from.

"Not only that, but I've been getting death threats. Can you believe it?"

Before I could respond, a man strode over with papers in hand. "Good news, Bill. I just got your numbers in. Your listeners are up by 50 percent. Fifty percent! Tell your sponsors who dropped out to take that!"

Bill blinked. "What?"

"I know that what's happening isn't necessarily good for you personally, but listeners are tuning in. Give it time, and those sponsors will come back. This murder could be the best thing that's happened to you."

I blanched at the man's calloused words. I knew that business was business, but . . . wow. How coldhearted could you sound? I had a dark sense of humor at times to help me cope, but that was only because I was around death all the time. This man wasn't. Unless talk radio was considered some figurative type of demise.

"All the loyal listeners in the world won't keep me out of jail." Bill sobered.

"That is true. Let's make sure that doesn't happen. You do have a lawyer, right?"

"Riley Thomas has agreed to represent me—"

Riley? He had? When had this happened?

Bill's phone rang and cut him off. He looked at the screen and grunted. "It's Katarina. She's out shopping today, trying to find a new outfit for some dinners we'll be attending together. I think it's her way of coping, if you know what I'm saying."

I waited as he answered. His expression changed from relaxed to intense in 2.2 seconds.

"Calm down, honey," he murmured. "What do you mean someone tried to grab you?"

I could hear her sobs from where I was standing, and my shoulders tensed. Someone had tried to grab Katarina?

This really was getting ugly . . . and more and more curious by the moment.

CHAPTER
SEVEN

"I'LL BE RIGHT THERE." Bill rushed toward the door. "Ernie, you've got to cover my show when it comes back on. I'm sorry. Play repeats or commercials. I don't care which."

I quickly followed after him. "What's wrong?"

"Someone tried to abduct Katarina. She's shaken up. Really shaken up."

Abduct Katarina? This wasn't good. "I'll go with you."

This time Bill had no problem pushing through the protesters. They yelled ugly things—really ugly things. Things I couldn't say in church.

But he didn't seem to hear. It was probably better that way.

We didn't say anything until we were in Bill's car. As soon as he accelerated I realized that I should have offered to drive. He was going way too fast for my comfort. My fingers dug into the armrest.

"What else did Katarina say?" My teeth clenched in fear as Bill wove in and out of the lanes on the interstate.

"She was leaving Macy's, getting into her car, when a man approached her. He asked for money. She ignored him, but he became aggressive. He grabbed her arm and tried to pull her into his SUV."

Someone asking for money. So this wasn't connected with Emma Jean's death. Not by first appearances, at least.

"How did she get away?"

"She jammed her heel into the man's shin. Some people leaving the mall came over to help, and the man ran away."

Thank goodness for that. "Did she call the police?"

"I told her to. Maybe I should call also." He went to grab his phone and nearly sideswiped a pickup truck in the next lane.

"I'll do it!" I snatched his phone before he could even be tempted. "You just drive."

With Bill's phone safely tucked away where he couldn't reach it, I pulled out my own cell and dialed Detective Adams's number. He promised to meet us at the scene.

Five minutes later, we pulled up to a mall located in downtown Norfolk. Bill grabbed a ticket stub at the parking garage and drove at breakneck speed around the corners in order to reach the third floor—where Katarina was waiting.

I reached for the roof, trying to steady myself before momentum rammed my head into the window. *Please don't kill me! At least let me enjoy being a newlywed first.*

Finally, we spotted Katarina. Bill didn't bother with a parking space. He stopped behind her car and jammed the gear into park. Before I could say, "I'll-never-ride-with-him-again," he was already out and racing toward Katarina.

A group of strangers lingered around her. Actually, of

the crowd, three were guys, and they were the ones trying to help. Their significant others stood in the distance with scowls.

Interesting.

As soon as Katarina spotted Bill, she abandoned her admirers and collapsed into his arms. "I so glad you here. I fear my life."

"It's okay. I'm here now." Bill stroked her back.

Blech.

I wasn't sure why seeing Bill involved in PDA grossed me out so much, but it did. Maybe it went back to the time I accidentally saw him in his tighty whities. My thoughts had been forever stained with that image.

I wanted to talk to Katarina before Detective Adams arrived, but I didn't have that chance. I couldn't get a word in between the sobbing and drama. Instead, I eavesdropped as Detective Adams questioned her. It gave me the opportunity to carefully watch her expression as she answered.

"Can you describe the man who tried to abduct you?" Detective Adams said, pen and paper in hand.

"He tall with short, dark hair. He have tattoos on his arm. Lots of tattoos." She motioned with each description, as if playing charades.

"Do you remember what any of these tattoos looked like?"

She quickly shook her head. "I no say. They designs. Points and angles. No pictures. You understand?"

Detective Adams nodded, seeming halfway mesmerized by Katarina himself. She obviously had that effect on men. It was her superpower. "I think so. How old was he approximately?"

She shrugged and ran a finger under her eyelid. Was

she really crying? Or did she just want to look like she was? "Thirty something. He strong."

"Did he have any accents or any other distinguishing features?"

"No, I don't think so. He not Russian, if that what you ask."

He shook his head. "Just a standard question, I assure you."

He was wondering about the Russian mafia too. I knew it!

"Who came out into the parking garage and stopped him?" I asked, looking at the crowd that was still gathered nearby.

Katarina snapped out of innocent victim mode for long enough to give me a dirty look. I really had gotten on her bad side quickly. Or maybe every woman had.

"Him." She pointed to a man with light hair, who looked to be her aesthetic equal. He was tall, buff, and beautiful.

While Detective Adams continued to question her, I walked toward the man. I wanted to get his side of the story. Because it was good police work to do so, not just because I didn't trust Katarina.

The man's eyes were fastened on Katarina as I approached, and he looked a little too worried for a stranger. His muscles were still tight, his jaw flexed, and his eyes narrowed.

"Excuse me," I started.

He pulled his gaze away from the Eighth Wonder of the World of Beautiful Women. "Yes?"

"I heard you were in the garage and helped to scare the man away before he could harm the victim."

He looked me up and down. He must have seen me with the detective and assumed I was with the department. I didn't correct him. "That's correct."

I needed a pad and paper. And those aviator sunglasses. They should remain in my purse as a basic part of my detective/Secret Service disguise, depending on the assignment.

"Can you tell me what you saw?"

"It was weird. At first, I thought it was just a guy and his girlfriend arguing. But then it became obvious there was more to it. The guy grabbed her wrist and began pulling her. She looked terrified, and I knew I had to do something. As soon as I called to him, the man ran away like a scared, little rabbit." His chest puffed out.

"Did you see where he went?"

"He jumped into a SUV."

"Into the driver's seat?"

"No, the passenger seat."

So the guy was working with someone. Good to know. "Did you get a license plate?"

He shook his head. "I was too concerned about her. I had to make sure she was okay."

I bet you did.

"The SUV did have a smashed back bumper. I noticed that as it squealed away."

I stored that information in the back of my mind.

"Was there anything else distinguishing about this man?"

He stared in the distance and rubbed his jaw, looking a touch like a modern-day Greek statue come to life. "He looked kind of scary. I felt so bad for that woman, though. It was close. Too close."

I glanced back and saw Detective Adams coming my way, so I thanked the man and scooted away. I joined Bill and Katarina, ignoring the knowing glance Detective Adams gave me. I was overstepping my bounds like a klutz playing hopscotch. I figured he would be used to it, but maybe not.

Katarina and Bill were still canoodling, so I blessed my eyes by looking away for a minute and observing the parking garage. There was a camera above the exit to the mall, and I was certain Detective Adams would take a look at that. If I really wanted to, I could probably weasel my way into seeing it myself, but I wasn't sure it was worth my time.

My gaze stopped at Katarina's car. On second thought, it was just far enough away that the camera may not have picked up much.

Why had she parked so far away? At the current time, there were plenty of spaces closer to the doors. Had there been a mad rush earlier? On a weekday? I couldn't see it. It wasn't like her car was super nice, the kind that people parked in the back of the lot so they didn't get any dings from other careless drivers.

Maybe I was reading too much into this. I wasn't sure.

I glanced back over at the man I'd interviewed. He was talking to the detective, but his gaze continually went back to Katarina. That was odd. Was he that taken with her good looks? Was he an overall concerned kind of guy? Or was there more to it?

I couldn't be sure. There were a lot of pieces to this mystery already. Perhaps the biggest one was: was this possible abduction attempt connected with the murder of Emma Jean? There almost seemed to be two separate crimes. First was the murder of Emma Jean, the second the animosity toward Bill.

I needed to find the area where the two circles of crime intersected . . . if they intersected.

CHAPTER EIGHT

AS I DROVE BACK to my apartment, my phone rang. Even if I hadn't looked at the number on my caller ID, I would have known right away who it was from by his British accent. Garrett Mercer, the man I'd dated while Riley and I took a break. He was a coffee mogul, philanthropist, and all-around good person. And he was handsome, to boot.

"Garrett, what's going on?"

"It's good to hear your voice, Gabby St. Claire. I see you're still in trouble, as usual."

I almost corrected him on my name, but the second part of the conversation seemed more urgent. "In trouble, as usual? What do you mean?"

"You were on midday news. Guarding that talk show host who lives downstairs from you. I believe you muttered, 'What are you people? Freaks?'"

Someone had caught that on camera? I thought I'd only mentally said the words. I had no clue I'd voiced them aloud.

Lord, help me. Help my mouth. It doesn't do me very many favors.

My stomach sank. I thought I was doing better with controlling my tongue, but apparently not. "That was on the news?"

"You know it. The good news is that you looked quite ravishing."

I laughed but quickly sobered. Did Garrett know that Riley and I had gotten married? He'd used my old last name. I needed to be careful and make sure my friendliness didn't sound like flirting. "Well, thank you. At least something good came out of that invasion of my privacy."

"You've always known how to make headlines. Just one more thing to love about you."

"It's one of my many talents."

The teasing tone left his voice. "Listen, I'd like to talk to you sometime, Gabby. Would you be available to meet?"

My stomach squeezed. Was this a romantic thing? A professional thing? I wasn't sure how to wade through these waters. Being a married lady was new territory for me.

I'd meet with him, I decided. But if he made any moves, I'd have to flash my wedding ring around . . . a lot. Garrett was the type who respected boundaries, so we'd be okay.

"My schedule is pretty full for the rest of this week," I finally said, speaking truthfully.

"Next week, then?"

"Next week works. You've got me curious."

"You should be." He chuckled. "I know how you love a good mystery. I just handed you one. I'll keep you in suspense."

"You're so mean."

"I try. I'll be in touch next week. Don't forget about me."

"I won't."

Interesting. I wondered what that was about. I supposed I would find out next week.

When I got back to my apartment complex, I halfway expected to see protesters there again.

Instead, my brother, Tim, was waiting on the front steps.

I hadn't talked to Tim in at least three months. We had a long, hard history that included him being abducted as a child and then returning to my life two years ago. We'd been steadily rebuilding our relationship since then.

Until June, when he'd met a girl and decided to hitchhike across the country. It had seemed like a horrible idea to me, but this was Tim's life, and I had to let him live it as he saw fit. I could only assume he had some great stories to tell me since he'd made it back alive.

Tim was a freegan, which meant he only used things that were free, including food. At least, that's the way he operated most of the time. He also looked homeless, maybe because he kind of was.

As he sat on the front stoop now, his beard looked dry and stretched down to his chest. His hair hadn't been brushed and appeared greasy at the roots.

He looked like a mess, and I was surprised no one had called the police on him yet.

He nodded aloofly when I walked up, but made no effort to move.

Something about him made my senses go on alert. What was different about my brother since I saw him last?

"Long time no see." I felt like I should hug him, but not

until I pinpointed what was going on. Until then, a feeling of dread grew in my stomach.

"Hey, Sis. I'm back."

I sat down on the concrete step beside him. Even though it was no longer garbage day, the scent of trash still lingered in the air. Traffic zoomed by. A neighbor somewhere blared "Bittersweet Symphony" by The Verve. "I can see that. How did hitchhiking across the country go?"

He shrugged. "We had to cut it short. Whitney got a kidney stone."

Whitney was his new girlfriend, and she was just as strange as he was. "A kidney stone. Ouch. Where is she now? Is she okay?"

"I dropped her off at a friend's apartment. She thinks she can wait it out without going to the hospital. She's had them before."

"I'll call her She-Ra if she does. I heard kidney stones can be a beast."

Silence stretched between us a moment. An unspoken question lingered in the air. I could sense it. I waited for Tim to ask it, but he remained quiet.

So I gave in. "Let me guess: you need a place to stay?"

For free. I kept that part silent.

He still didn't look at me, but instead stared straight ahead stoically. "Do you mind?"

How could I say no to my brother? A small part of me would always feel guilty because of what had happened to him as a child. And that guilt would push me to make retribution by appeasing him in every way possible. He'd been kidnapped. While I'd been watching him. And he'd been gone from my life—no matter how horrible my adolescent years had been at times—for years.

I felt like I needed to make it up to him. To make things right. To ensure he didn't suffer anymore.

But something wasn't right with him now.

I narrowed my eyes, trying to pinpoint what was different about my brother. Either he was depressed, he'd taken chill to a whole new level, or . . . "Tim, are you on something?"

He blinked and made a face. Finally, he turned toward me, a bewildered look in his eyes. "What? No, of course not."

"Tim . . ." I didn't want to question him, but I'd seen people on drugs before. Tim had all the markers for it.

"What?"

"You're not acting like yourself. What are you taking?" And why couldn't the people in my family get their acts together? At least my father seemed to be doing well after struggling for years with alcoholism. But it always seemed to be something with someone. I'd had my turn, if I were to be honest.

"It's no big deal."

Anger flared inside me. "Drugs are a big deal."

"You're so uptight, Sis. Just chill. I'm a big boy."

"And I'm your big sister. How do you think I'm going to act?" I sounded like a shrew, and I didn't like it. But I'd lost my ability to control the emotion in my voice.

"You're more worried about this than you were about me when I was kidnapped."

My jaw dropped open. A mix of emotions punched me in the gut. Guilt. Outrage. Regret. And that was exactly what he'd been going through.

"That's not true, Tim. You have no idea what we went through. My childhood ended the day you disappeared. Mom and Dad were never the same. Never. We thought about you every minute of every day. Your bedroom was practically a shrine as we hoped, day after day, that we'd find you. Your room stayed like that until Mom died and Dad was forced to sell the place because he couldn't pay the mortgage anymore."

That hit him somehow. He flinched ever so subtly.

"You're going to abandon me again?" he finally said.

It was another sucker punch. Not quite as strong this time, but it was enough to make me want to double over.

"You're trying to manipulate me, Tim."

"I just need a place to stay."

"You can't do drugs if you're staying in my place."

"I won't. It was just once or twice. The hitchhiking thing was stressful. So were the kidney stones. I just needed something to take the edge off. You catch my drift?"

I'd bet he was lying about that. "I mean it, Tim. You've seen what alcohol did to Dad . . ."

I hadn't even seen this problem as a distant blip on my radar. My brother taking drugs wasn't anywhere close to being a concern. Tim had always been kind of flighty and free-spirited. But he'd never expressed his feelings about his kidnapping like this before. It had always been with kindness and compassion.

Were the drugs making his real feelings come out? Had he suppressed them this whole time?

"I just need some help until I can get back on my feet. A place to stay. That's all I'm asking. Please."

I couldn't deny my brother a safe place to fall. We all needed that, didn't we? I'd just keep my eyes on him and, if there were any signs of trouble, I'd deal with them then and there.

I stood. "Come on up. You can stay at my old place."

He rose to his feet. "Your old place?"

"I got married," I told him, stepping toward the door.

"You didn't invite me?" He had the nerve to actually look offended.

"You were hitchhiking across the country with no cell phone," I reminded him. "It's not like we planned the ceremony in advance. What was I supposed to do?"

He shrugged, dragging his feet as he followed me inside. "Beats me. You could have tried a little harder, I'd say."

"Tim . . ." I warned. He was really pushing my buttons today, and I wasn't handling it well.

He raised his hands in surrender. "I get it. You don't have to talk about it anymore. Now, can I just go take a load off?"

"Sure thing."

I led him upstairs and opened the door to my old place. As I stepped inside, I realized it smelled stuffy and closed up. I'd been using it less and less frequently.

I really needed to give up my lease. Why was I having trouble letting go? It was so silly. Being with Riley was everything I'd dreamed about. Yet letting go of my past was harder than I'd thought.

"I'll let you do your thing. I'll be across the hall if you need me."

CHAPTER NINE

EARLY THE NEXT MORNING, Patton Patrick called me back and informed me his name was actually Patrick Patton. I'd told him, when I left the message, that I was calling concerning Greg Borski.

Apparently Borski was his nemesis.

"You have dirt on him?" the man asked, his voice too nasal to sound tough.

My eyebrows shot up at how quickly he got to the point. "I'm looking for the dirt, actually."

"If you find it, let me know."

"What's your beef with him?" I pulled the sheets up, making the bed. This was something new for me. I hadn't realized I'd been such a slob before. Living with someone else and trying to honor their preferences could be exhausting. Still, I wanted to respect Riley's desires. That meant being a little neater than my nature desired.

"He owes me a lot of money. I invested in his restaurant, and he promised to pay me back within the first three years. I haven't seen a dime of it yet. Meanwhile, the place seems like it's successful. I don't know where all the money has gone."

"Have you talked to Borski?" I fluffed a pillow and tossed it against the headboard.

"He won't call me back. I've stopped by, but he's never available. I have no idea where he's living now. If you talk to him, let me know, because I'd really like to have a long conversation with him."

Greg Borski was beginning to seem more and more like someone I needed to check out further.

After I got off the phone and finished making the bed, I sat down and did a quick Internet search on Borski. I was amazed at the results that came up. He was an award-winning chef. His food was called innovative. His restaurant had been featured in several magazines.

The man seemed to have everything going for him.

So why was he having so many financial troubles?

I needed to find out.

I'd seen a key card on his desk. It was from a hotel in a rough part of Norfolk. I'd assumed that someone else was staying there. But I wanted to check it out.

I pulled up there ten minutes later. This definitely wasn't known as a desirable area of town. No, it was old and not well maintained. The motel had siding falling off and trash lurking against the edges of the building.

I couldn't picture Borski staying here. But it was worth checking out.

I put my car in park and leaned back, taking a sip of my coffee. Stakeouts were never my favorite thing. They seemed so exciting on TV, but in real life they were usually a waste of time. Or they seemed like a waste of time for the first five hours. Only the last ten minutes really meant anything.

I glanced at the time. It was only 9:30. I assumed Borski would need to get to the restaurant soon to begin prepping for the day. Wasn't the morning when deliveries happened? When veggies were cut and soups were started?

I'd never worked in a restaurant myself, but that made sense to me.

The day was sunny but brisker than it had been earlier in the week. This was the kind of weather that beckoned a pumpkin spice latte. Later, I promised myself.

I stared at the faded red doors lining the two floors of the place. Black metal railing prevented anyone from falling off the second story. Crooked numbers graced each door. At the far end, a cleaning lady pushed her cart around the corner.

I didn't even know which room door to look at, I realized. I didn't know which car was his. I didn't know for sure that he was here.

This could be a colossal waste of time. I'd give it until eleven, I decided. Then I had other things to do.

At 10:30, I hit pay dirt. Borski exited one of the rooms on the second floor.

Was he living here? Why?

I'd have to sort that out later.

Borski was wearing his trademark bow tie again, along with tight jeans and a button-up shirt. He climbed into an oversized pickup truck—not what I'd expected—and began to pull away.

I put my car into drive so I could follow. I assumed he'd be headed back to The Crispy Biscuit. To my surprise, he turned toward Virginia Beach instead. And he kept going. And going.

This was going to be a total waste of time, wasn't it?

Knowing my luck, he was going to a Rogaine specialist or some kind of fitness boot camp.

Despite that, I kept going. I'd already come this far.

The suburban roads surrounded by neighborhoods and shopping centers gradually turned into country roads surrounded by farms and cornfields. If we went much farther out into the middle of nowhere, Borski would definitely notice me behind him, especially since the road was otherwise empty.

Finally, he slowed and turned down a gravel road. A sign reading "Farmer Farms" graced the curb. This was going to be harder to keep an eye on him without being spotted.

But I was determined to do it.

I pulled over into the next driveway, which just happened to be the entrance to a pumpkin patch. Working quickly, I parked my car in the gravel parking lot. I resisted the urge to buy some pumpkin ice cream or a pumpkin—especially one of those oddly shaped purple ones—or even take a hayride. All those things made me want a redo of the best moments of my childhood.

Praying I didn't get caught, I climbed out of my car. For just a moment, I listened to the happy sounds of school kids running through the pumpkin patch in the background. I heard the whistle of a teacher trying to get her students' attention. I heard more tires rumbling down the gravel road.

Against all of my better instincts, I cut through a field of dried corn.

I wasn't sure what I was thinking. I'd seen horror movies about this stuff, movies that included catatonic children with disturbing eyes and black-and-white clothing. But I did it anyway.

I stayed focused as I moved, which allowed less time for worst-case scenarios to flash through my mind.

Finally, I reached the other side.

I peered between the stalks, feeling very . . . stalkerish.

But I did have a perfect view of Borski. He was standing outside a barn, talking to another man. After a few minutes of chitchat, he carried out various bags of what I assumed were vegetables and put them in the back of his truck.

Interesting.

Maybe they didn't take deliveries at the restaurant. After all, the backside of the building was strangely configured, being that it was actually two buildings mashed together to become a restaurant. There were no delivery bays. Besides, if there were, someone might see the industrial freezer and leak it to the press.

Knowing that, maybe Borski picked up the vegetables himself. That seemed very persnickety and Borski-like.

I watched as he slipped the vegetables into awaiting boxes in the back of his truck.

A few minutes later, he slammed the door to his truck and pulled away.

Weird. That was weird.

I stepped back before anyone spotted me in the field.

I needed to get back to my car.

I took several steps back through the cornfield when I paused.

What was that?

Were the dry leaves simply rustling together? Or had that been the sound of someone else out here?

No, that would be crazy. I had no reason for anyone to follow me. Especially not cultish children with disturbing eyes and Amish outfits. I'd done stupid things before.

Stupid things that had given people a good reason to hate me and want to harm me.

But not this time. This time I was innocent.

I glanced around quickly. As I did so, I lost all sense of direction. What way had I been heading?

I couldn't remember.

I looked at the sun, hoping it would give me guidance. Nature people would be able to look at the sky and know exactly which way to go. Unfortunately, I wasn't one of those nature people.

Which way, Gabby?

My lungs tightened as panic threatened to erupt.

That way, I decided. I'd been headed that way.

I wish I didn't feel uncertain as I stepped in my chosen direction.

As I did, another twig snapped in the distance.

A squirrel, I told himself. It was just a squirrel.

I didn't convince myself.

I took off in a run.

The corn stalks seemed endless.

Or maybe I'd gotten turned around. What if I was headed farther into the heart of the massive farm instead of back toward my car?

Panic threatened to consume me, but I couldn't let it. Finally, I slowed long enough to hear children. Happy children. To hear a tractor cranking up.

I was headed in the right direction. I had to be.

Follow the noise, Gabby. Follow the noise.

And reward yourself with pumpkin ice cream.

Besides, you can always use your cell phone to call for help.

All wouldn't be lost. Mostly me, though. Mostly, I wouldn't be lost.

My meditative moment of wisdom made me feel better. For a moment.

Until I ran into a spider's web.

I swatted at my face, trying to combat potential arachnids that could be crawling on me like eight-legged freaks.

I suppressed a scream—but only because there were innocent children close by.

And I ran faster. And faster.

Finally, I emerged from Nightmare on Corn Street.

My car. I was at my car!

Thank You, Jesus!

My hands continued to flap when I felt something in my hair. Something big.

I held my breath, praying it wasn't a spider. Instead, I pulled out a dried cornhusk or leaf or something. I didn't hold onto it long enough to find out.

As I continued to feel imaginary insects all over me, a bus full of school kids pulled in right as I stepped out, my hands still flailing in the air and a leaf caught in my hair.

Uncountable kids had their faces pressed to the window, looking on in horror.

To makes matters worse, I'd worn a flannel shirt and jeans today.

I looked like a scarecrow come to life, didn't I?

Before I could recover, I saw kids raise their cell phones. Cell phones? Since when did school-aged kids carry phones with them?

It didn't really matter. I'd probably just become an overnight Youtube sensation . . . again.

I couldn't let an opportunity pass me by. So once I was in my car, I swung by the farm next door to hopefully talk to the farmer there. Three pumpkins now rested in my back seat, and I checked the mirror to make sure no ice cream lined my lips. I was good.

As I climbed out of my car, I glanced around one more time. I didn't see anyone watching me, and I really wished I could shake that feeling. I also wished I could stop humming "Somebody's Eyes."

There was absolutely no proof that anyone was following me. Maybe all my past investigations were making me feel a little crazy. It was the only explanation I could think of.

I stepped out and glanced around the farm. Earlier I'd only been focused on watching Borski, so I'd ignored the farm itself. But I was surprised to see that it looked rather dirty. There was lots of clutter against the barn, almost like a mini junkyard. The house in the distance looked old, and it also had clutter around it. Four broken-down cars were parked between the two buildings.

Interesting. Clean eating didn't mean clean farming, I guessed.

The same man who'd spoken with Borski approached me as he was leaving the barn. Something about his body language instantly told me that I couldn't dive in to this using only the truth. He wouldn't tell me things just to tell me.

I needed a cover.

"Can I help you?" The man was thirtyish, with a ball cap and a sweaty white shirt, dirty jeans, and work boots.

"I'm looking to buy some produce." That seemed like a good start.

"You have a restaurant?"

"No, but I'm having . . . a harvest party. I need to add the 'harvest' to the 'party,' if you know what I mean." I did a little shimmy with my shoulders, which I realized in retrospect was a horrible idea.

Lame, Gabby. Lame. And slightly inappropriate.

He stared at me a moment before nodding and tugging at his John Deere ball cap. "Well, I've got the harvest, as you call it. How'd you hear about me?"

"From . . . Jenny."

"Jenny? Jenny from Jenny's Produce?"

"The one and only." I had no idea who Jenny was.

He nodded. "Great gal."

"Absolutely. So, could I get a price list from you, by chance?" I needed to change the subject from Jenny before I got caught.

"I can run and get you one of those. I'll need some advance notice to make sure I have enough. Crops aren't as strong this year due to that frost we had back in September. When is this party?"

"Two weeks."

He nodded again. "That should work."

"Fabulous. I've been looking for some all-organic farmers for a while now, so I'm thrilled to find you."

He stared at me. A weird stare.

I cringed and almost did a shoulder shimmy again as a nervous twitch.

That could *not* become my nervous twitch.

What had I said that was wrong? Had I given myself away somehow?

My mind scrambled to find answers.

"Lady, this isn't organic produce. Why would you think that?"

"Don't you supply The Crispy Biscuit with their

produce?" Maybe I shouldn't have asked that. But I did it because I desperately wanted the answer.

"I've heard of the place. I don't supply anything to them, as far as I know."

He didn't realize that Borski was associated with The Crispy Biscuit. He didn't seem like the type who kept up with trendy restaurants or Norfolk nightlife.

"Oh, well, I'm sorry for the confusion. I thought I saw Greg Borski pulling away as I pulled in. He owns The Crispy Biscuit."

He made a face. "That was Rod Brown who just left. He has a place in Norfolk."

"Oh, yeah? Which one? I always like trying out new restaurants—especially ones that use local produce."

He tapped his finger on his lip a moment before shrugging. "You know? I'm not really sure. And he always pays with cash, so . . ."

All I knew was this: something was rotten. Really rotten.

CHAPTER
TEN

BORSKI WAS REALLY GETTING under my skin, and I couldn't let it go.

I'd read that he started as a chef under a mentor at Darcy's Fine Cuisine, and I wondered if anyone at that restaurant would talk to me. I decided to find out.

I headed toward Virginia Beach. Though the restaurant was known as being upper crust, it was located in a worn down building in an old, rather boring part of town filled with dated shopping malls and electrical lines still strung above ground instead of buried.

I asked at the hostess stand to speak to someone about Greg Borski. I was led back to an office several minutes later and introduced to Garfield Darcy himself.

Garfield Darcy was the opposite of Borski. He looked . . . normal and unassuming. Calm and thought-out. He had a neat beard, short hair, and he wore a white chef uniform. His kitchen was clean and orderly, quite the change from The Crispy Biscuit.

He directed me into his office, and I sat in a comfortable chair on the opposite side of the desk from him.

I introduced myself as a private detective investigating a case whose details I couldn't disclose.

"You think Greg Borski killed that woman, don't you?" He said the words calmly and without much emotion.

I nodded. "How'd you know?"

"I knew Borski's temper would catch up with him one day," Garfield said.

"What do you mean?"

"He was an excellent chef—creative, daring, even spicy. But he could be explosive. He was such a loose cannon that I knew I had to part ways with him or I'd regret it one day."

"Can you give any specific examples?"

He launched into it right away, not even taking time to think. "There was this food critic that tore apart one of his creations. Borski went ballistic. It was bad enough here at the restaurant as he was yelling and throwing things. But it got worse."

I was on the edge of my seat. "How?"

"He went to this reviewer's home and began threatening him. He stalked him on Facebook and left nasty messages. He began critiquing this man's reviews on every online forum possible."

"That's . . . over the top."

"To say the least. I was afraid I would somehow end up getting sued simply because of my association with him."

"What ended up happening?"

"Borski came to his senses and apologized. I severed our professional relationship. He went his way, and I went mine. He was out of my hair, so I really didn't care what he did at that point."

"I see. Do you, by chance, remember this food critic's name?"

"Will Eason."

"Is he still in the area?"

Garfield nodded. "Yeah, he's at the cemetery out in Princess Anne. He had a heart attack two years ago."

As five o'clock grew closer, a crowd began forming outside the apartment complex again. Someone must have known Bill's schedule because this was the exact time he usually arrived home. Today, however, he was doing yoga with Katarina. The thought of Bill doing yoga wasn't a pleasant one, but . . . at least he was doing something to keep himself in shape.

I peered out the window, taking in the "Kill Bill" signs, listening to the chants, and wondering why these people didn't have anything better to do. The building was otherwise quiet. Riley was at work. Sierra was probably working from home. Rhonda, Chad's mother, had left with Reef just as I'd arrived back, and Mrs. Mystery was out of town.

I used the time until Bill arrived to hop on my computer. I was going to try and work until Riley came home from the gym.

The first thing I checked out was *Godfrey Gossips*. The words on the page exploded like fireworks on the Fourth of July. He was urging his fans to go to Bill's home and let him know how they felt about his self-righteous double standards. This man really was behind this protest.

It just seemed so . . . dramatic.

If Godfrey had his way, thousands of people would be gathered outside this apartment complex soon. And it wouldn't be the cool, crowd-surfing type of group. No, it was the guillotine-toting type.

I looked back out the window. Some news vans had also shown up. This was crazier than I could have ever imagined.

Out of curiosity, I Googled "Katarina Sokolov" next. I was surprised by the lack of results that showed up about her. The way Bill talked, she was practically a celebrity. But, according to what I found, she'd done a few modeling gigs for some department store catalogs—nothing that would launch her into supermodel status.

There was also a surprising lack of information about her background. I couldn't find anything to confirm where she was from or any details of her past.

Mafia . . .

I couldn't get Sierra's words from my mind.

Speaking of Sierra . . . I stood and stretched. Maybe I should take a break from all of this and check on my friend. I hoped her knee was doing better. I hoped she was surviving having her mother-in-law here to help out. The woman seemed perfectly nice, but I knew having two women in one house could be explosive.

I clacked down the stairs, my flip-flops especially noisy on the distressed wooden steps—they were distressed before distressed was cool. I could hear the crowd outside, but I didn't want to address them right now.

I knocked on Sierra's door and heard a "come in!" from the other side. So I went in.

Sierra was sitting on the couch with her leg propped up. She frowned and stared at her phone, barely looking at me. This wasn't a good sign.

"Hey, Gabby."

"What's going on?" I glanced around, noticing how the apartment seemed unusually quiet.

"Rhonda took Reef shopping. The noise outside kept waking him up."

Something else was missing . . . "And your cats. Where are your cats?"

Sierra had at least three or four at any given time. She was addicted. And softhearted—but only when it came to animals.

"I had to take them to the office while Rhonda is here. She's allergic. It was just easier to let them stay there."

I plopped down next to her. "So you're here all by your lonesome, huh?"

She frowned. "I couldn't make it walking at the mall. I figured it was better if I stayed here and let my leg rest a little more. No more slaughterhouse reenactments for me."

"What are you doing?" I peered over her shoulder, wondering what she was so preoccupied with. She wasn't usually a technology junkie.

She shook her head and continued to frantically jab the screen of her phone. "This isn't working."

"What's not working?"

Her gaze remained intensely focused on whatever she was doing. "One of my employees decided to make this new app that we hope will help promote awareness of animal rights in a fun, relevant way. Users literally get to save cartoon animals from destruction. Animal lives matter and all."

I loved her latest campaign theme. It made me smile every time she said it. "Not a bad idea. So what's wrong?"

"We've spent a lot of money on developing this, and I can't get this lizard to work like it should!"

I looked at the screen. A cartoon lizard refused to move

out of the way of the toxic substance flooding his swamp. "You know what they call that, don't you?"

She jabbed the screen one more time with a frustrated grunt. "What?"

"E-reptile dysfunction."

She actually paused for long enough to look at me and groan. "That was bad."

"It was, wasn't it?" I was about to say something else witty and funny when I noticed the commotion outside seemed to get even louder.

I peered outside and spotted Bill pulling into the parking lot. The crowd mobbed his car. They'd really have a fit if he emerged wearing men's yoga pants. And I would cease any further affiliation with him.

Did I even attempt to help him? Or did I mind my own business?

Male yoga pants, I reminded myself.

I'd never been good at minding my own business.

With a mental sigh, I stood. "Sierra, I'll be back. Sorry to cut this short."

"If you're leaving to try and silence the people squawking outside my door like a bunch of rabid monkeys, then go right ahead. I'm going to do as the gorillas do soon and start throwing dung at them."

My eyes widened. My friend was grumpy. Very grumpy.

I didn't want to know where she planned on getting the dung.

And she was right. The sooner these people got away from our house, the better. They weren't only a disruption to Bill, but to all of us.

I opened the front door just as he emerged from his car wearing . . . sweat pants.

My eyes thank you.
I released my breath.
I rushed toward him, ready to walk him inside. He'd need help to get through this angry mob.

Just as we reached the porch, a loud bang cracked the air.

Gunfire, I realized.

Someone was shooting at us.

CHAPTER
ELEVEN

"GET DOWN!" I shouted.

Everyone either scattered or seemed to fall to the ground collectively.

Except Bill.

I ran toward him and jerked him onto the asphalt. My heart raced out of control. Where in the world was that gunfire coming from?

It all seemed very JFK assassination-like. Minus the parade, the pomp and circumstance, the Secret Service, and gobs of supporters.

Okay, so this was nothing like that.

I raised my head just enough to glance around. Almost all of the protesters were on the ground or they'd run for their lives. The buildings on either side of me looked clear, as did the coffeehouse across the street.

But there was a shooter somewhere.

In the middle of the chaos, a car eased into the parking lot.

Rhonda's car, I realized.

My heart pounded even harder.

I could hear Reef wailing in the car. He'd obviously distracted his dear grandma and taken away her good sense. She had no idea what she'd just driven into.

Without standing up, I tried to motion for her to stay put. She didn't see me.

Her door opened.

"Rhonda, no!" Just as I said the words, another gunshot rang out.

The glass on Rhonda's door shattered.

Had someone lost his or her mind? There was a baby in that car!

Just then, movement across the street caught my eye. Someone was fleeing from the scene!

It was the shooter. I was certain of it.

I pulled myself to my feet and darted after him before anyone could stop me. I dodged the minefield of protesters lying on the ground. Nearly tripped on a "Kill Bill" sign. Vaguely thought I really did see a foam guillotine.

I didn't have time to examine everything.

I had to catch this idiot.

I didn't have my gun with me or anything else to protect myself. But I couldn't lose this guy now.

The figure wore all black. Was thin. Fast.

A black mask covered his face.

Or was the person a woman? I honestly couldn't tell.

For all I knew, it could be Greg Borski.

I jerked to a stop at the street as cars zoomed past. At the first break, I rushed across. But that roadblock had allowed too much distance.

The shooter was farther away.

As the shooter disappeared around the corner, I stopped. My chest heaved as I tried to drink in air.

I hadn't been able to catch up with him . . . or her.

But the stakes in all of this had just become a lot greater.

Detective Adams came by to get everyone's statements about what had happened. He'd already questioned Bill, Rhonda, and several protesters. I was hanging around until the end so I could talk to Adams privately. After all, we were practically BFFs.

As the sun set, I stood outside in the almost-deserted parking lot, waiting as Adams talked to another detective. A CSI collected the stray bullet and searched for the bullet casing. Another team of officers searched for the shooter.

Riley was still at work and probably didn't know what was going on. Chad had rushed home a few minutes ago to check on his family. Thankfully, they were all okay.

A news crew had shown up and were setting up cameras on the edge of the property. Gawkers lingered on the sidewalk, wondering what the commotion was about. Cars slowed as they passed, rubbernecking to see what was going on.

Finally, the other detective headed across the street to check for camera footage from the businesses there. I only knew that because I'd overheard Detective Adams talking to him.

A lot of criminals weren't smart enough to avoid cameras. My gut told me that this one was.

When a natural pause in the conversation came, I broached the subject that had really been on my mind. "Anything new on the case that you can tell me about?"

Adams raised an eyebrow and propped an elbow up on the stair railing. "You mean since I talked to you last?"

I nodded, hoping he didn't feel the question was unreasonable. "Yes, exactly. I've been trying to sketch out the timeline for Emma Jean, but I haven't had much luck. My best guess is that she died on Monday. I just can't figure out where she died or how she ended up in the freezer."

"That's what we're trying to figure out also. I can tell you this: we don't believe the freezer was the initial scene of the crime."

Interesting. "You don't know where the initial location is?"

He shook his head.

I wasn't finished. "Do you know what she was hit with?"

"Something round and thick."

"A rolling pin?" I wondered aloud.

"That would be too easy, right?"

Maybe it would be. Again, it just went back to how smart this criminal was. It also went back to if Emma Jean's death was connected with the threats against Bill. I hadn't found the connection yet, other than Bill. Maybe Bill was enough.

What else would fit the description of the murder weapon? "A baseball bat?"

"We're trying to figure it all out."

"What about the contents of her stomach? What did that tell you?" Such as time of death . . .

"I'm waiting to hear back from the medical examiner. They're backlogged with cases still. Certainly you know better than most people that they're short-staffed."

Did I ever. I'd been let go because of budget cuts. I wondered if I could call down to a few friends there myself . . . it was something to consider. I only wanted to play that card when it was an absolute necessity.

"Do you have any suspects?" I continued.

"You're full of questions, aren't you?"

"Nothing's really changed."

"That's for sure. We do have our eye on someone."

I leaned forward, wishing I had another donut to offer him. "It's Greg Borski, isn't it?"

He blinked. "Why would you say that?"

"Because he had motive and means. He couldn't stand Emma Jean. He obviously had access to the freezer at the restaurant. He could have kept people away from that area."

"Theories aren't reason enough to arrest someone. You know that."

"That's right. You need some hard evidence."

"You got any?"

"Not yet."

"Let me know if you find anything. I need a weapon. I need a crime scene."

"I'll see what I can do."

He smiled. "I know you will."

CHAPTER
TWELVE

JUST AS DETECTIVE ADAMS left and I stepped inside to check on Reef, the door upstairs opened and Tim rambled out. I blinked. I hadn't even realized he was here. Maybe that was because he didn't have a car and he hadn't shown his face since he moved in.

"What's going on?" He leaned on the post at the top of the stairs. His eyes looked dazed, his hair even messier than usual, and I was pretty sure he still hadn't showered. "It's been loud out here."

I slowly climbed the steps to reach him. "You missed all the excitement."

Had he really slept through everything that happened?

Deep inside, I was worried about him. He was a grown man, capable of making his own choices. I didn't think I would ever truly understand him. When he'd returned from his abduction, he'd been a different person. I figured his experiences had changed him, as had his new upbringing with his kidnappers. Being a freegan was his way of coping, just as crime scene cleaning had been my way of coping. Could we ever regain what we'd lost?

"I didn't realize how tired I was." He yawned and stretched, as if to prove his words were true. "I guess hitchhiking across country was more exhausting than I thought."

He scratched his head.

"You know you can use my shower, right?" I imagined him sleeping on my sheets with that itchy head and squirmed. Lice? I didn't even want to think about it.

But that was okay because I needed to get rid of my furniture anyway. For that matter, I needed to get rid of my apartment. Maybe this would get the ball rolling faster.

"Oh yeah, yeah. I will. Totally. I just needed to sleep a little bit first."

"How's Whitney?"

He squinted. "Whitney?"

"Your girlfriend?"

"I don't know if I'd call her that."

I suppressed a sigh. "How's her kidney stone?"

"Oh, that . . . I guess it's fine."

"You haven't talked to her?" What had he been doing for the past twenty-four hours?

He shrugged, acting like I'd just asked him something casual, like if he'd seen a new TV show. "Not in a couple of days."

"Aren't you concerned with how she's doing?" *Don't nag, Gabby. Don't nag.* But really?

He stared at me, snapping out of his earlier stupor. "What's with all the questions? I just woke up. Can't I just chill for a minute?"

Irritation pinched at me. "I see. Anything else new?"

"Nah, not really."

"So, any idea how long you'll be staying here?" I hoped he didn't hear the tension in my words.

"Not really. Since you're not using the place any more, I didn't think it was a big deal." He scratched his head again.

Lice. I really hoped he didn't have them. Ew . . .

"I didn't say it was a big deal. I was just curious."

"As soon as I know my next move, I'll let you know."

I could accept that—for now. But eventually, like by the end of this month, I would most likely need to give up my lease. He would need to be out, and I didn't care what kind of guilt trip he gave me.

He straightened. "Alright, Sis. I've gotta go. And could you ask people to keep it down out here?"

My irritation turned to anger, but I held it back. "Of course."

"Thanks. See ya."

Riley and I were tired, to say the least, when we arrived at church the next day. The excitement of the previous night had kept us up talking into the early morning hours. Who would go so far as to shoot at Bill? It just didn't make sense to me.

Maybe we were looking at two different crimes: The murder of Emma Jean, and someone else who was intent on attacking Bill and, by default, Katarina. Or had someone killed Emma Jean and tried to frame Bill? Everything didn't quite make sense yet.

It had taken everything in me to concentrate during worship and the sermon and not to think about this case. When church was over, we had to tear down the chairs, tables, and sound equipment.

The church we attended met at a school. We arrived

early every Sunday morning so we could set up and stayed late so we could tear down. I wasn't going to lie—I loved my church, but I was ready to not do the set up/tear down thing anymore. Until we could find a permanent building, though, this was how it had to be.

As I finished putting away a table, I paused when I saw a friend from Bible study coming my way. Leona Hemsley. I smiled—until I noticed the stormy look in her eyes.

"Hi, Leona," I started, sliding the table onto a cart. "How are—?"

The thirty-something woman raised her finger. In my face, at that. Her eyes were buggy and her nostrils flared.

"If you support Ed Stead and the people who support Ed Stead, then you can't possibly call yourself a Christian," she snapped.

I blanched. There were very few things that could take me by surprise or throw me off-kilter. But her words cut so deep that I had no idea what to say for a brief second.

Then indignation blared to life inside me. I tamped it down and remembered I was in church. Unlike Leona, who apparently knew no boundaries. "Say again?"

Certainly, I hadn't heard her correctly. I should at least give her the benefit of the doubt. To keep my hands occupied so they wouldn't fly in the air to drive home my point, I grabbed a chair and folded it. Then I squeezed the metal, willing myself to remain level-headed as I waited for her to explain.

"I can't believe you would support the viewpoints of someone like Stead. I thought more of you."

"What are you talking about?" I was seriously not following this. Nor was I following how someone who seemed so sweet and genteel at Bible study was acting like someone who'd contracted mad cow disease. Or maybe politics made people act slightly demon-possessed.

"I saw you on that video protecting Bill McCormick. I can't believe you're on board with someone like him. Viewpoints like his set America back by a hundred years."

"Whoa, whoa, whoa. Trying to help someone and keep them safe doesn't mean my viewpoints and his align with each other." I squeezed the chair tighter.

"Your friendships say a lot about you. That's in the Bible. And if you're friends with Bill, then we're obviously not friends." Her finger flipped from me to her and then back again.

Had this woman lost her mind? She still looked bug-eyed and crazy. Maybe that was just what politics did to some people.

"So you're essentially telling me right now that this election and politics are more important than our friend-ship?" I finally said. One of my hands slipped free and flew up in agitation, almost like it had a mind of its own. "I've never said who I supported politically because that's no one's business."

She narrowed her eyes, apology nowhere to be seen. "You've made it obvious whom you support."

"I can't even have this conversation with you right now." I couldn't. I was going to say something I regretted —and at church nonetheless. It was better if I just kept quiet until my emotions simmered down. The old Gabby would have given her a piece of her mind.

"Well, I've said all I needed to say. I'm disappointed in you, Gabby Thomas. And your husband, too, for not keeping a better rein on you."

I watched her walk away, my mouth gaping open. It wasn't that I necessarily cared that she was disappointed in me. I only cared that she had the nerve to just have that conversation. And did she really expect my husband to keep a rein on me? That took some nerve.

Riley joined me, his gaze following Leona. "You okay?"

I pulled my eyes away and grimaced. "I'll tell you later. But you may have to rein me in."

His forehead wrinkled. "I'm not really sure what that means, but how about we talk about it over lunch?"

I nodded. "Over lunch."

"You want to go with Pastor Randy?"

"Can it just be us this time? I mean, I love Pastor Randy and everything, but life has been so busy lately with everything. It would be nice to just hang out with you."

"Of course." He laced his fingers with mine as we walked toward the door.

Thrills still ran through me at his touch. I hoped that never changed.

"Mexican?" he asked.

"Sounds scrumptious."

Ten minutes later, we were seated at our favorite Mexican restaurant, The Red Burrito, a place with live mariachi music and festive paper lanterns strung across the ceiling. As soon as we ordered, I rehashed my conversation with Leona to Riley.

"She really said that?" Riley said.

He looked as dumbfounded as I felt.

I nodded first in confirmation, then I shook my head in disgust. "I was pretty stunned. I mean, why are politics so volatile?"

"People get fired up and passionate. Other people see the injustice of the process with media bias and people in power pulling strings, making deals. People are fed up.

They're taking a stand . . . but not always in the right way."

"You can say that again. It's bringing out the worst in people and making me lose my faith in humanity."

"Our faith was never supposed to be in humanity to begin with," Riley said.

I just got owned.

But Riley was so entirely correct.

I nodded. "True enough. Okay then. Enough about Leona. Let's talk about something else."

"Do you know what I find interesting?" He poked his straw into his ice water.

"What's that?" I grabbed a chip, unable to resist their salty goodness.

"The very first case you were working when we met involved Detective Adams and a politician. Not so dissimilar to this one, no?"

"I guess you're right. I never thought about it. It's kind of funny how it's all coming full circle."

And it was. And I was so glad it was coming full circle with Riley by my side.

Riley nodded toward the TV in the corner. "It looks like The Crispy Biscuit being a crime scene is no longer a secret."

I turned and watched the news story, which featured the headline: "The Crispy Biscuit and The Frozen Corpse." Clever.

The reporter talked about Emma Jean's death. About how she'd been found at her place of employment. How the police still hadn't named any suspects but that many speculated about her former husband, Bill McCormick.

My bets, at this point, were on Greg Borski. I just needed to find some more evidence against him. The whole organic/non-organic thing was very interesting. However, was it worth murdering over?

I wasn't sure. Nor was I sure why he was in so much debt. Had Emma Jean discovered something about his finances?

I needed to get into that restaurant again. Talk to some employees. Investigate more.

The waitress came and took our order. I ordered a pumpkin burrito, and hoped I didn't regret it. I mean, I loved pumpkin just as much as anyone else, but really? I ordered it anyway.

I turned back to Riley. "I heard you're representing Bill."

He shrugged. "Unofficially, I suppose. He called and put me on retainer, just in case he needs me."

"What do you think? Were you able to review anything?"

"There's no evidence, right now at least, to prove he's guilty. It's like Detective Adams said last night—there's no murder weapon. We don't know where the murder occurred. Last I heard, we don't even know when the murder happened. Unless the police discover something new, I'm not sure he needs representation." He leaned closer. "What do you think?"

I sighed, trying to sift through my thoughts. "The only person I'm leaning toward at this point is Greg Borski, the owner of The Crispy Biscuit."

I explained what I'd discovered about him.

"Anyone else?" Riley asked.

Well, since he'd asked . . . "I feel like Emma Jean was holding a lot of information over a lot of people. That means any one of a number of people could be guilty."

"Even Bill?"

"Maybe. You threaten people and risk ruining their relationships or career or reputation? That will make people mad. Mad enough to kill."

"So you're not convinced it's Borski?"

"I'm trying to trace his footsteps. And Emma Jean's."

"Have you considered that Borski and Katarina might be connected?"

"Why?"

He shrugged. "Well, they both share Russian surnames."

Brilliant! Why hadn't I thought of that? "You're amazing."

He shrugged again. "I have to feel useful sometimes."

I leaned across the table and gave him a quick kiss. "All the time. I'm going to put this all together yet."

"You will. You always do."

I smiled. "Thanks."

I was at home, contemplating how to find out more dirt on Borski or if there truly was a connection between him and Katarina. Riley was working out, and the gunshot yesterday seemed to have scared the protesters away. For now, at least.

I sat on the couch, trying to get into the right headspace to think this through, but I really felt like I needed to go back into my old apartment to properly muse. However, Tim was most likely there. Possibly with lice, which I just couldn't even handle thinking about.

Give me blood and guts to clean up any day.

I missed seeing my crime scene cleaning knickknacks— the fake blood on the table, the crime scene tape pencil holder, the pad of paper that looked like a body outline. Most of the items had been gifts. They were quirky, but they fit me. They didn't, however, seem to fit the motif of a married, professional woman.

As I stared at a piece of paper on my lap with various circles and arrows and scribbled words, my phone rang.

"Gabby, we got the call," Chad said.

"The call?" My mind was in a different place. A political polling call? A call from the doctor about Sierra's knee? To serve overseas as a missionary?

"To clean the crime scene. Emma Jean's."

I sat up straighter. "Oh. Emma Jean's. You did?"

"We did. The bad news is that the owner wants us to clean it today. And to use tact. He doesn't want anyone to know why we're there."

"Everyone already knows." We'd just seen it on the news two hours ago.

"If it makes this Borski guy feel better to think we're being especially discrete, then so be it. He seems tightly wound, to say the least."

"Understood. When are you leaving?" I glanced at my watch, even though I didn't have any real plans for the rest of the day. I'd drop them to get back into that restaurant.

"In about an hour."

"Borski liked Clarice, didn't he?" I knew he would. They didn't call me the master people reader for nothing.

Okay, so no one actually called me that—except maybe me.

"No idea, but I'm going to let you and Clarice handle this. Are you okay with that?"

"Me and Clarice? It's been a while. Sure. We can do this." With any luck, I wouldn't end up strangling her.

An hour later, Clarice and I showed up at The Crispy Biscuit. Greg Borski's truck was out back, which presented an interesting problem for me. Of course, he'd recognize me if I went inside, which could make things very awkward.

The last thing I needed was to start doing a shoulder shimmy again to break the tension.

"What are you thinking?" Clarice turned toward me with wide, doe-like eyes.

The answers were clear to me. For now, at least. "You go in first. I'll organize stuff out here and kill some time until Borski leaves."

Her eyes widened even more. "What do I do? I've never been the point of contact before."

I patted her shoulder, trying to ease her out of Bambi mode. "You'll do fine. Just introduce yourself, explain that we'll be cleaning and that the job should last about three hours, etc."

She nibbled on her bottom lip. "What if this guy doesn't leave? I can't do this whole job by myself. Remember that paint thinner incident?"

That would be a problem. "We don't need paint thinner for this job—or paint. Let's just take this step-by-step. We'll figure it out."

———

An hour later, Borski was still there. I really should have thought this plan through a little better. I knew I had to dive into Plan B. Clarice had already been back out to the van several times, asking for my advice on what to do, what to say, and to grab a few supplies.

She'd given me updates each time. So far, she'd talked

to the staff, signed a contract, brought in equipment, and prepped the area for our work.

It was time for me to move in. Otherwise, it really wasn't fair to her.

Just as I'd suspected, Borski had already gotten Clarice's number and wanted to ask her out, which didn't do much to put Clarice at ease.

"He's a creep, Gabby. And I'm dating Nate!" she whispered to me in the back of the van.

I raised a hand, urging her to calm down. "Just stay on his good side. I'm coming in."

"But he'll recognize you!"

"I've got a plan."

I grabbed one of Chad's old hats from the back. It had sweat stains on it and smelled disgusting, but I couldn't think about that. I pulled my hair up, concealing it, and shoved the Norfolk Tides—a local baseball team—cap on my head. Then I climbed into a white Tyvek suit. As the final touch, I pulled on my goggles and a facial mask. It wasn't flattering, but it would work.

Even Riley wouldn't recognize me in this getup, which always left me feeling half like an astronaut and half like a Teletubby.

Something about wearing the Tyvek suit made me feel like I was waddling instead of walking. When I stepped inside, everyone seemed to stop.

I waved, a little too widely.

The good news was that I didn't do any shimmies.

"This is my associate, Gab—" Clarice cleared her throat, and her gaze shot across the room to a propane tank. "Gassy. This is Gassy."

Gassy? Really? You couldn't think of anything else?

"My mom had a wicked sense of humor," I said with a weak laugh and slight scowl toward Clarice.

I quickly observed the people staring at me. First, there was Borski, who looked disgusted at my complete lack of style and my name. Then there was the blonde cook I'd seen when I was here before. Selena was embroidered on her lapel. She didn't look any happier today than she had earlier as she stomped around, tossing pots and pans back into the cabinets. Perhaps the dishwasher had quit?

Finally, I spotted a new person wearing a traditional chef's uniform. He had to be the sous chef. What was his name? Julian, if I remembered correctly. He appeared to be in his early thirties and had spiky black hair and multiple earrings. A tattoo crept up the side of his neck and he held a knife in his hand.

He might look scary if it wasn't for the friendly smile on his face.

"You need to sign this." Borski thrust something toward me, looking away as if I made his eyes hurt. "Gassy."

I glanced at the paper. My voice was muffled by my facemask as I said, "What's this?"

"A nondisclosure statement. My recipes are proprietary, as are the practices of this restaurant. If you share anything you've seen here, I'll sue you. That's what it boils down to."

"O . . . kay." I picked up a pen and signed my fake name. I mean, I couldn't really sign my real name, since I'd just introduced myself as Gassy. And there was the fact that I might very well share something I'd seen here today. Was that how he'd kept it quiet that his organic produce was anything but?

He took the paper back, examined my signature, and stomped into his office.

Somehow I needed to get in there. I wanted to look at his books. I had to wait for just the right opportunity, though.

I quickly slipped into the freezer. I paused inside and shivered. Though Clarice had already cleaned out a lot, the space was still stark. There, right in front of me, was a gigantic bloodstain.

The sight of it made me want to get out—and fast. I quickly secured the door with several boxes, just to make sure it didn't slip shut and result in Gassy turning into Ice Cube-y.

This was where Emma Jean had been placed. She'd continued to bleed until the cold had stopped it. Despite the localization, the whole place had to be sanitized. Everything inside here should be thrown away. The freezer really should be thawed and scrubbed from top to bottom, but Borski hadn't turned it off in time to properly defrost.

I guessed he'd never heard of blood-borne pathogens.

I started by pouring hot water on the floor to loosen the ice. Then I poured some bleach. Clarice helped me to wipe it all up and helped by bringing more hot water.

It wasn't a pretty job. I wasn't pretty when Clarice and I emerged from the freezer an hour later. My nose was red like I'd been outside in the freezing cold, yet my hair had the humidity effect going on and sprigs had started to spring from my baseball cap. My shoes were wet, despite the covering I'd put on them.

I needed to step back, let the freezer dry, and then reassess everything we'd done.

The good news was, Borski was nowhere to be seen.

Instead, Selena and Julian were staring at us, watching us like they had nothing better to do.

"Not busy?" I asked, wiping my forehead.

"Not since the news leaked information about what supposedly happened here," Selena said, giving me a death stare.

"Bummer." I set a mop down and pulled my goggles off.

"Tell me about it." She pursed her lips. "The only thing that's worse than being busy is not being busy."

That was deep.

"Mr. Borski left?" I asked.

"He said he needed to take a mental health day," the sous chef said. "Gassy."

I think people liked saying my name a little too much.

I wanted to give Clarice a dirty look, but I couldn't without raising suspicions.

"He's looked stressed to the max lately." He flipped the knife in the air and caught the handle. He was obviously bored also.

The blonde finally sighed and disappeared to sit on a couch in Borski's office.

"Impressive." I pulled off my hat and facemask too. Without Borski here, I didn't have to worry so much.

Clarice stepped out of the freezer also and rolled her neck. She unzipped the top of her Tyvek suite, which seemed to grab Julian's attention.

He shrugged, smiling at Clarice. "I try. My dream was to be a carny at one time."

"For real?" Clarice asked.

He nodded and flipped the knife again, obviously in impress mode. "Life is too boring to settle down, you know? I've already been a gardener, and a lifeguard, and a nanny. I figured I'd be a sous chef for a while. Who knows what the future holds for me? Bull rider? Tattoo artist? The possibilities are endless."

"Endless," I echoed.

"That's the great part about America—the dreams we can dream and accomplish," he continued. "At least, that's true of the country as it now stands. We'll see what happens after the election, right?"

"It's like the fate of the world hinges on it," I muttered.

Wherever I went, people wanted to talk about the election. And my conversation with Leona still left me perturbed. At least this conversation was better suited than the one I'd had when I was getting a cavity filled. The dentist went on and on about his choice of candidate. Actually, he'd gone on and on about the other guy: someone who would destroy our nation. I was afraid he might end up giving me a root canal just because he was so angry.

It was exhausting, in all honesty.

Julian slid his knife back into the butcher block. "Can I fix you something to drink? I make a killer smoothie."

"Sounds great," Clarice said. "I'll take anything you can give me."

I shrugged. "Why not?"

"So you guys are crime scene cleaners?" he asked, his gaze still on Clarice as he began to pull various fruits from the bowls on an island in the center of the kitchen.

Clarice smiled up at him. "That's right."

"How do pretty girls like you two end up in a career like this?"

Everything in me wanted to share my list of accomplishments and how I'd risen above my blue-collar career into a more prestigious one. After all, I had worked hard to get where I was. But I knew I'd only be shooting myself in the foot if I shared my affiliation with law enforcement. I needed to seem disconnected to all of this. It was honestly the best way to get information—most of the time.

Clarice and I exchanged a glance, and I nodded toward her. She was supposed to be the lead today, so she should act like it.

"I was just looking to make some extra money," Clarice said. "I stumbled into it, I guess. But I've met some super great people. And I do feel like I'm making a difference, in my own way. People need closure, and what I do helps them."

Her answer surprised me. Sometimes she came across like an airhead who only skimmed the surface of life. Other times her depth amazed me. She usually surfaced fast enough to give me the bends before plunging down deep again.

"Sounds noble." He began chopping some bananas and strawberries.

"These are organic, right?" I asked, trying to work the subject in. "That's all I eat."

He smiled but said nothing, just kept chopping.

"Uh oh. You're avoiding my question." I wasn't letting him off the hook that easily.

"I'm just not answering it."

"I see."

He chopped silently for a few minutes before nodding toward the boxes. "You see those boxes over there?"

I glanced in the direction he pointed. There were several cardboard containers, all stamped with ORGANIC. "I see them."

"That's what our fruits and vegetables come in. That should answer your question."

Interesting. That's what Borski had done. Transferred the produce from the bags into these boxes. Then he'd delivered them to the restaurant himself. No one had questioned him.

Except maybe Emma Jean. Or did Julian suspect it also? I couldn't read his grin.

I crossed my arms. "So, how do deliveries work here? I mean, this setup isn't traditional. I imagine trucks would have trouble getting back here because of the narrow alleys. Our van even found it tight."

He threw some fruit into a blender. "Greg hand-chooses everything himself. He insists on picking it up from local growers and brings it in every couple of days."

"Wow. That's dedication." And a lie. How many lies had Borski told?

"That's Greg for you. He even picks up the meat, poultry, and fish from local farms and fishermen. Some things we can't get in this area. He has a friend from up north who brings certain kinds of fish down for him."

Sure he did.

I glanced at Julian as he turned the blender on. He definitely seemed to have a talent and flare. He'd cut those fruits up like a pro. My finger would have come off by now.

I wandered to the other side of the room to the lockers there. One of the doors had photos taped to the front. It obviously belonged to Julian. One showed him playing some hippy-looking instrument around a bonfire. Another had him suspended over train tracks as if levitating. Still another featured him squatting beside some kind of white plant with pruning shears in his hands.

Interesting that all of his photos were of himself, but maybe these pictures just made him happy.

I needed to find out what he knew. Because he knew something. He'd threatened to cut off Emma Jean's fingers, according to Borski. A moment later, he handed Clarice and me our smoothies. I wasn't going to lie: they looked good. Really good.

I took a sip and let the fruity flavors wash over my taste buds. Perfection.

"You should make a pumpkin one," Clarice said, peering over her straw like a pinup girl.

Did she do that on purpose? Or did she try to be sexy and coy? I honestly thought it came naturally to her.

"I love pumpkin," she murmured. "It's super yummy."

"Everyone loves pumpkin," Julian said with a grin. "It's the watermelon of the fall."

She giggled. "I like that."

Julian's eyes warmed, and he looked pleased that Clarice was giggling. What about poor Nate? He wasn't my favorite person, but still . . .

I took a few more sips before broaching the subject I really wanted to talk about.

"So, it's crazy what happened here, isn't it? I'm sure the lady who died will be missed at The Crispy Biscuit. I'm surprised there's no memorial set up in her memory."

He chopped up some more fruit, obviously making a smoothie for himself now. As he did so, he glanced up at me. I waited for him to slice his finger open. He didn't.

"Not really," he deadpanned. "No memorials or wakes or times of mourning here."

Ouch.

"How do you think she ended up here in the freezer?" Clarice jumped in before I could ask about his morbid assessment. "That's what I can't get over. It's super weird."

"Your guess is as good as mine. I think it's all crazy."

I took another sip of fruity goodness before a new thought hit me: I hoped none of the nonorganic fruits had been anywhere near that blood spatter. After all, the killer had only left her in the freezer. Who knew what happened between the time she died and the time she ended up in the freezer. Where was the health department?

I set my smoothie down. "I heard she had a lot of enemies."

He glanced back at me again, slicing a pineapple as he did so. "How'd you hear that? Did you know her?"

Careful, Gassy. Don't show your hand.

"It was on the news." I tried to say it like it was no big deal. "Or maybe it was a blog."

Julian gave me a sideways glance. "Do you always read up on the murders you're cleaning up after?"

I decided to go with the truth. "I do. Unfortunately. I guess you could call it morbid curiosity."

"I think I would do the same thing," Julian said. "But, yeah, Emma Jean wasn't the most friendly person. She had a talent for rubbing people the wrong way."

"Even here at the restaurant?" Clarice asked.

Clarice and I shared the trait of having unquenchable curiosities, which worked in my favor at the moment because she rounded out the conversation nicely. We seemed like three friends—one with a bad name—standing around, shooting the breeze.

Julian chuckled sardonically. "Especially here at the restaurant. I'm not saying someone here finished her off because of it or anything. I'll leave that for the police to determine."

"I didn't say that," Clarice said. "The whole situation is just fascinating."

"She was an opinionated know-it-all. She wasn't afraid

of anyone. People didn't like that." He stuck more fruit in the blender, casually glancing toward the door leading outside the restaurant. There was still no action there. Customers had deserted this place.

"I see. So . . . like, what did she do?" Clarice asked.

She couldn't have done a better job if I prepped her.

He snorted. "Well, when she was here on Monday, all I can say is that she was extremely agitated."

"Why?" My pulse spiked as I anticipated what he might say. This could be the missing puzzle piece I'd been searching for.

I only hoped Julian shared before Selena came back in here and stopped all my snooping.

"Well, apparently her ex-husband came in here with his new girlfriend." He poured his smoothie into a tall glass.

My eyes widened. No they didn't . . . Bill and Katarina? Funny how Bill had never mentioned that. A lie of omission? That made my neighbor look guilty. Very guilty.

CHAPTER
THIRTEEN

"HER EX BROUGHT his new girlfriend here?" Clarice's bottom lip dropped open in soap opera worthy shock. "That takes a lot of nerve."

I had to agree with her. That took nerve. Like, a lot of nerve. Why would Bill do something that tactless?

"He came in quite a bit," Julian said, eating up all the attention. "I guess this was his favorite restaurant."

My jaw dropped open this time. "No . . . "

He leaned back and sipped his drink. "Oh, yeah. I heard about it every time he came here with his super hot girlfriend. Emma Jean was going out of her mind with jealousy."

"I can imagine." I shook my head, picturing it playing out in my mind. "That just seems so rude."

"According to Emma Jean, her ex was rude all the time. But he especially liked to flaunt his new girlfriend."

Clarice shook her head. "If I was the super hot girl-friend, I definitely wouldn't want to be flaunted."

What? That sounded like the Clarice I knew and loved. I didn't have time to even wonder about where those words had come from. Julian was still being chatty, and that was the most important thing.

"You know who her ex is, don't you?" Julian shook his glass, urging any parts of his wayward smoothie downward. "He's that obnoxious radio talk show host. Bill McCormick."

"You know—I think I heard that. He *is* obnoxious." And Bill had kept that detail from me. The realization made anger simmer inside me. His omission only made him seem guilty.

"It's not just on the radio. Bringing his new girlfriend here just shows how much of a jerk he really is. It's not just for show."

"I'd say so." I pressed my lips together, choosing my words wisely. "I even heard the police are looking at him as a suspect."

"They should." Julian took another long sip.

But why? Why would Bill kill Emma Jean? That's what didn't make sense. What would he gain from it? After all, he had everything going for him.

Unless Emma Jean had something hanging over him also. Because Emma Jean liked to have things hanging over people. Maybe she had something that could ruin Bill's newfound success.

Bill and I needed to have a serious talk. Soon.

"This was delicious." Clarice set her empty glass, smeared only with some leftover pink smudge on the edges, on the stainless steel counter. "I guess we should finish the freezer."

As she said that, Selena the cook stepped out, clanking some keys in her hands. "I'm outta here."

"What do you mean out of here?" Julian asked.

"I'm done. This place is done. I have better things to do with my time."

"Are you going to tell Greg first?" Julian continued, his eyes nearly bulging now.

"Frankly, I don't care if he knows or not. He dug himself into this hole." She offered a wave, dropped her uniform on the floor, and left out the backdoor.

"I can't believe that," Julian ran a hand through his hair, not looking quite as laid-back as he had earlier.

"She makes it sound like this place is doomed," I said, trying to take as long as possible to finish my smoothie so I could prolong this conversation. "Is the restaurant really doing that badly?"

Julian frowned. "I don't know. I think she's exaggerating."

"I mean, this will pass, right? As soon as they find this woman's real killer, everything will go back to normal. The Crispy Biscuit will be the 'it' restaurant again for health-conscious foodies in the area."

He nodded a little hesitantly and averted his gaze. "Right."

Okay, that really hadn't given me any answers. I needed some definitive proof about what was going on here. That meant I needed to somehow get Julian out of here so I could snoop. So I could *really* snoop.

Clarice was the perfect person to help me with that task, but I somehow had to get that message to her. Did she know me well enough to read my cues? I was going to find out.

I flung my gaze toward the outside door, careful not to move my neck. Clarice watched me, her eyes full of questions. Finally, she nodded.

"You need to go outside?" she muttered.

I gave her a look and shook my head, hoping Julian didn't see me.

"You have a head twitch?"

I seriously wanted to strangle her. I shook my head again. I flung my gaze even more dramatically toward the outside door and then at Julian.

Her lips formed an O. "Julian, I could use help getting some of this equipment back outside. Would you mind helping me while Gab—Gassy, I mean, finishes up in the freezer? Then we'll get out of your hair so you can finish . . . making smoothies and stuff."

I resisted the urge to roll my eyes. Finish making smoothies? I supposed that was what he was doing. But . . .

"Sure thing. I don't have anything better to do." He grabbed an air scrub and began hauling it from the freezer.

As soon as he disappeared from sight, I ducked into Borski's office. I opened a few drawers but saw nothing.

How did people keep books? Was it on paper?

No, of course not. Even I didn't keep my books on paper.

It would be on the computer.

I tapped his keyboard and his screen popped on. Apparently, Selena had been playing Minecraft. Interesting.

I closed that screen and scrolled through the other applications until I found some accounting software. As I heard Julian and Clarice coming back inside, I ducked under the desk.

"Where's your friend?" Julian asked.

"Probably in the bathroom. She has some digestive issues," Clarice said. "It was like a premonition that her mom named her Gassy."

I scowled.

"Enough said," Julian muttered.

I waited until their voices passed before going back to the computer. I remained low as I hit the keyboard. A moment later, the ledger appeared.

I didn't have to look very far to see that this restaurant was clearly in the red. Like, really in the red. Hundreds of thousands of dollars in the red.

Had Emma Jean known this? Had she threatened Borski as a result?

How was this place even operating at all?

Maybe this explained why Borski was living in a hotel. Had he lost his home?

As I heard the voices approaching again, I darted from the office.

Julian glanced at me when he entered the room again. "Everything okay? Actually, never mind. I don't want to know . . . Gassy."

Clarice and I left an hour later. I'd purposely "forgotten" some duct tape and a utility knife, just in case I needed an excuse to go back.

When we arrived at my apartment, I was dismayed, to say the least, to find the beautiful pumpkins I'd purchased on Saturday were now smashed in the parking lot.

"Who would do this?" Clarice asked, her doe-like eyes appearing again.

"Maybe some kids were being mischievous. Or it could be someone sending a message." Man, I liked those pumpkins. They added a touch of autumn to the place and made me feel grown-up.

"I'm sorry, Gabby."

"You know what this means? I'll be singing 'Bullet with Butterfly Wings' for the rest of the day."

Clarice stared at me.

"Smashing Pumpkins? The alternative rock band?" How could she not have heard of them?

She shook her head, blinking like headlights were headed her way.

I took a step away, but Clarice remained in place. "Never mind. Anyway, thanks for your help today. You did great."

"Gabby, do you think I'm going to be a good forensic investigator one day?"

My heart squeezed, and I paused, realizing I had the opportunity to encourage someone who needed encouragement. "Of course. You did a great job reading my body language and helping me out. And the line about the bathroom? It was brilliant."

She frowned. "But I really thought you were in the bathroom . . . "

"I've never had bathroom issues—" I stopped and shook my head. "Never mind."

"Goodnight, Gassy."

I caught her smile before hurrying upstairs to take a shower. It was the first thing I always did after cleaning a crime scene. Even though I wore protective gear, I still felt dirty . . . and like a walking biohazard. In fact, my Tyvek suit had to be put in a special bag and sent to a biohazard center for safety and health reasons.

No sooner had I gotten dressed than Riley called.

"I was hoping we could do something tonight," he started. "Just you and me."

I did have a few ideas that had been simmering in my mind . . . "Sure thing. You mind if I plan it?"

"No, that sounds great. I'll be home in fifteen."

His idea of planning and mine were bound to be different. But I knew he loved me, and I hoped that wouldn't change when he heard about my idea for tonight.

I knew I had to separate my professional and personal life. But that was hard to do when a case was pressing on me. I mean, someone had smashed my pumpkins, for goodness sakes! That was so 1979.

I packed some sandwiches, some pita chips, and hummus. Riley's sandwiches were actually turkey rollups with cheese, lettuce, and no bread. I also threw in some bags of nuts and beef jerky for him. Riley was doing this high-protein thing as he prepared for his big competition.

Right on time, I met Riley outside with a picnic basket in hand.

"A picnic?" he said. "I like it."

I smiled. "I have more than this in store . . ."

He wiggled his eyebrows. "I like the sound of that." He glanced around as we walked back to his car. "What happened to your pumpkins?"

I really should clean them up before they began rotting. When they rotted, flies would start swarming them. The flies made me think of maggots, which made me think of lice, which made me think of my brother.

I really should check on him.

"At least there are no protesters," Riley said.

"Those gunshots seemed to have scared them off. Temporarily, at least."

"That's good, at least." He opened the door for me and I climbed inside.

The clean, piney scent of his car always calmed me. It

reflected Riley: neat, organized, well thought out. Gentle music floated through the speakers. He carried a first aid kit, an extra blanket, and even kitty litter in the winter in case it got icy.

It was unlike my car, which had straw wrappers, crushed water bottles, and notes I'd scribbled on napkins. My radio was usually blaring. More often than not, my tires needed air or my windshield wiper fluid needed refilling.

"Okay, so where to?" Riley asked.

I cleared my throat, bracing myself for his reaction. I decided instead to delay it for a little longer. "How about if I tell you as we go?"

"If that's what you want."

As we drove, I filled him in on my day. I glanced behind me a few times as we cruised down the road, a paranoid habit I'd developed recently.

Was that car following us? The roads were busy, so perhaps it just happened to be headed in the same direction we were.

But I wasn't sure about that. Not sure at all. Not after the things I'd experienced.

"What's wrong?" Riley asked.

I stole another glance behind me. "I think we're being followed."

"Why would someone be following us?"

"I have no idea. It's all very confusing. It can't possibly have anything to do with me sticking my nose where it doesn't belong."

"Of course. It can't possibly." He threw me a knowing look. "Can you tell anything about the vehicle? All I can see are the headlights."

I shifted for a better glance. After we'd been run off a

mountain road in West Virginia last month, I felt more cautious about the whole being followed thing. It was no joke.

The glaring headlights did make it harder to tell much about the make and model. "I think it's a SUV. That doesn't really help."

Riley's muscles clenched. "I'm going to turn and see if they keep following us."

At the next cross street, Riley veered off the main highway. I held my breath, watching to see if the vehicle would follow us. To see if this would turn ugly.

To my relief, the driver kept going straight.

But as I stole one more glance at it, I noticed a dent in the back bumper.

Just like the vehicle that had pulled away after Katarina had nearly been abducted in the mall parking garage.

CHAPTER
FOURTEEN

"YOU BROUGHT ME TO AN OLD, rundown hotel?" Riley asked, peering out the windshield with a frown. "I mean, if you really wanted to get away for the evening, certainly there are other places . . ."

"Overnight dates are always welcome. But that's not why we're here. I have a little more class than this."

"So why are we here?"

I heaved in a deep breath. "I thought it would be an interesting change of scenery to have a picnic in the shadow of part of our city's history—"

"Gabby . . ."

I shrugged, knowing good and well that he could see through my tongue-in-cheek excuse. "Greg Borski is staying here."

He gave me a knowing look. "You could have just said that."

"It wouldn't have been nearly as fun."

He clicked off the ignition and leaned back. "Okay, then. Let's make the most of this. It's not exactly the romantic location I'd conjured up in my mind."

"Darling, anywhere with you is romantic to me." I said it in my best Southern belle drawl.

He smiled, leaned toward me, and planted a kiss on my lips. For a moment, I felt like a teenager making out in the driveway. Not that I had ever done that . . . but it actually wasn't a bad idea. Except, that wasn't why I was here.

When I collapsed back into my seat, I reached down and opened the bag beneath me. I began pulling out the various goodies I'd packed for him. "Okay, let's eat."

He took a deli meat rollup. "Do you know if Borski is even here?"

I nodded toward his truck. "He should be. And that's his room." I pointed to 289.

"You've been here before."

"Of course." I pulled out my own sandwich and unwrapped it. The bread was semi-stale, but it would do.

"What do you think we'll see?"

"No idea. But I know that Borski is the only one I've encountered who has motive, means, and opportunity."

"Why would he leave the body in the freezer at his restaurant and implicate himself?"

I pressed my lips together. "That's a good question. I do know that he handles all of the produce and meats himself. Maybe no one else used the freezer. There was a lock on the door."

"But still . . . he could have left her somewhere far away from anything associated with him. Then no one would be looking at him. Not so quickly, at least."

"That's . . . true." I had no rebuttal for that. Either he wasn't smart, or he'd been set up. "What if someone set Borski up?" Riley seemed to read my thoughts.

"Why would they do that?" I knew the answer, but I needed to talk it out.

"Why would they do it to anyone? Because they disliked him. They wanted to frame him. They want to see him suffer in some way. Probably for one of many reasons."

I remembered the food critic Borski had threatened. But that seemed desperate. Why not just kill Borski and let Emma Jean live?

I had so many questions and so few answers right now.

"Let's think about this." I began ticking reasons off, counting them finger by finger. "Borski is in major debt. I can only assume that's why he's living here at the hotel. His restaurant is about to go under. He has an explosive temper. And Emma Jean could get under the skin of the most levelheaded person. She was probably holding something over his head."

Riley finished his turkey rollup and grabbed the bag of almonds. "How does this tie in with Bill then?"

That was the question of the hour. "It doesn't make complete sense that the crimes are separate. While I know that coincidences happen, the timing on this one is too uncanny. But I still have no idea what the connection is."

"Keep sifting through the pieces, and eventually some answers will emerge."

"I hope so. Because this one has me puzzled." I took a bite of my turkey sandwich. I hadn't realized how hungry I was.

Riley flipped on the radio. Bill wasn't on at this hour, but another talking head was. And, of course, the topic was the elections. Everyone was worried that this third party candidate would split the vote and effectively give the election to Ed Stead."

I spotted someone walking toward Borski's hotel room. I squinted.

Was that . . . the Nordic god who'd saved Katarina from the bad guy in the parking garage? It was! Why was he here?

He paused at Borski's room. A moment later, he slipped inside. Borski glanced around, scanning his surroundings as if to spot anyone spying on them, and then shut the door.

"What is going on?" I muttered. "That's not a coincidence. I won't believe it."

"Who is that guy?"

I filled Riley in.

"And the plot thickens," He muttered.

"He's the connection in these cases right now. But it doesn't make any sense . . . He saved Katarina at the parking garage."

"Okay . . ."

"But if Borski killed Emma Jean, and this man is friends with Borski, how is Katarina in this at all?"

"That's a great question."

"I should go confront them." I grabbed the door handle.

Riley's hand circled my bicep, and he pulled me back. "No, you shouldn't. If he's guilty, what makes you think he won't kill you too?"

I bit my bottom lip. "That could be true, but . . . how am I ever going to find answers?"

"You always do, Gabby. Always."

I fought a sigh. I had to do something. The answers were probably all waiting for me in that hotel room. If only it was as easy as charging inside and demanding the truth.

"Let's wait until the man emerges and follow him," I finally said.

"That's a plan I'm more comfortable with." Riley

leaned back in his seat again, finally convinced I wouldn't dart out of the car at any moment.

We waited ten minutes. Then Nordic god emerged, climbed into a gray sedan, and took off down the road. Riley counted ten seconds and then eased the car out of the lot.

I'd trained him well.

We cruised down the highway, keeping Mr. Nordic in our sights as he wound down various Norfolk roads.

"He's onto us, Riley," I murmured.

"Why would you say that?"

"Look at how he's driving. He's obviously not going anywhere. He's just seeing if we're following."

"What should we do?"

"Keep following. We don't have anything to lose at this point."

"As you wish."

At that moment, Mr. Nordic accelerated—rapidly.

"Uh oh," I muttered. "This will be interesting."

We stayed behind him. Ahead, I saw a traffic signal turn red. The great equalizer, I realized. We'd catch up with him there.

But instead of slowing down, the driver sped up. He dashed through the intersection, leaving an army of cars honking and slamming on brakes.

Riley slowed to a stop and sent me an apologetic glance. "Sorry, Gabby. I couldn't risk it."

"I didn't expect anything less." I pressed my lips together, fighting my frustration. His decision had been a smart one. But I'd really wanted to figure out who the man was and why he was meeting with Borski.

"What now?"

"I guess we head home." I leaned back, letting my

thoughts wander. "What if the real connection all along was between Katarina and Borski? What if Katarina wanted to kill Emma Jean?"

"Why would she want to kill Emma Jean?"

"Kill the competition?" My words were unconvincing.

"I really don't think Katarina felt threatened by Emma Jean."

"No, me neither . . ." I chewed on my fingernail a minute. "Maybe both Katarina and Borski are secretly a part of the Russian mafia like you suggested."

"I don't think I ever said mafia."

"You suggested they were connected because they both have Russian surnames."

"That's a far cry from suggesting they're a part of the mafia."

"True . . ." What was it with me and politically incorrect conversations lately? That was just one more thing I could check off my list of possible careers in the future, along with Secret Service: politician.

But I needed to keep those ideas in my mind because you never knew when they'd come in handy.

———

Bill didn't get home until after ten o'clock, but I waited up for him because we had to talk. As soon as I heard him open the front door, I rushed downstairs to confront—I mean, meet—to *meet* him.

"Gabby, you'll never believe this," he started, either ignoring the agitated expression on my face or not noticing it. "Guess who mentioned me today?"

I crossed my arms, not really caring. "Who?"

"The President."

I squinted. "The president of what? The radio station?"

He looked like a kid at Christmas who'd just gotten everything he asked for. He was absolutely giddy. "POTUS. Yes, you heard it correctly. The President of the United States."

"No way." I didn't believe him.

Bill pulled out his keys and switched his briefcase into his other hand so he could unlock his door. "He was stumping for Munich at a campaign rally in Cleveland. Of course. And he went off on this tirade about the negative attention and false rumors Munich was getting. He said it was all because of talk show hosts like me. Me! Can you believe it? I've made it to the big time, Gabby."

"That's . . . great." What was I supposed to say to that? It was exciting, but that didn't change the fact that I was annoyed with him.

He paused from unlocking his door long enough to spread his arms in the air. "Soon, living here will be a distant memory. It's been nice, but I need a house that represents my success, don't you think?"

I felt slightly insulted. "Only if you can afford it."

"My income has tripled in the past few months."

"But will you be able to sustain it?"

"Why wouldn't I? It's all about exposure. I've been exposed!"

Most people wouldn't be delighting in that kind of exposure, especially given his current circumstances.

He paused from his rambling and stared at me. Then his face tightened, as if realization had struck him. He finally realized I wasn't acting like my normal self and that I had something to say.

His shoulders slumped ever so slightly, and he let out a

breath, as if preparing himself for the confrontation that was going to happen.

"What's going on?" He shoved his keys back in his pocket.

"We need to talk."

He pushed his door open and extended his hand in what looked like a begrudging motion. "Come on in."

I went inside and stood by the door with my arms crossed.

I didn't waste any time. "You and Katarina frequently went to eat at The Crispy Biscuit, even though Emma Jean worked there?"

He paced into the kitchen and poured himself some hard liquor into a shot glass. Normally, I wouldn't encourage that. But Bill's lips became even looser when he drank, so I didn't argue—this time.

"We did. It's Katarina's favorite restaurant."

"Come on, Bill. That's crass."

He ran a hand over his face, jangling the glass in his hand. "I know, okay? I wasn't really in favor of it. But The Crispy Biscuit has really good food. We tried to go in the evening when Emma Jean wasn't working. But she was a workaholic. She was always there."

"There are plenty of other restaurants."

"Katarina likes that one. Always fresh, never frozen."

"Yeah, we see how that worked out," I muttered.

"I don't know what else to say." He threw back the shot.

I shifted. "Does Katarina know Greg Borski?"

"No, not that she's mentioned him. Why?"

"They're both Russian."

He snorted. "Next thing you'll be saying she's a part of the Russian mafia."

I almost affirmed his statement but decided it was better if I didn't.

"Something isn't fitting, Bill." I narrowed my eyes. "What was she holding over you, Bill?"

He poured himself another shot of caramel-colored liquid. "Who? Katarina?"

"No, Emma Jean. She had leverage over everyone, it seems."

He snorted again and took another swallow of liquor. "She wasn't holding anything over me."

I doubted that. "But if she was, that would give you motive also, wouldn't it?"

"I asked you to help me, not to find me guilty, Gabby." His eyes clouded and he toddled across the room, drink in hand, and plopped on the couch. "If you're going to point the finger at me, then you're fired."

"I'm trying to get answers, but that's hard when you're not being truthful with me. Besides, you can't fire me. You haven't even paid me."

He ran a hand over his face again. "It's nothing. Not really. I mean, she was going to release some of my tax records."

I jammed my hip against the wall and crossed my arms. "What's the big deal about that? I mean, other than the fact that it wasn't her place."

He sloshed his drink around the glass again. "The thing is that when Philip Munich was first running for office— for senator back then—I gave money to his campaign."

"But you hate Munich."

"I do now. But I've evolved over the years. Emma Jean thought that factoid would ruin my success because people would think I was a hypocrite. If she ruined me, then I'd lose money and then I'd lose Katarina. Emma Jean thought that when that happened, I would come back to her."

"She had it all thought out, didn't she?" Conniving. That summed up Emma Jean in a nutshell.

"Emma Jean had everything thought out."

I mulled over that fact a moment. "Why did you give to Philip Munich's campaign? When did you donate . . . Didn't he run for office for the first time ten years ago or something? Weren't you doing your show back then?"

His face fell even further. "Sometimes life and politics can get messy, Gabby."

I chewed on his words a moment.

Bill downed another shot before slamming his glass on the table. He stared at me, his eyes already bloodshot and his words slurring. "I didn't kill Emma Jean for it, Gabby. I know that's what you're wondering. But I didn't do it."

CHAPTER
FIFTEEN

I HAD a workshop the next morning. Thankfully, it was only a few cities south in Elizabeth City, North Carolina.

In between my sessions, I had lunch at a local deli with a few of the officers I was training. I downed a turkey club and delicious homemade potato chips in between chatting up Gray Tech, my company, like a good, little employee. While they began talking about things privy to their city, I escaped to the waiting area for a moment to check my messages.

I wanted to make sure my boss hadn't emailed me and that there were no updates I'd missed. Plus, I didn't really care about city parking violation codes. Not in the least.

When I glanced at my phone, I was surprised to see one of my social media feeds blowing up. What in the world . . .?

I began scrolling through the posts that had been made on my pages. They were all . . . hateful.

You're an idiot if you're friends with Bill McCormick.

People like you make me sick.

If you support someone who's hateful, that makes you hateful. And a bigot. And a generally bad person.

My mouth dropped open. Oh. My. Word. What had happened to instigate this?

"I'm sorry. I didn't mean to do that to you."

I swirled around and saw a man standing there. He wore a fedora, glasses, and had a dopey grin on his face. I'd never seen him before.

He extended his hand. "Godfrey Arnold."

I narrowed my eyes when I recognized the blogger's name. "What are you doing here? Are you following me? And what exactly didn't you mean to do to me?"

"One at a time!" He chuckled, not the least bit bothered by our conversation. "I'm here because I'm following you. And I didn't mean for so many people to post so many ugly, nasty messages on your social media profiles. Not really."

My eyebrows shot up. I didn't even know which of his faults to address first. "Why are you following me?"

"I want a quote on Bill."

"You're out of your mind. I'm here with police officers, for goodness sake!" I glanced over at my table full of trainees. None of them were paying a bit of attention to this situation.

Traitors.

Godfrey shrugged, seeming to notice their disinterest also. "Not really worried about it."

"And you're saying that you did something to incite your rabid fans to post hateful messages?" The longer I talked to this guy, the more outraged I felt. There should be a social media jail that would ban people from being on the Internet as their sentence. Maybe I'd start a GoFundMe campaign to get that initiative off the ground.

He shrugged again, still unbothered. "My latest blog post may have encouraged people to be vigilant in their beliefs by taking a stand against anyone who stood in their way. There's a lot at stake during this election. We must use whatever means necessary."

"How is threatening me on social media at all necessary? How am I standing in your way? I didn't do anything!"

"If it wasn't for you, Bill McCormick may not be here with us right now."

I could not have heard this man correctly. I shook my head, hoping my ears would start working properly again. "Were you the one who tried to shoot him?"

Finally, his glib façade cracked. He glanced at the cops, as if nervous they'd heard me. "No, of course not. How could you think that? I shoot arrows with my words."

"But you wish the man had gotten shot? How am I supposed to interpret that?"

"I didn't say that." He frowned. "I only implied he would have been shot if it weren't for you."

I stepped toward him and lowered my voice. "You, little man, are a smug, sad excuse for a human. You need to start talking right now and tell me exactly what you're planning before I start talking really loud."

All his glibness scampered away liked a scared rabbit. "Okay, okay. Do I need to remind you that there are cops over there?"

"They're on my side. Not yours. Believe me, you little weasel." I wasn't sure I'd actually ever called anyone that before. I kind of liked it.

He raised his hands as he took a step back and hit the wall behind him. One of the framed newspaper articles about the place rocked back and forth on impact. "I may have shared your social media links on my website. I would have just given your email address, but I couldn't find it."

"Why would you do that?" I felt so exposed. Bill might enjoy the feeling—thrive on it, even—but I didn't.

"Just to put more pressure on Bill McCormick."

"Why?"

"Because he stands to ruin Philip Munich, of course."

"What in the world are you talking about? How could one talk show host ruin a presidential candidate? He has outlandish theories that no one believes, but it makes for good ratings."

"He knows something." Veins popped out on Godfrey's neck.

"What does he know?"

His hands went up higher. If the situation was different, I might think he was using jazz hands. "I don't know. But it could apparently ruin Munich's chances."

"The info is that juicy?"

Godfrey nodded. "That's what I hear."

"And where did you hear this?"

"I have my sources."

I stepped closer and lowered my voice to a threatening growl. "Godfrey . . ."

"Someone who works at the radio station told me. Okay? Bill is waiting until two weeks before the election to reveal it. He hopes Munich won't have time to recover and he'll lose. Are you happy now?"

"I'm thrilled," I deadpanned. "You need to tell people to stop posting on my social media."

"It's a free country."

"We'll see how free you feel when you end up in jail."

"You're being a bully."

CUNNING ATTRACTIONS   141

"You're the one who followed me here. Need I remind you of that?"

He sneered but rolled his shoulders back. "I guess you won't be giving me a quote?"

"Over my dead body."

"You keep defending Bill McCormick and your wish may come true."

CHAPTER
SIXTEEN

IRONICALLY, I had a parking ticket when I left the deli. Go figure. I'd briefly considered begging for leniency, but I hadn't.

After the workshop, as I drove home, I mulled over what I knew.

All the signs pointed to Borski as Emma Jean's killer. But that didn't explain who shot at Bill, who was potentially following me, or who had attempted to abduct Katarina. Whether the cases were related or not, I wasn't sure. Bill and the violence around him seemed to be connected with the election. I saw no connection with Emma Jean and politics except Bill. Altogether, it was a big, confusing mess.

Jerry called me right as I hit the strip of highway beside the Great Dismal Swamp—a dark, haunting place where I'd almost died at the hands of a serial killer. I was glad for the distraction of talking to him.

He informed me that Emma Jean's house had been cleared, and I was now free to check it out. He asked if I could wait until tomorrow because he had a meeting with his lawyer tonight. I supposed that was just fine.

"One more thing, Jerry. Did Emma Jean have any friends?"

He was quiet for a long minute. "Maybe try Sarah Babble. I don't know if they were friends, per se, but Emma Jean talked about doing things with her. It's more than I can say about most people Emma Jean knew."

After I hung up. I pulled over and did a quick Internet search for Sarah Babble. There was only one woman by that name who popped up in my area, and she worked at an old drive-in restaurant in Norfolk named Lunar's. I knew where I was headed next.

It took me nearly an hour to get there and, thankfully, by the time I arrived, I was hungry. The challenging part would be parking . . . um, booth? . . . where Sarah would be my server. If she was even working today. There were a lot of ifs in this.

I pulled into the lot and fought the blaring sun as I looked around. Finally, I spotted a carhop on roller skates who resembled Sarah's social media photo. She glided toward a truck parked at a spot to my left.

I steered that way and pulled into the one empty space in that section. At once, memories hit me. Memories of the good days of my childhood when my mom would bring me here in between working her many jobs. She'd clerked at a drugstore and cleaned houses and delivered newspapers and sold Avon. But every once in a while, she would tuck away enough money after paying bills for a treat.

We'd come to Lunar's, and I'd always order a barbecue sandwich, fries, and a milkshake. My mom would get water and a hot dog and claim it was because that's what she liked. I hadn't put it together until I was older that it was because money was so tight.

Pushing the memories aside, I lowered my window, pressed a button on the screen beside me, and waited for Sarah to skate on over. She did exactly that two minutes later.

"What can I get for you?"

The woman was nothing like what I'd expected a friend of Emma Jean's to look like. Perhaps it wasn't kind, but this woman looked too normal to be friends with Emma Jean. She was in her thirties; she was fit; and she had a great smile that emanated positivity. Her long hair was braided on each side. She wore blue eye shadow and pink lip gloss. I couldn't see any similarities to Emma Jean except they were both women.

"I'd like one barbecue sandwich and as many answers you can provide to some questions about Emma Jean," I started with an innocent flutter of my eyelashes.

Her bubble gum smile slipped. "Emma Jean? How'd you connect me with her?"

"Long story . . ." I shook my head as soon as I heard the flimsy excuse leave my lips. "Actually, it's not. Jerry told me about you."

"Her ex?" She twisted her lips in surprise.

I nodded.

"Who are you?"

"Someone who's trying to figure out what happened to her," I said. "I heard you might have some answers."

She glanced around. "I have a break in five minutes. I'll bring you your sandwich, and we can talk. Sound good?"

"Sounds perfect. Oh, and can you add some fries to that?"

"Sure thing. And a pumpkin shake too?"

I grinned. "I can't resist pumpkin."

Five minutes later, Sarah was seated beside me in my car. Sure enough, she'd brought a sandwich, fries, and shake with her, and the tangy smell of vinegar-based barbecue tantalized my senses.

"First of all, I'm really sorry for your loss."

She nodded. "Thank you."

"How did you two know each other?" I had to get that question off my chest first.

She frowned. "Emma Jean and I met in anger management class. She was my mentor."

Anger management class? I wasn't surprised, now knowing what I did about Emma Jean. But Sarah, on the other hand, seemed like the antitheses of Emma Jean.

"I see. Do you have any theories about what happened to her?"

She sighed and stared out the window. "I have no idea. Honestly, there are so many people I can think of who would want her dead."

Hearing that didn't even faze me anymore. "Like who?"

"Greg, to start with."

Good old Borski. "You're not the only one who's mentioned him. Do you know him through Emma Jean?"

"You should say that."

"Why do you suspect him?"

"Greg is just vindictive and arrogant. He lives in his own little world where everything he does is perfect and everything everyone else does is flawed." Her voice lost its perk and replaced it with bitterness.

"You have strong feelings." I couldn't wait to eat any longer. I took a bite of my paper-wrapped sandwich and let the tangy vinegar mixed with sweet coleslaw delight my taste buds.

"I went out on a date with him once. It didn't go well." She rolled her eyes.

"I see." Scorn could explain a lot of things. Just like a good barbecue sandwich could make everything better.

She locked gazes with me, and I paused from chowing down. "You know how she got the job there, right?"

"No idea."

"The two of them met at anger management class."

I shook my head. "What? Really? That's how you know him also?"

She nodded. "Yeah, we all three met there. I'm not sure how she managed to get a job from him still because the two never liked each other. I'm sure she used leverage."

"What do you mean?"

"Emma Jean was always holding things over people's heads. She had a way of digging up dirt and then using that to get what she wanted."

"Including Borski?"

Sarah shrugged. "I can't say that for sure. But I know she was always griping about the restaurant. I couldn't blame her. I mean, Greg would switch out regular produce and put it into organic bins so that everyone wouldn't know how he was cutting costs. He bought frozen meat. Sometimes he even bought stuff from China. For people who are immersed in the world of natural eating, the last place they want their food from is China."

"That is the ultimate sin for food purists." Actually, I wasn't a food purist, and the idea of food from China turned my stomach. Speaking of food . . . I took a sip of my pumpkin milkshake. Autumn came alive in my mouth.

Colorful leaves, hayrides, and mountain streams sprang up.

Not really. But it was yummy.

"I do know she recently got a raise."

Now *that* was interesting. "But Borski was having money troubles."

She nodded and snitched one of my fries. "I know. I suspect there was more to it."

"I'd say." I shifted, rattling my milkshake back and forth to get more of the dairy goodness within reach of my straw. "Is there anyone else who comes to mind who might have had a beef with Emma Jean? Or that she had some serious information on?"

Sarah stared out the windshield and twisted her lips together. "I thought what she was doing to Jerry was wrong."

Jerry? She was doing something to Jerry? "What was that?"

"She kept threatening to tell the judge that Jerry had cheated on her with his new girlfriend. She wanted to get custody of AJ."

I blinked. "Really? She'd go as far as to lie?"

"I'm not sure. Maybe. Or maybe she really believed it. I just know that Jerry loves AJ. He was furious. Said nothing would get in the way of him and his son."

Jerry did, huh? Maybe the biker dude wasn't as innocent as he'd pretended to be.

And maybe, just maybe, my suspect list was finally growing.

After all, I needed to keep my options open in case Borski fell through.

CHAPTER
SEVENTEEN

DESPITE WHAT HAD HAPPENED last night, I decided to check out Emma Jean's house the next morning. Riley decided to go with me since it was before work, and we hadn't seen each other the day before. I knew he'd be going to do some more training after work today, so I was grateful that I could spend some time with him now.

Jerry didn't say much when we arrived. He simply let us inside and asked us to lock up before we left. He seemed more somber today and less angry and abrasive. Perhaps reality was kicking in. Grief could take on so many ugly forms. I knew it because I'd lived it.

Emma Jean's house was a small bungalow in an area of Norfolk known as Colonial Place. I'd expected the residence to be a wreck, just as her life seemed to have been.

Instead it was orderly, and simple. Based on the pictures all around the house, she'd really loved AJ. That realization made my heart ache.

Before this, she'd been only a caricature of a person. Someone Bill liked to talk about. Someone I imagined in my mind.

But seeing her home made her real. She may have been flawed, but she'd loved life in her own way.

"What are you thinking?" Riley asked as I stared at a photo.

"About how I shouldn't make assumptions about people. There was more to Emma Jean than her opinions and abrasiveness."

"Kind of like the lady who confronted you at church on Sunday? We make a lot of assumptions. Let a lot of things define other people in our minds. But people are complex."

"Agreed." I set the photo back down and glanced behind me. "Where to start? Isn't that the question?"

"Why don't you check her desk and I'll look through the kitchen?" Riley suggested.

"Seems like just as good a plan as any. Hopefully, the police left something for us." I strode across the room and sat down in her office chair. The only thing that caught my eye atop the desk was her calendar. As hard as I studied the dates there, nothing stood out.

I went through all the drawers and found nothing. No incriminating notes, unusual appointments, or strange and mysterious bills.

We moved through the rest of the house, but halfway through I'd found nothing of value to the investigation.

"I'm going to keep looking since I only have one room left," I told Riley. "I just want to be certain."

"Knock yourself out."

The last room I reached was Emma Jean's bedroom. I sat down on the edge of the mattress and picked up another picture of AJ. As I went to set it down, the bottom slid out. Pictures escaped.

Carefully, I pulled them out.

They were pictures of Katarina. And it didn't appear the woman was aware the photos were being taken. In one she was standing on the street corner with a phone to her ear. In another she was driving somewhere, sunglasses over her eyes.

I dug deeper and saw some older photos, including one of Katarina with a man, probably college-aged. They had their arms around each other and dopey smiles on their faces.

I quickly took my phone out and took some snapshots of the photos, just in case they came in handy later.

Things had just taken an interesting turn.

I was tired of beating around the bush. It was time for me to talk to Greg Borski.

I dropped Riley off at the apartment so he could get to work, and then I headed to the motel where Borski had been staying. I didn't mention that to Riley, however.

When I got there, Borski's truck was nowhere to be seen.

In what felt like an exercise in futility, I headed back to The Crispy Biscuit. Sure enough, his truck was parked behind the building, despite the gigantic CLOSED FOR BUSINESS sign hung out front.

Had he decided to shut the place down? For good? Or just until things blew over?

Emma Jean's death may have been the straw that broke the camel's back. They were already in dire straits, and now this. If word leaked about Borski's food ethics, this place would definitely be done.

I needed to talk to Borski.

I paused at the backdoor. I wondered if I should let someone know that I was here—just in case.

Then I decided that would be overkill, which was a terrible word to use when thinking about a murderer.

I could handle myself here. I grabbed the handle but paused again.

No, I couldn't just charge inside and confront a potential killer. The old me would have. The new me tried not to be so impulsive. I should be smart.

With that in mind, I dialed Detective Adams's number. He didn't answer. After a moment of contemplation, I left a message.

"Hi, Detective Adams. This is Gabby. I have some information on Emma Jean Lewis's death. Could you call me back? Thanks."

With that done, I knocked on the backdoor. No one answered.

I wiggled the doorknob, surprised when it turned.

It was unlocked.

I pushed it open and stuck my head inside. "Hello?"

Silence answered.

Cautiously, I stepped inside. After all, that's what the quiet was practically inviting me to do . . . right?

The place looked unchanged from when I'd been here last. But it looked empty. I was surprised no one was packing up or restocking or prepping for future business.

I didn't hear any sign of movement. Which was strange since the place was unlocked.

I took another step and then another until I was standing in the center of the kitchen.

I still saw no one. "This is Gabby . . . I mean, Gassy. I left my duct tape here and wanted to pick it up."

Taking another step, I peered into Borski's office. It was also empty.

Everyone could be in the dining area, I supposed.

The door to the freezer, I noticed, was open. Was someone inside?

I walked toward it, opening the door farther so I could see inside. I pushed through the plastic tabs at the entrance and glanced around.

No, it was empty also.

All of this working myself up so I could talk to Borski appeared to be for nothing. He wasn't here. I, at least, needed to grab my duct tape.

I started to turn to leave when something hit my shoulder. The next thing I knew, I was on the icy cold floor of the freezer, and the door slammed behind me.

CHAPTER
EIGHTEEN

MY PALMS BURNED against the freezing floor as I pushed myself up. I rushed toward the door, desperate to escape.

Just as I threw myself against the door, I heard the lock click in place. I pushed the safety release, but nothing happened.

Someone had intentionally locked me in here.

I banged on the door, knowing I was wasting my breath. But my survival instinct wouldn't let me stop. "Let me out!"

The only person who could hear me was the person who'd locked me in here. I doubted he'd be letting me out.

Who would have done this? Only one person came to mind.

Greg Borski. Again. Why did everything seem to point to him?

I couldn't worry about that now. I had to worry about getting out of here before I froze to death. The whole Gassy turning into a solid state of ice joke I'd made when I'd been cleaning this area suddenly didn't seem so funny.

I glanced around. The light above me was dim, making it hard to see. Frost drifted around me, adding an unwelcome atmosphere.

I shivered. Already. My nose tingled and my fingers burned with cold from their encounter with the frigid floor and wall.

I studied the space around me. Shelves lined the sides. Most of the food was gone, but a few boxes remained. I glanced at the ceiling, knowing there was no escape hatch, but hoping there would be one anyway. What was I going to do?

That's when it hit me. My phone! I could call for help.

Relief flushed through me, along with embarrassment. Why hadn't I thought of that before?

But when I looked at my screen, I realized I had no signal. The thick walls of the freezer blocked any cell-phone reception.

My relief, which had caused my stress to melt like a puddle inside me, instantly froze with tension again.

This wasn't good. It wasn't good at all. No one knew I was in here except the person who wanted to harm me. He wouldn't be rushing to help any time soon.

Dear Lord, please help me now. Again. I know I ask this a lot.

At least I'd worn a sweatshirt.

As I shivered again, I realized that this sweatshirt wasn't going to keep me warm enough. Especially not my feet, which were clad with my customary flip-flops.

Okay, think, Gabby. Think. There has to be a way to get out of this.

I needed to stay warm until someone came looking for me. By my best estimations, that would be at least six hours from now. That's when Riley would try to call. I wouldn't answer. He would get worried and start looking for me.

Except he would go to work out at the gym tonight. What if he didn't call me like he normally did? After all, we had seen each other this morning for an extended time. He might decide it was okay to wait.

No, I couldn't think like that. I had to stay positive.

I looked around again. All the walls and the floor and ceiling were made with galvanized metal. It was cold and frosty. Just like I'd be in about an hour.

I needed to trap my body heat before it escaped from my feet, arms, and head.

Thankfully, I'd left my utility knife and duct tape. I'd had no idea how that would come in handy now.

I had to be careful not to move so much that I would start sweating. Perspiration would only make me cooler in the long run.

With that thought, I cut down some of the plastic slats hanging in the doorway. I used the duct tape to strap the plastic around my feet.

It wasn't pretty, but it would keep me warm for a little while. I then taped the bottom of my jeans 80s peg style. If I wasn't careful I'd start singing some Debbie Gibson or Tiffany. I knew one thing: No one would be getting lost in my eyes or wanting to be alone with me if I was dressed like this.

Everything about me was already cold, I realized with a shiver.

Okay, you still have to keep your hands warm. And your head.

I cut down another one of the plastic slats, made a circle out of it, and taped it together. Then I used another slat to cover the top, and I taped it there.

My breath came out in icy puffs around me. As I worked, my fingers became more and more numb.

Of all the things I'd expected to happen today, this was not one of them.

When I finished, I took my creation and placed it on top of my head. It was a hat. Of sorts. At least my body heat should escape from me more slowly this way.

Watch out, Project Runway. There's a new player in town.

I taped another slat around my neck loosely.

I looked like a frozen mummy. Or Madonna in one of her strange outfits.

It wasn't a good look. But this was no time to be vain.

Now I need to stay still.

I glanced around. The boxes were my best hope. I grabbed a couple and stacked them in each other to make them stronger. Then I set the boxes in the center of the freezer—being too close to the walls would only make me chillier. I plopped myself on top.

All I could do now was wait it out . . . and maybe make some duct tape mittens. At least it would help to occupy my thoughts.

Before I did that, I glanced at my phone.

Had it only been forty minutes? That couldn't possibly be right.

I was already so cold. How would I make it five hours or more?

I wasn't sure I would.

I sat on the little box chair I'd made on the floor and tried to remain calm.

How can I stay calm? I need to do something I enjoy and distract myself.

Like by singing.

But the only song that came to mind was "Do You Want to Build a Snowman?" from Frozen.

I was going to be a snowman by the end of this, if I wasn't careful.

The song didn't give me the warm fuzzies I'd hoped for.

Why would the killer, presumably Borski, have left Emma Jean here?

Either he thought he was brilliant enough to get away with it.

Or . . . he'd put her here with the intentions of moving her.

The idea hit me like a lightning bolt.

Maybe he had plans to move her. To put her somewhere else. To implicate someone innocent.

The more I thought about the idea, the more sense it made.

I needed to explore this possibility.

But I had to get out of here first.

I'd been watching the time for the past three hours. With my luck, my phone was going to die, and then I'd really feel lost. I couldn't even get Internet, but maybe it was better that way because I might be tempted to read all the nasty messages people were leaving me on social media.

At least it would be something to pass time. Then again, my makeshift duct tape mittens made it hard to do anything.

Was all of this really worth it?

Yes, it was, I decided. Bringing a killer to justice brought me immeasurable satisfaction.

Being a victim? It wasn't my first choice.

I glanced at my phone again, as if it would magically hold the answers.

I'd been in here for three hours and fifty minutes. I tried to mentally calculate how long I could last in here, and the number I kept coming back to was six hours.

That gave me approximately two hours until I . . .

No, I couldn't think like that.

Someone was going to find me. But had I told Detective Adams where I was? For a smart girl, that hadn't been a smart move.

I drew my knees toward me. As I did, I heard movement outside.

Was it Borski? Had he come back to make sure I was well on my way to dying?

Or was it someone who could help me?

I decided to take a chance. If I was going to go out, I was going to go out fighting for my life.

I stood and began pounding on the door. "Help me! I'm in here!"

"Gabby?"

My heart surged. Was it actually my husband? "Riley? Is that you?"

"Stay put. We're going to get you out of there."

Suddenly, it seemed like the cold factor tripled. I was going into hypothermia, I realized. If I wasn't careful, my extremities would get frostbitten.

Riley had arrived just in time.

Now if only he could get me out of here in time.

Keep calm. If you panic, you'll breathe too fast. It won't help your cause right now.

"Gabby, do you know where the key is?"

Someone else asked me that question. Was it Detective Adams?

"I have no idea," I called. "Someone locked me in here."

"How long have you been in there?"

"Four hours," I said, my teeth chattering uncontrollably.

"An ambulance is on the way," Adams said. "As soon as you're out of there, we're going to get you taken care of."

"Okay. No pressure, but hurry. I can't feel my hands." Or my nose or toes or brain.

"We're going to get some tools and see if we can pry this open," Riley said.

Go get tools? That meant they were leaving me.

That thought caused the panic to kick in.

My breaths came faster. Which meant my oxygen was running out in here.

I'd tried to avoid that thought.

But I could no longer do that.

I knew that the freezer was approximately twenty-by-ten feet, which left me with about 1600 cubic feet of air. When I first became locked in the space, it contained 20 percent oxygen and no carbon dioxide.

Without breathing too quickly, the average person when resting used 2800 cubic feet of air per day. Since I was exhaling, I was turning part of the already-limited oxygen into carbon dioxide, and it was happening at a rate faster than I'd like to acknowledge. When the carbon dioxide became greater than 5 percent, it would become fatal.

All that was to say I was on borrowed time.

"We found something, Gabby." Riley's voice filled me with comfort again.

He was back. Thank goodness.

My head was starting to swim.

If I let myself, my eyelids would droop. But if that happened, I probably wouldn't be waking up.

Against my better senses, I leaned against the door. It was cold. Really cold. My skin stung as I touched it.

But I was fading. Fast. I just wanted to be out of here. To be with Riley.

To catch the person who'd done this.

But, before I could, I slid down onto the floor. I closed my eyes and surrendered to my exhaustion.

CHAPTER
NINETEEN

"GABBY! Don't you go to sleep on me!"

I pulled my eyes open and saw Riley standing there. No, he wasn't standing there. He was holding me. His gaze looked urgent, alarmed . . . worried.

I was on the floor, I realized.

Not in the freezer.

I didn't think so, at least. I thought I was in the kitchen at The Crispy Biscuit. Had they rescued me in time? Reality blended with delusion.

Or was I dreaming? I wasn't sure.

Before I could ask any questions, medics surrounded me. An oxygen mask was strapped over my nose and mouth. Warm blankets were piled on top of me. I was hauled onto a stretcher. It all seemed like a blur.

Riley stayed at my side the entire time, even in the ambulance.

"I'm fine," I muttered on the ride to the hospital. My body rocked back and forth in cadence with the vehicle. Paramedics stared at me like aliens who'd beamed me aboard their spacecraft in the middle of the night before doing experiments on me.

"You need to be checked out," Riley said, gripping my hand. "Just in case."

The cold flashed back to me. The moments of hopelessness. Despair that felt more frigid than this election season.

"That was close, Riley," I whispered.

He peered at me and nodded. I saw the worry in his eyes. He'd been afraid of losing me.

"I know."

"How'd you find me?" My voice sounded as frostbitten as my fingers felt.

"I just happened to check my Friend Finder app."

I smiled, and my cracked lips rebelled with pain. We'd had some tense conversations about that app. It seemed invasive, yet oh-so-helpful.

"I showed up? My cell signal was blocked."

"It showed your last location before the screen went blank. When you didn't answer, I became concerned. I decided to swing by and make sure everything was okay."

"I knew that app was a great idea."

He grinned. "I think you said it was like an electronic leash."

"But as much trouble as I get in, I was a fool to argue."

"Yes, you were." He kissed my forehead.

I wished my limbs would stop trembling and shaking and jerking. But they wouldn't, so I had to deal with it.

"Where did Adams go?"

"He's looking for Borski."

Our gazes locked. "He tried to kill me, Riley."

His eyes softened. "I know, sweetie. I know. But you're safe now."

"Only because of you."

He kissed my hand. "I'll always keep you safe, Gabby. Always."

So far, I'd been at the hospital for four hours, and I refused to let the doctors admit me to a room to keep me for observation. From what I understood, I'd be able to go home within the hour, but until then I had to stay put. Until then, I remained in my little curtained off room in the ER.

The sounds and smells of the ER caused a rush of bad memories. So many bad memories. Of my mom dying. Of Riley being in a coma. Every beep and blip made my muscles tighten. Every time I inhaled antiseptic cleaner, I felt like I might throw up.

No, I'd be much better off healing somewhere else. Not here.

Talk about a day.

Riley sat beside me.

Part of me felt slightly guilty because I knew he needed to be training. His competition was only a few days away, and he'd been working so hard. But he refused to leave me.

"By the way, I really liked your outfit," Riley said.

I glanced at him and snickered, wondering when he might bring that up. "I thought I had a certain sense of style that would make the most fashion conscious among us jealous."

"It was like Eskimo meets bag lady meets Heidi Klum."

"You know, it's funny. That was the exact look I was going for."

He shrugged with a grin. "You know what they say about great minds . . ."

At that moment, Detective Adams appeared through the curtain. "How are you feeling, Gabby?"

"I'm ready to get out of here."

He smiled. "That doesn't surprise me. You've always been stubborn."

"I'm just thankful to be alive." I shivered again. I really had wondered for a moment if that freezer was where I'd die. Thank goodness, Riley had been keeping tabs on me.

Adams paused beside my bed. "I got your voicemail. Next time, leave a location."

My cheeks warmed. Not one of my best moments. "Will do. Oh, by the way, Borski killed Emma Jean."

His eyebrows shot up. "You have definitive proof?"

"He locked me in the freezer, didn't he?"

"Did you see him with your own eyes?"

I scowled. "No."

"I do have an update."

I sat up straighter at that announcement. That already made me feel better. "Okay."

"Greg Borski claims he's innocent."

"Doesn't every criminal?" I rushed.

He raised his hand to slow me down. "He did admit that the company was in the red. He even admitted to having a temper and that Emma Jean had threatened to go public with his less-than-ethical food practices."

"That should say a lot!"

Adams grimaced. "He also claims he wasn't at the restaurant today."

My shoulders tightened. "But his truck was there!"

"He said he dropped it off this morning and met up with a friend. He's not sure why the backdoor was unlocked. No one was supposed to be working."

"And you believe him?" Certainly Adams was smarter than that.

"We're still trying to get in touch with his friend and verify the alibi."

"Did you arrest him in the meantime?"

He clucked his tongue. "We're holding him."

"How much more proof do you need? Does he even have an alibi for the night Emma Jean died? From what I've been able to ascertain, she was killed on Tuesday."

"That's also what we've determined. And, no, Mr. Borski doesn't have a strong alibi for that evening. He was at the office when she left on Tuesday. He departed about thirty minutes afterward. His employees have verified that."

He left? Did he follow her and kill her, then return to the restaurant after it closed? "Where did he go?"

"He ran errands."

"Did he list specific shops?" I knew I was hyper, but I felt like we were on the verge of discovering important information that could potentially change this case.

"He did. We will be checking his bank statements and security cameras at the stores for that time, but it's going to be a long process."

I nodded, wishing police work was faster than a speeding bullet. It was more like a slug.

He patted my hand. "So just hold tight. Get some rest tonight. You'll need it after what you went through today. Maybe by tomorrow afternoon we'll have an update for you. Okay?"

I nodded again.

"You did good work. As you always do."

"Thanks, Detective Adams. That means a lot."

CHAPTER
TWENTY

I WOKE up the next morning, grateful to be alive. To feel my husband's arms around me. To live in this apartment, surrounded by people who felt like family to me.

I did a quick assessment, wiggling my fingers and toes. As far as I could tell, I was back to normal. I could feel all of my extremities. I could breathe. And Riley's arms around me kept me warm.

"What are you thinking about?" Riley murmured beside me.

"About how grateful I am for another day. It could have been very different."

"Yes, it could have been. Please don't do that to me again." He pulled me closer.

"I wish I could promise that."

"But it never quite works out, does it?" Resignation strained his voice.

"No, it doesn't." I'd almost been killed more times than I could count at this point. And, as long as I stuck my nose where I shouldn't, that probably wouldn't change.

"Anything I can do for you?" He kissed my shoulder.

Heat rushed through me, and I turned around until we faced each other. "You can stay home today. Maybe we just stay here. Both of us. It can be like a staycation."

He offered a sleepy-eyed grin. "I wish I could. But this isn't one of those days I can miss work—unless it's an absolute emergency. I have to be in court in two hours."

I frowned and let out a slow breath. I studied his face and ran my thumb over his cheekbone, his jaw, his neck. My desire to explore the possibility of staring at those wonderful features all day had been short-lived but strong. "Are you sure?"

"You're making me less sure by the moment."

Secret delight rippled through me. "I can keep making you less sure, if you'd like."

His eyebrows flickered up. "You are very tempting."

Just as he drew me closer and our lips met, my cell phone rang on my nightstand. I tried to block out the sound. I wanted to ignore it. I really did. But . . .

Riley let out a soft sigh as I rolled away. "You should get that."

"One minute," I muttered.

"Take all the time you need. I've got to get ready for work." He climbed out of bed.

I frowned, wishing reality didn't trump desire. But it did. When I looked at who was calling, my spirits lifted. Detective Adams.

"Gabby, I hope I didn't wake you up," he started.

I glanced back at Riley as he disappeared into the bathroom. "No, I was awake."

"I have an update that I knew you'd want to hear."

I pushed myself up in bed, tugging my down comforter higher to ward away the morning chill. "Shoot."

"Greg Borski has an alibi during the time you were locked in the freezer."

I gave myself a moment to let those words sink in. "What?"

"It's true. We called the man who picked him up yesterday, and he verified they were together."

"He could be lying."

"And more than one person saw them at a restaurant they were checking out."

I pressed my lips together, unwilling to accept his conclusion "But what about during the time when Emma Jean died?"

"Some of my best men were up all night working on this. Borski's credit card purchases verify that he left the restaurant that evening and did several errands during the time we believe she was killed."

No, no, no. That was too easy!

"What if someone else was using his card?"

"Security camera footage verifies it was Borski." Adams paused. "I'm sorry, Gabby. I know this isn't what you wanted to hear. But I assure you that we're still working this case. The answers are coming slowly, but they'll come."

"No crime scene or murder weapon still?"

"No, not yet."

The crime scene would hold some answers we desperately needed. I could feel it in my bones.

"I appreciate the update," I told him.

But if Borski wasn't guilty, who was?

After Riley went to work, I did a couple of errands, including dropping off Lucky, our pet parrot, to have his nails trimmed.

I'd started back to the apartment complex, but the protesters had returned, and I didn't want to deal with them. Apparently, no one else at the complex did either because the lot was empty.

I knew Sierra was attempting to work at the office today—probably because she wanted to be with her cats. I'd seen Rhonda, leaving with Reef around the same time I'd departed earlier. Bill was at work, and Mrs. Mystery was in Florida.

How quickly those protesters had forgotten about the gunshots that had happened here over the weekend. They must not have gotten the memo that Bill was innocent, either.

Instead of dodging them, I slipped inside The Grounds and ordered a pumpkin spice latte and a pumpkin muffin. I chatted with my friend Sharon, who owned the place, for a few minutes, and then sat at the window to review my notes for an upcoming workshop.

But my mind wasn't on the workshop. My thoughts were skipping and scampering everywhere but work.

There was still a lot that didn't make sense. Maybe I was losing my touch, because every angle I examined this from didn't make sense.

Like why had Borski met with the man who saved Katarina in the parking garage?

Were these protesters truly not connected with Emma Jean's death?

I wanted this to be neat and tidy, but not all crimes were. There could be more than one thing going on here.

Focus, Gabby. Focus.

I forced myself to focus on the notes in front of me. The next two hours, I concentrated on new lighting techniques. I had to be an expert on these things if I was going to teach other people.

"I was hoping you might be here."

I looked up and did a double take when I spotted Sarah Babble standing there.

"Sarah . . . what a surprise."

She sat down across from me, reminding me of a roller derby girl. She wore a fitted baby-blue football jersey with bubble gum makeup that included glossy pink lips and sparkly blue eye shadow.

"I didn't have your number or I would have called," she said. "Sorry."

"How'd you know I was here?" My qualms rose. I'd never told her where I lived.

She opened her mouth and then shut it again, as if she'd been caught. "Truthfully?"

"Yes, please."

"You told me you were neighbors with Bill McCormick."

"Correct . . ." That still didn't explain how she knew where Bill lived.

She frowned. "Emma Jean brought me here once. I figured if you weren't home, you might be at the coffee shop."

I was obviously going to have to draw every little detail out of her. "Why did Emma Jean bring you here?"

"She was spying on Bill."

"Why was she spying on Bill?"

Sarah shrugged and then sighed. "I guess she's dead now, so it doesn't do any harm to share. As I mentioned before, Emma Jean liked to dig up dirt on people."

"I've noticed."

"She was following Bill."

"Why were you with her? To dig up dirt?"

She nodded. "We were having a mentoring session. She asked if I would ride with her. Then we showed up here. She said her ex-husband was acting suspicious lately, and she was trying to figure out why."

Apparently, Emma Jean was stalking Katarina and Bill. "Did she figure anything out?"

"She never told me."

This wasn't getting me very far. I leaned toward her. "Sarah, did Emma Jean like to do anything besides work, be a mom to AJ, and spy on people?"

She thought about it for a moment. "She started doing yoga."

I blanched. What was it with everyone doing yoga lately? "She didn't seem like the type."

"She said it helped with her anger management issues."

"I see. And where did she do yoga?"

"The Yoga Tree, I think. I figured if it would help her, then she should go for it."

I glanced across the street. Was that Riley's car? When had he gotten home? Maybe he'd come home for a work break before going to do his training tonight. For that matter, maybe I'd go to the gym and watch him this evening. Nothing was sexier than watching him go across adult-sized monkey bars.

I began packing up my stuff, hoping I could catch him. I always had time for Riley. And I hoped that never changed.

"Why'd you find me?" I was still unsettled by her appearance here.

"I remembered that Emma Jean said she felt like she was being followed, but she wasn't sure."

"You just remembered that? That seems pretty major." I finished collecting my things, ready to wrap up this conversation.

"She always had so much drama in her life. It's a lot to sort through."

I could see that. "She had no idea whom it might have been?"

"No idea. Not that she told me, at least."

"Thanks for sharing." I slung my bag over my shoulder and stood.

Sarah began walking with me toward the apartment.

Just as I crossed the road, an explosion rocked the street. I flew back and hit the ground from the force of it.

When I looked up, I realized my apartment building was ground zero.

CHAPTER
TWENTY-ONE

SHARDS OF DEBRIS hit my face, my arms.

I sucked in a breath as I processed what had happened.

Even from twenty yards away, heat hit me. Flames blinded me. Fear pulsated inside.

The apartment building.

My apartment building.

It was on fire.

The top floor was demolished. Flames quickly consumed the rest.

"Are you okay?" I asked Sarah.

She lay sprawled on the ground beside me.

She nodded. "I think so."

"Call 911."

I pushed myself to my feet and took off in a sprint toward my home.

Riley was inside.

Riley. A gasp caught in my throat.

I had to help him. He was okay. He had to be. I just had to find him.

My chest ached as my heart pounded into my ribcage.

The closer I got, the hotter the air became. Debris still rained around me, along with ashes. I could hardly keep my eyes open as smoke burned them. But I wasn't turning my back on my husband.

Just as I reached the front stoop, arms wrapped around me and pulled me away from the flames.

"Gabby, it's okay."

I froze, but only for a minute. I twirled, needing to match the voice with the face. I needed confirmation. To know my mind wasn't playing tricks on me.

My heart turned into a puddle.

"Riley!" I buried myself against him.

He continued to pull me away as more pops sounded, more debris rained down, and more flames ate away at my home sweet home. We finally stopped right against The Grounds. The windows of the coffee shop had been blown out in the explosion, and the patrons inside milled around looking dazed and off-kilter.

The next thought slammed into my chest, making me lose my breath.

"Sierra. Reef. Chad." They all ran through my head and rushed from my mouth. I started to jerk away from Riley, but he pulled me back. They'd left . . . right? But what if they hadn't?

"They're safe, Gabby. They weren't at home."

I buried myself into his arms again. "How did you get out? I thought . . ." I couldn't finish my sentence.

Riley stroked my back. "I'd just stepped out the backdoor to take the trash to the dumpster. I started talking to our neighbor behind us. It may have saved my life."

"You weren't even supposed to be home." I sniffled, trying to compose myself, but I was having trouble holding myself together. I thought I'd lost everything.

Everything. Not just my physical possessions but my heart.

He'd only recently come back into my life. This time as a permanent fixture. I couldn't lose him.

"I was going to surprise you and make lunch," he murmured. "I got done with the case early, and I know we've both been really busy lately. I wanted to spend some time with you."

"Well, your timing is awful." I sniffled again.

"I'm so glad you're okay." He kissed the top of my head before wrapping his arms tightly around me.

I glanced over, staring at the quickly disappearing remains of our place. The fire was devastating the building. The second and third floors were nearly gone and only a skeletal reminder of what had once been there remained. Orange flames still invaded the downstairs walls

I bit back a cry.

No sooner had I done so than I heard the sirens begin in the distance.

"No one else was inside, right?" I mentally reviewed everyone again. Mrs. Mystery was down in Florida. Bill was at work. Katarina was probably at the spa again, but certainly not here.

Everyone should be safe.

Another thought slammed into my mind. Tim.

What if Tim was inside?

The Grounds became a meeting place for the displaced while firefighters continued to put out the flames. Sharon had given out drinks to everyone there. Sarah was helping her, seeming to do better by keeping herself occupied.

Riley rubbed my back as I stood, leaning against a wall. I could sit. There were seats available. I just didn't want to. My adrenaline was pumping too hard. Even my pumpkin spice latte couldn't cheer me up.

I'd left messages for the rest of the residents. Sierra had actually cried. Chad had let out a few choice words. Mrs. Mystery hadn't answered.

But the main person on my mind was Tim.

What if he'd been in my apartment? What if I lost him again?

How had this happened? A bomb? Had someone done this to send a message?

I straightened as Detective Adams stepped inside. He walked over to Riley and me, bringing the scent of smoke with him.

"There was no one inside the building when the explosion occurred," Adams told me.

My muscles went limp with relief. Thank goodness, Tim was gone. I didn't even care where he was, as long as he wasn't here. "Do you have any idea what happened?"

A bomb. That was all I could think about. Someone had planted a bomb inside the apartment building.

Riley had just been talking about all of the similarities between this case and my very first real case. Strangely enough, that one had also involved a bomb being left outside my apartment. Did someone know that? Were they trying to mimic that investigation?

I held my breath as I waited for his verdict.

"I'm going to need to take you down to the police station to ask you a few questions, Gabby," Detective Adams said, not even one hint of amusement in his gaze.

Those relaxed muscles tightened again.

"Why?" I said.

"I'll tell you at the station."

"No, please tell me now. What's wrong?"

He tried to take my arm, but I didn't budge from the wall.

"I know what you were doing inside your old apartment, Gabby." Detective Adams let out a long breath before clenching his lips together in . . . was that disappointment?

"What I was doing inside my apartment? What are you talking about? Yes, sometimes in the morning I sneak over there just because I like my old couch—"

"You do?" Riley said.

I half shook, half nodded my head. That wasn't exactly the way I wanted him to find that out. But this was not the time or place to discuss it.

"Yes, I was easing myself away from it." Like a drug user weaning themselves from their addictions. "But that's all I was doing over there."

"I think we both know that's not true." Adams gave me a little tsk tsk.

All of the camaraderie I'd felt with the detective disappeared. "Why would I do something illegal? Anything inside was planted. You know better than anyone about everything that's been happening lately. I almost froze to death yesterday, for goodness sake! When that didn't work, someone went the opposite direction and tried to kill me with fire."

Adams sighed. "Gabby, must we do this here?"

I crossed my arms, knowing I had nothing to hide. "We must."

"Fine. We know about the meth lab in your apartment."

My jaw came unhinged. "Meth lab? Are you crazy? Do I look like a meth addict?"

"The money's good. It can tempt the most level-headed of persons."

"Detective Adams, you know me better than this." Then I realized what was really going on. I nearly doubled over at the thought of it. I dropped my head and my shoulders sagged. "Oh my word."

"What?" Adams asked.

I began pacing and shaking my head. I hoped my thoughts weren't correct . . . but I knew they were.

Could I speak the truth aloud? I knew I couldn't withhold what I knew. There was too much at stake.

"My brother was staying at my place," I muttered. "I suspected he might have been doing drugs. I had no idea he'd created a lab . . ."

"Your brother?"

I nodded. Riley rubbed my neck, but it did little good. My world was spinning.

"Do you know where your brother is?" Adams continued.

"I have no idea. I was afraid he was still inside . . ."

"We'll need to talk to him."

"Of course." I squeezed the skin between my eyes. "I just can't believe Tim would do this."

"You'll stick around here in case we have any questions?" Adams continued.

I nodded, wishing I could disappear. "Of course."

I turned to Riley, and he pulled me into a hug. I melted there, relying on his strength to keep me standing.

"I'm sorry, Gabby." His voice sounded low and soothing.

"How could he do this to me? How could I not have seen this?"

"Who would have ever thought he would create a meth lab? None of us saw it."

"This could have turned out so much worse, Riley. And it would have been my fault. Someone could have died."

"It wasn't your fault."

I barely heard him. "Our home is gone."

"Homes can be replaced. People can't. We'll find somewhere else to live."

I stared out the window at the smoldering building across the street. The structure was beyond fixable. There'd be no rebuilding.

Reality as I knew had just changed.

Tears pushed from my eyes. Again.

At that moment, a rundown fifteen-passenger van pulled up right outside the crime scene tape. Tim hopped out and gave the driver a laid-back wave.

I stormed toward the door, ready to give my brother a piece of my mind.

CHAPTER
TWENTY-TWO

"HOW COULD YOU?" I didn't want to think that the screeching voice assaulting my ears was mine. Nor the finger that I jabbed into my brother's chest.

He blanched, looking from me to the apartment building as we stood on the darkening sidewalk with neighbors gawking all around. "What . . . ?"

"I trusted you. I let you use my apartment to help you out. How could you do this? Someone could have died!"

"Gabby—" he started.

"Don't even try to make up an excuse. You have no idea what you've done."

Riley pulled me back. At his touch, I realized that I was in Tim's face. There in the shadows of my ashen apartment building, I was on the verge of losing control, much like the flames that had consumed the building.

Before I could lash out anymore, Detective Adams interceded and escorted Tim toward a police cruiser. The sound of his rights being read drifted toward me on the autumn breeze.

Tim glanced back at me, and, just for a moment, he

looked like a broken, scared little boy—like the brother I'd lost so many years ago.

My heart ached. Literally. My hand flew over it.

Maybe I shouldn't have been so hard on him. But . . . how could he?

Riley placed a hand on my arm, pulling me back toward the coffeehouse. "I'm sorry, Gabby."

I collapsed into his arms. "I can't believe this."

I felt like I was saying the same thing over and over. My brain was struggling to keep up with reality. Maybe it didn't want to keep up. If it didn't, maybe I'd cross some kind of threshold into madness.

"I should have checked on him more to see what he was doing in there," I murmured into Riley's chest.

"No one would have guessed he was creating a meth lab."

"I should have been more observant. I thought he was doing drugs. I warned him not to. If I were a good sister, I would have followed up more. Given him more accountability. I would have been there for him."

"No one is blaming you, Gabby."

"Well, they should be."

I looked up as Bill's car screeched to a halt on the other side of the police line. He stepped out, shaking his head as he stared at the carnage of his home. Katarina joined him, grasping his arm like a lifeline.

"Is this because of me?" He sounded more sober than I'd heard him in a long time.

My heart twisted with regret again. "No, unfortunately, it's not."

Riley pulled me closer, as if afraid I might collapse.

"Unfortunately?" he questioned.

I shook my head. "Never mind."

I couldn't say it yet. I wanted more proof. Then I would try to make amends. Speaking of which . . . I needed to call Garrett. He'd bought the building so I could keep my home. Did he know yet?

Bill stared at what was left of the building, his face growing paler by the moment. I followed his gaze. Fire trucks and police cars surrounded it. A couple of protesters were being treated by paramedics. I'd gotten through with just a couple of bruises and cuts.

Crews would be out here for a while managing the scene. The road was blocked, and smoke hung in the air.

"It looks like I'll be getting that new place I talked about whether I want to or not," Bill said.

"Yeah, me too."

Riley tightened his arms around me.

"Man, I can't believe it. This place has so many memories," Bill continued. "I was the first resident here, you know. We've become like family over the years."

I wiped beneath my eyes. I hadn't even realized I was crying. "We have."

I couldn't believe that era was ending.

Where would we all go? What if I didn't see my neighbors—my friends—anymore?

I felt another major life change coming. The little safety net of my community had been snatched away.

Thanks to The Red Cross, all the residents of the building were provided rooms in a hotel until we could find somewhere else to stay. The accommodations were located in downtown Norfolk, right across from the Scope Arena, a large, dome-shaped entertainment venue.

Thankfully, my car had survived, probably because I'd parked at the coffeehouse to avoid the protesters. Riley would need a rental until we could figure out if his was salvageable. His car windows had busted, two tires melted, and that was only what we could see on the surface. The heat and flying debris could have caused other issues also.

Our hotel room was simple but nice, I supposed. I had to overlook the fact that it smelled like someone had sprayed too much air freshener to cover a bad scent. The fantastic view of Norfolk and the Elizabeth River made up for it.

Sierra and her family were staying at the house of someone from her work who was on a month-long vacation to Europe. I hoped she was comfortable there. Bill was next door, and, right now, Katarina was with him.

Riley and I had gone to the store together and picked up enough supplies to get through a few days, at least. I'd had to buy everything: clothes, underwear, a toothbrush, shampoo, makeup. I tried not to let the thought of it all overwhelm me.

I sat in a stiff accent chair in the corner of my room and crossed my arms. I still felt like I was in shock. But now that I'd had some time to let it sink in, I was thankful no one was harmed. Even Sierra's cats and Lucky hadn't been there.

Tim's image fluttered through my mind, especially the look he'd given me as he was led away by Detective Adams. I wondered how he was doing. If he was sitting in a jail cell.

I couldn't bring myself to go see him yet. Not until my anger died down.

But I'd called my dad and his fiancée, Teddi, and they

were dealing with Tim. It was the best I could do at the moment.

All of my things . . . The things my mom had left me. Mementos from when Riley and I first started dating. My equipment for my job. My silly coffee mugs and obnoxious crime scene knickknacks. They were all gone. I'd never expected to feel grief at the loss of possessions, but I did. All I had was Riley and the clothes on my back.

"Gabby . . .?" Riley came back into the room with two cups of coffee. He paused in front of me and kneeled down. "Are you okay?"

I shrugged, setting my coffee on the table beside me. "I don't know what I am. I'm mourning what we've lost. I'm angry at my brother—to put it mildly. I'm thankful to be alive."

"I know you're disappointed in Tim."

My jaw hardened with welling emotions. "More than disappointed. I let him into my home. I trusted him. This was so . . . irresponsible, to say the least."

He laced his hands with mine. "We'll get through this, Gabby."

"I know. We always do."

He stood and pulled me up with him. "What do you want to do? Stay up here? Check out the hot tub downstairs? Maybe that will help you relax."

"The hot tub could be nice. Except I don't have a bathing suit."

He leaned closer and his lips lingered on mine. "I'm sure we can find something else to do."

For a moment, my problems started to disappear as tingles overtook my gloom.

Until someone knocked at the door.

"Gabby? Riley? Are you in there? It's Bill. We need to talk."

I sighed and stepped back. Had he heard my brother was responsible for this? Was he coming by so he could tell me off?

I deserved it.

As soon as Riley opened the door, Bill charged inside. He began pacing near the window, his body language screaming "distressed!" I waited for Katarina to follow him inside, but she didn't.

"There's something I should have told you from the start." Sweat sprinkled Bill's forehead.

Riley and I exchanged a glance as we sat across from Bill on the edge of the queen-sized bed.

"What's that?" I finally said, partly relieved to avoid the whole Tim conversation.

"I've been sitting on a key piece of information. I couldn't tell anyone. Timing was everything for me."

"Why is timing everything?" I asked.

"For the election, of course."

He'd gotten a taste of life at the top, and now he wanted more. How far would he go to get ratings? Had he staged some of the events of the past few days?

He raised a hand, as if he could read my thoughts. "Hear me out before you jump to conclusions. You've got to understand. This is big information."

"What is it?" I hardly wanted to hear this "information." I was so over all of this. I was over the secrets. Over the lies. Over the vile contempt people had for opposing opinions.

"It's about Philip Munich," he continued.

"What about him?" As a wave of exhaustion came over me, I finally sipped the coffee that Riley had bought me.

"Let me guess: he has a body double and is the product of his political party. A mindless robot. A Manchurian candidate."

"No."

"He was secretly born in another country, and the fact that he's one of the final two candidates is a scheme of other world governments to overthrow our country," I continued.

"No."

"He secretly dodged the draft and did drugs? Inhaling only?"

Bill let out his breath and narrowed his eyes, obviously not as amused by my theories as I was. "He killed someone, Gabby. He killed someone."

I actually snorted. "Come on, Bill. Really? I mean, I thought my theories were outlandish. Great conversation starters and fascinating to think about. To write books about even. But they're out there—well, except for the last one, I guess."

"I'm not kidding, Gabby. Munich killed someone. I have evidence."

I set my coffee down before I spilled it. "You better not be yanking my chain."

"I'm not, Gabby. Ask Riley."

I looked at Riley, my eyes widening. Riley knew about this information? He hadn't told me.

Riley shrugged, his gaze apologetic. "I couldn't share, Gabby. I'm legally bound to remain quiet about it. You know that. Client confidentially is most definitely not a conspiracy theory."

His words may have been true, but they didn't make me feel better. This was big. Why wouldn't he have shared it with me with a promise that I'd keep quiet? I knew the answer, but my emotions were colliding with my logic. I was dog-tired and everything was getting to me.

"Start talking, Bill."

"I've been sitting on this information for a while. I wanted to make sure it was true. And I was trying to gauge the timing of when to release it."

"What happened?" I was losing patience.

He raised his hands. "I'm getting to it. I'm getting to it. When Munich was in college, he was quite the party boy, as were the rest of the guys in his fraternity. Then one of his fraternity brothers died."

Now he was getting somewhere. "What happened?"

"This guy—his name was Frederick Mason—had an asthma attack. A fatal one."

My lungs deflated at his revelation. I'd been expecting something big—another bludgeoned body left in the freezer or something. "That hardly sounds like murder."

"Wait." He raised a finger and sweat dripped off the end of his nose. "There's more to it. Munich was with Frederick when he died."

This still wasn't making sense. I crossed my legs and tried to do some deep breathing before I lost my patience. "He wasn't able to save him? Was there no inhaler?"

"No, there wasn't an inhaler. But instead of getting help or calling 911, Munich left him to fend for himself. Apparently, Frederick couldn't even speak because this attack was so bad. He couldn't call for help or anything."

"So Munich basically left him there to die?" I asked.

"Precisely," Bill said.

My gut felt tight as these new details emerged. "Why would Munich not help?"

"Frederick apparently had information to prove that Munich had cheated on one of his exams. That's all hearsay, of course. But the theory is that Munich feared his frat brother would take that information to the dean. His academics were already rocky. Getting kicked out of college? Well, that would never work for a future president."

I paused as his story ended. "Okay, I could see why that would be a reason for concern. But why hasn't this information ever come out before? I thought you said it happened at a fraternity."

"It did. But it was over Christmas break. Hardly anyone was there. He could have easily gotten away with it because everyone thought it was a terrible tragedy but not anything malicious. That's because no one knew Munich was there and could have saved Mason."

My exhaustion was quickly fading as this rollercoaster adrenaline ride continued. "So how'd you find out?"

"I said hardly anyone." His eyes gleamed with satisfaction.

I shifted, wondering exactly where this would go. Was this the puzzle piece I'd been missing?

"One of the guys in the fraternity—his name is Steve—was a real smart aleck. He left his web camera on to pick up any . . . well, you know, funny business. Only no one knew it was there. When he watched the tape, he realized Munich had been there the night their frat brother died."

"Did he go to the police with that information?" I asked.

Bill shook his head. "No, he went to Munich, whose family paid him off. I mean, technically, Munich wasn't at fault. But it looks bad. It looks really bad."

"I agree that it looks bad," I said. "What kind of proof do you have? Just one person's word against the other's?"

Bill's gaze locked with mine. "I have the video of

Munich leaving the room. It's time stamped and every-thing. I also have a copy of the check Munich's family gave Steve for his silence."

I drew in a deep breath. That could definitely be incriminating. "Steve came out of the woodwork during the election? That's suspicious in itself."

"You have to understand that Munich has been hand-picked for this role of presidential candidate for a long time. Even back in college there was talk about him running for office one day. Steve knew he could hang on to that evidence about Munich and that timing was everything."

"I guess he didn't like Munich very much?" I asked.

"No, not at all. Munich stole his girlfriend. It was part of the reason he'd set up the web cam in the first place. He wanted to find evidence against Munich to break him up with the girl he stole. He ended up finding something much bigger."

"And he came to you with this information?" I rubbed my forehead, feeling a headache coming on. This was all too much. Out of my league. If Bill was right, the scope of this was bigger than everything I'd ever encountered in any investigation before.

Bill shifted, and I could tell he was contemplating how much more to say . . . or how to best frame his lie to his advantage.

"Bill . . ." Warning stretched through my voice.

"Okay, okay. You know that book advance I got?"

"Yes . . ." I already didn't like where this was going.

"I spent most of it on this information." Another bead of sweat dripped from his nose.

"So you bought it?" I heard the judgment in my voice, but I didn't feel bad about it.

He raised his chin, as if determined to save face despite his confession. "That's right. And it was worth it. I'm going to shake up this election once and for all."

"Why did he come to you? Certainly some of the networks would have paid him more?"

"He doesn't trust the mainstream media. In fact, he's my biggest fan. Or so he says."

Before I could ask any more questions, a scream sounded in the hallway.

I'd recognize it anywhere. It was Katarina.

CHAPTER
TWENTY-THREE

WE ALL DARTED into the hallway—because why would I want a break from the circus my life had become? No, I needed more excitement to fill my days and nights.

To my surprise, Bill reached Katarina first.

She was in the hallway. On the floor. Against the wall. Dazed but alive.

In the distance, a man darted away.

Since I could tell Katarina was shaken but okay, I darted after the man instead. Riley was right on my heels. Then he passed me. He got to the stairwell an entire thirty seconds before I did.

All of his working out was paying off. Maybe I should look into training also, for moments just like this.

The guy—he was wearing a black ski mask, like any good criminal would—darted over the stair railings, moving faster than I could comprehend.

Riley stayed on his heels.

Until a family walked into the stairwell, right between the intruder and us. Riley rammed into the wall to stop himself before he ran them over.

The mom, dad, and two kids didn't seem to notice the chase. Instead, the mom argued about how taking the steps was healthier than getting a free ride on an elevator. The kids whined about it. The dad looked like he'd signed out.

"Excuse us," Riley muttered, trying to skirt around them.

They looked up at us like we were weapon-wielding clowns.

I glanced down, trying to keep my eye on the man. But he was out of sight. The sound of this family's argument drowned out any other noise.

By the time we reached the first floor, the man was long gone. He'd most likely blended in with a huge tour group of dancers who all wore matching lime-green shirts.

"He got away," Riley said when I caught up with him. His chest rose and fell with healthy exertion.

Unlike me. I heaved air in and out like a dying woman.

I definitely needed to start training with him.

"Did you notice anything about him?" I asked, leaning forward to open up my airways. It didn't work.

He shook his head as people milled around us, towing luggage behind them and gazing at the building's tall atrium. "No. Nothing. He was dressed in black from head to toe. I'm guessing he lost that gear as soon as he got down here."

Of course, he did. He was no dummy. "Let's go see if Katarina saw anything."

Katarina sat in my accent chair. Bill handed her a glass of water. She fanned herself with a paperback novel I'd purchased at the store. Every once in a while, she let out a little whimper that sent Bill scurrying to comfort her again.

Riley and I stood, waiting for Adams to arrive. He was going to be thrilled to see me again. He probably hadn't gotten a good night's sleep since I'd "run into him" with that sprinkle-covered donut at the station.

"What happened?" I asked Katarina.

"I walk in room and man there," Katarina said. "I get back from hot tub. No relaxed anymore."

"What was he doing when you walked in?" I asked.

"He look through suitcase."

Could he be looking for the video Bill claimed to have? Had word leaked that Bill had it? Was that what all of this was about?

"Is anything missing?" I asked Bill.

"Not that I can tell."

"Could you tell anything about him?" I asked Katarina.

She swung her head back and forth. "No, nothing. He wear black. He push me down and run out."

Great. So we still didn't know anything. That was about on par for the course of this investigation.

Someone knocked at the door. Detective Adams.

"Hello . . . again." I started. I wanted to ask about Tim, but I didn't. Adams looked tired, had coffee breath, and crumbs hung suspended in his chin scruff. His clothes had more wrinkles than usual, and he still smelled like smoke, which made me wonder if he'd come from the fire.

It was 2 a.m. We were all tired.

While CSI techs checked the neighboring room for evidence, Adams questioned Katarina and then Bill and then Riley and me.

When he finished, he stood. "I'll check the security footage also and see what I find out. You all are making me want to retire early, by the way. I haven't slept but eight hours since all this started."

"Sorry . . . ?" Did he want an apology? He had to know that none of this was my doing. Well, most of it wasn't, at least.

I walked him to the door. "Any updates on the fire?"

He shook his head. "It needs to cool more before we'll know anything for sure. There was definitely a meth lab there. We're just not sure if it was the cause of the explosion. The flames are out, though. The building is nothing but ashes. I'm sorry, Gabby."

I nodded, my heart heavy. "Can you tell me anything about Tim?"

I'd told myself I wouldn't ask, but I had to.

"We've charged him with the manufacturing and distribution of methamphetamine."

My heart fell. "I see."

"If he's found guilty, he may have to pay the city the cost of cleaning up this mess."

"That will be interesting since he has no money . . ."

He paused, studying me. "Your dad came to visit."

"Did he post bail?" Speaking of no money . . . my dad hardly had money for his bills, so I doubted he could afford to get his son out of jail. Maybe Tim deserved to stay there for a while to learn his lesson.

"No. It would be one thing if Tim had just made and distributed the drugs. But his actions put people's lives on the line. He could be charged with arson and child endangerment, just to name a few."

"I know. I still can't believe it." My stress returned like a floodgate opening. I didn't even have a song for it, which meant I was really, really stressed.

"He's lucky to have a sister like you."

I hadn't expected to hear that. "What do you mean?"

"You're the type who doesn't give up on people, just like you don't give up on finding answers. He needs that now."

Guilt flashed through me. I had thought about giving up, if I were honest. That's not to say I would. But I'd seen the cycle of addiction with my father's alcoholism. I didn't want to go through that again with Tim.

"Of course," I finally said. "He needs people who will always be there for him."

I wasn't sure I was ready to offer anything still except anger.

"Stay safe, Gabby. Stay safe."

Riley and I grabbed breakfast at the restaurant downstairs the next morning. Unbelievably, I was getting burned out on pumpkin, so I chose a cranberry muffin to have with my three cups of coffee. Riley got two hard-boiled eggs and some Greek yogurt. Protein, protein, protein.

Riley shifted in his seat, and I knew our conversation was about to move from the daily news to something much deeper. "So, Gabby, you do understand that there are things I can't share as an attorney, right?"

I was wondering when the subject would come up. Last night we hadn't had a chance to talk. After Bill and Katarina left, we both passed out from exhaustion.

And I understood that he couldn't share everything. Yet, at the same time, I hated knowing he was keeping things from me.

Boundaries are essential.

I'd shed a fresh round of tears this morning when I'd

woken up and remembered my house was gone. I knew it was just stuff, but it was still harder than I'd imagined it would be. That apartment had been my safe place, and I had so many memories of my time there.

I set my coffee down. "Yes, I understand. But that doesn't mean I like it."

"If I can share anything with you, I will. I don't like keeping things from you."

I raised my hand, guilt now rushing in like the tide. "Really, I know. And I know I'm having the wrong reaction. Give it some time and I'll come to my senses."

He leaned back. "So what are you doing today? You don't have a workshop, right?"

"No, that's tomorrow. This morning I thought I would call the insurance company, probably go shopping for a few things, possibly check on Tim. Is there anything you need me to do?"

He pressed his lips together. "I don't think so. I will need to purchase a few things to wear while training."

"That's right. You had those expensive tennis shoes, and they had to be broken in just right." He'd mentioned that several times, but I hadn't given it a thought until now.

"It's okay. I'll make do with whatever I can get. No big deal." He grabbed my hand. "I know this is hard, Gabby."

"I feel like I'm showing a lack of faith by mourning after this." The words felt raw but honest.

"It's only natural to mourn. It's loss. And that doesn't say anything about your faith."

"I keep thinking about the people I look up to. When I imagine them being in this situation, I imagine them spouting words of wisdom and inspiration."

"You mean, people like Leona?"

I let out a soft breath, realizing the irony of this conversation. "Yeah, like Leona."

"We're all human. We all make mistakes. We laugh. We lose. We mourn. We just can't let those emotions get the best of us."

I smiled. "Thanks, Riley. You always know what to say."

"I wish I did. Sometimes there's nothing you can say . . ."

I squeezed his hand. "I'm glad this happened, by the way. And by 'this,' I mean you and me. Not the fire, of course."

Rambling, Gabby. You're rambling.

"Me too, Gabby." He shifted. "You still thinking about seeing Tim?"

I shrugged, my appetite waning. "Yeah, I just don't know if I'm ready to face him yet. That also makes me feel like a bad person. I should forgive and want to help him and utilize all the fruits of the spirit that are supposed to be ripe in my life. Instead, I want to throttle him. It's like all my fruit is rotten."

"Give it time. It will come. You want to do right. That's the first step." He glanced at the time on his phone. "I really should take today off work."

I waved it off. "No, go. I know you have a lot going on, and I have a free day. I can handle things by myself for a while. I'll call if I need anything."

He stood and kissed me goodbye, tossing his trash into a nearby trashcan. "The rental car should be waiting downstairs. They just texted me. I'll check in with you later."

I nodded as I watched him walk away. I knew I should

go upstairs and start making phone calls. But I wasn't quite ready to do that yet.

Instead, I grabbed my car keys. I was going to find a little closure. I drove to the grungy hotel where Greg Borski was staying.

I stared at it a moment. His truck was out front, so he should be here.

Was I stupid for stopping by here alone? The man had an alibi, so he was innocent, according to Adams. And I wouldn't be abrasive. I would just ask questions. It would be more like a friendly conversation.

With determination pulsing through me, I opened my car door. It was brisker outside today than it had been, and I wished I had my favorite sweater. Too bad my favorite sweater no longer existed.

I strode up to Borski's room. I pounded on his door, and he pulled it open a moment later. When he saw me, a puzzled expression came over his face.

"You," he muttered. "You're . . ."

"Gabby. The PI looking into Emma Jean's death."

He started to close his door. "I don't have to talk to you."

"I was locked in the freezer at your restaurant two days ago."

He paused and observed me again. "I didn't do that."

"I didn't say you did. In fact, I heard you have an alibi."

His shoulders relaxed ever so slightly. "Why are you here?"

"I just have a few questions. Can I have ten minutes of your time? Please?"

He gave me a hard stare and finally opened the door

wider. "Ten minutes. But only because I have nothing better to do."

I slid inside the dingy hotel room. I wasn't sure this was a good idea anymore. But I had brought my gun, just in case. Thankfully, it had been in my purse and not in my apartment.

"Is The Crispy Biscuit done?" I asked.

"In essence. Who's going to want to eat there again?" He closed the door and stood in front of it with his arms crossed like a security guard who wouldn't let me leave.

Bad idea, Gabby. Bad idea.

"Why did you pretend to have organic fresh food?"

"My bills got out of control. I felt like I had no choice. If the restaurant closed down, it wasn't just me who'd pay the price. My employees would be without jobs. I know it was low, but I was desperate." He waved his hand around. "As you can see, I've done without a paycheck for a while now. I can't even make ends meet."

"Yet you gave Emma Jean a raise."

He narrowed his eyes. "How did you know about that?"

"Sarah Babble told me."

He muttered something underneath his breath. "Sarah. Of course. Emma Jean was threatening to go public about my hypocrisy if I didn't give her a raise."

"That sounds like motive for murder to me."

Shouldn't have said that, Gabby.

"Maybe it was. But I didn't do it. I certainly wouldn't have hidden her body in my own restaurant. It's clear to see that I'm being set up."

I couldn't argue with that theory. "Any idea who killed her?"

He shook his head. "I've thought about it over and

over, and I have no idea. I mean, people didn't like her, but that doesn't mean they'd kill her."

"Is that the same reason why you didn't fire her? Because she was holding something over your head?"

He let out another breath. "Yeah, you could say that. You know what they say about keeping your enemies closer? She definitely felt like an enemy. She'd been slightly more pleasant since she started doing yoga."

"Funny, you're the second person who's mentioned yoga. Did that surprise you that she did that?"

He nodded. "Yeah, she was too lazy to walk while she was at work. She'd scoot her chair all over the kitchen instead. But whatever worked for her . . ."

"There's one more thing I don't understand."

He glanced at his watch. "You have four more minutes."

"Who's the man who came here to visit you? The tall, pale guy who looks like he stepped off the pages of an Abercrombie catalog? How is he connected with Katarina?"

His eyes widened. I'd caught him, and he knew it. But then the flames ignited in his gaze. "Have you been watching me?"

"How else would I know you were here?" Wasn't it obvious?

He flung his head back and forth. "That's none of your business."

"You're getting very fired up. That usually means you're hiding something."

"You're out of line." Veins bulged at his neck, and I knew I needed to back off.

"I'm just looking for answers." I kept my voice soft and free of accusation so I wouldn't accelerate the situation.

He only stared at me.

"Look, I saw that same man when Katarina Sokolov was almost abducted from the mall parking garage. Then I saw him coming to your hotel room. What aren't you saying?"

"He's a friend. That's all I know. The rest of it? It's a coincidence."

"I don't believe that."

"Believe it."

"Can you give me his name, at least, so I can talk to him?"

"Absolutely not. You need to keep your nose out of it, if you know what's best for you. Now this conversation is over." He moved from his security-guard stance and opened the door.

I wanted to keep talking, but, if I valued my life, I should get out of here.

"One more question?" I paused outside.

He growled.

"Do you know where Emma Jean did yoga?"

"The Yoga Tree in Virginia Beach." He slammed the door.

I was more curious now than ever. I glanced at my watch, knowing I needed to get back to the hotel and make some phone calls. Despite that, I headed to the radio station. Priorities, you know?

I skirted past protesters—their numbers had thinned— and waited until Bill had a break, so I could talk to him. His show blared on the speakers overhead. Apparently, Philip Munich had mentioned Bill in his remarks earlier today, which made Bill have an overinflated sense of self again. All of this drama was making his ratings skyrocket.

Bill stepped out of the booth ten minutes after I arrived and stared at me, his gaze skittering nervously. "What's going on? Did something else happen?"

I got right to the point. "Where was Katarina when Emma Jean died?"

He blanched, glanced around, and then took my arm. He pulled me into his office and shut the door. "You think Katarina killed Emma Jean?"

"I'm just exploring every possibility."

"Why would Katarina kill her?"

I shrugged, knowing that people could rarely see beyond their own emotions. Especially when it came to love. "Maybe she felt intimidated."

"Katarina? Over Emma Jean?" He sounded like I'd just told him that the election would be postponed this year.

I knew the idea seemed absurd, at least on the surface. "Look, I don't know. I'm not sure. I don't have the answers yet."

He shook his head and glanced at his watch. "I have to be back on the air in three minutes, so let me make this clear: it wasn't Katarina. She was in Atlanta when Emma Jean died."

"Doing what?" I wasn't nearly as convinced.

"There was some kind of gala there for one of the magazines she works for."

I quirked an eyebrow, hating to burst his bubble, but . . . "You mean one of the department store catalogs?"

"She's done other work also."

I doubted that. "For which magazine?"

He broke eye contact. "I don't know."

"Bill . . ." He was such a bad liar.

He let out a long breath and ran a hand over his face. "I think it was the Harrison Group. That's all I know. But she didn't get back into town until you saw her show up that day at the apartment. Are you done now? Because I've got to get back on the air."

"One more question. Maybe two. First, are you still going public with that information you discovered?"

"Of course. Why wouldn't I?"

Oh, I don't know. Because people's lives are on the line over it?

"And also: did you tell anyone else that you had information on Munich's frat days?"

He stepped toward the door, avoiding eye contact. "Only one."

"Who?"

"Katarina."

I didn't waste any time. As soon as I got back in my car, I pulled up the Internet and did a search for the Harrison Group. The company ran a chain of low-end department stores. Interesting.

I just happened to find a charity gala they hosted in Atlanta on the exact night Emma Jean was murdered. And there were pictures. Tons and tons of pictures.

I scrolled through them. All of them. I searched for Katarina's image. I didn't see a single one.

I'd think someone like Katarina would want to be included in the shots.

At the bottom of one of the pages, I spotted a media contact number. On a whim, I dialed the number. A perky woman answered three rings later.

"I'm calling in regards to the gala you hosted last week for the Harrison Group," I started, staring at the protesters in the distance and their "Kill Bill" signs.

"Yes, ma'am," she said with a Southern drawl. "What can I do for you?"

"I'm with a local newspaper in Norfolk, Virginia. We were interested in doing an article on one of your models who's living here now."

"Well, of course," she said. "Who's that?"

"Katarina Sokolov."

"Katarina?" Her voice instantly changed from sweetly Southern to fussy debutant. "Oh, I'm sorry. But Ms. Sokolov is not with us anymore."

"She's not? I understood she was up at the gala last week."

"No, she parted ways a good year ago. We haven't seen her since then. I'm sorry someone gave you wrong information." She lowered her voice. "It was probably Katarina herself, though. It wouldn't surprise me."

The conversation had taken an interesting turn. "You don't think highly of her?"

"I'm in PR. I'm supposed to talk highly of everyone—everyone I represent, at least. I guess since I don't represent her any more, I can say whatever I want. But that woman acted like a diva. Everyone was glad to see her go."

"I see. Well, thank you for that information."

"No problem." She paused. "Oh, and by the way, I'd stay away from that woman if I were you. She's trouble with a capital T."

I decided to be a good girl after I left the radio station, and I went back to the hotel and began making calls. It went against everything in me. All I wanted to do was investigate and not leave this case unfinished. But my housing situation was pretty serious, and it needed to be addressed.

While sitting cross-legged on the bed with a notebook and pen in my lap, I called the company providing my renter's insurance. Then I called the car insurance company. Then I tried to call Mrs. Mystery, who still didn't answer.

Finally, I tried to call Garrett Mercer again—but he didn't answer his phone. He was probably out of town again on business of some sort. He traveled a lot.

I could only imagine how he would feel when he heard about the house. Guilt pressed in on me again, and I squeezed the skin between my eyes. This was my fault, whether anyone said that or not. I'd invited my brother into my home, and he'd abused that privilege. But it was still my responsibility ultimately.

I let my head drop back on the headboard behind me. A meth lab. I mean, really? Was Tim stupid? And where had he gotten the money to do something like that? He only believed in free. Last I heard, pseudoephedrine was not free.

I stared at my phone. Should I call my dad and check on Tim? See if he had any updates. I put my phone down. No, I couldn't do it. Not yet.

Instead, I did my normal "let's try to sort this out" list instead. I needed to keep my thoughts occupied and fill my insatiable desire to find answers.

Borski: supposedly innocent, but still keeping secrets of some sort.

Bill: has a secret about Munich. But how was that connected to Emma Jean's murder?

Katarina: alibi doesn't check out. But why would she want Emma Jean dead?

Jerry: Emma Jean threatening to lie about his love life in order to get custody of their son.

Nordic god: were he and Katarina connected through modeling? Secretly dating?

Was there anyone I was missing? I tapped my pen on my notebook, waiting for another idea to strike like lightning.

Seriously, you're losing your touch, Gabby. None of this makes sense. What are you missing?

Did this crime go all the way up to Munich? Was this about politics? Had Emma Jean discovered something she shouldn't have while stalking Bill, and that had ultimately led to her demise?

It was a possibility.

But it seemed so unlikely.

There was only one thing I knew to do in order to proceed. I had to go to yoga class, whether I liked it or not.

CHAPTER
TWENTY-FOUR

THERE WAS NO BETTER person to go with me to yoga than Clarice Wilkerson. Pretty, lithe, sometimes airheaded Clarice.

We drove together, and she chatted nonstop on the way. She went on and on about the fire. About how she couldn't believe it had happened. How her aunt Sharon, who owned The Grounds, would be out of operation for at least a week until she could get the place cleaned up and the windows repaired.

Then she moved on to talking about her college classes. She'd gone back to school part-time to get a degree in criminal justice. It was super interesting, and some of the cops she'd met through her lectures were super cute and brave.

At a break in the conversation, I asked, "How are things between you and Nate?"

I instantly knew I'd probably regret bringing up the subject.

She'd met Nate when we went to West Virginia at the beginning of September to fix up an old amusement park turned resort destination. For the record, I was against their union before I was for it. Now I was just waiting to see what happened between the two strong personalities.

"I'm supposed to go see him in a couple of weeks, but he's been super busy with opening Mythical Falls."

"Is it going well for him?"

"He seems super excited."

What was with her using super so much lately?

"I'm glad. I hope things work out for him. And for you two together, for that matter." But was she ready to settle down? I mean, she'd just been talking about how super hot the cops she'd met were.

"Me too." She turned her attention to the strip mall in front of us. "Here we are."

I frowned as I put the car in park. As I stepped out, I tugged at my yoga pants. I'd had to go to Walmart to buy some. They weren't my favorite item of clothing, but I'd worn a long shirt over them. Yoga was nowhere near the top of my bucket list.

"Are you looking forward to this?" Clarice asked at the door.

"Like using a Porta Potty on a humid day."

She wrinkled her nose. "What?"

I shook my head. "Never mind. Let's do this."

We stepped inside, and I blanched. "Speaking of Porta Potties . . . it smells like a paper factory in here."

Apparently, I said that out loud. And a little too loud. Because a woman at the counter launched into educating me.

"When we relax our body's muscles, our organs also relax. As a result, flatulence can occur. I assure you that it's healthy and a sign that the participants here are doing the exercises correctly."

Ew. I could have lived without that explanation.

"Thank you," I finally said.

I paid for Clarice and me to take the class. Then the woman behind the front desk started into her spiel about how The Yoga Tree was only open in the evenings because the owner was a dermatologist by day. There were monthly and yearly memberships available. Blah blah blah.

I needed to ask her about Emma Jean, but I was going to wait until after the class. Instead, I glanced around quickly as she droned on and on. Large windows created the walls at the front and back of the building. The offices and bathrooms were on the side, which made the set up slightly unconventional but pleasant. The place reminded me a bit of a gypsy's lair with draped purple fabric on the walls, rustic wood floors, and low lighting.

I followed Clarice's lead and grabbed a mat from a bin against the wall. She unrolled it, lowered herself to the floor, and began stretching. I tried to stretch, but compared to her I was merely moving more than stretching. She was like Mr. Fantastic, and I was like the Thing, the rock-studded superhero.

Note to self: must work on becoming more limber.

"Did you know some people consider yoga New Age?" Clarice drew in a deep breath through her lungs.

"Don't tell Leona that." If she knew I was friends with Bill *and* that I did yoga, she'd really think I didn't love Jesus.

"Who's Leona?"

"Never mind. I'm just talking to myself." I tried to grab my foot again but couldn't quite reach it.

I was really glad I didn't have to do this by myself

because I had no idea how to proceed. Give me jogging any day over this.

I figured when the lights were lowered even more and soothing music came on overhead that it was time to start. And someone finally lit some incense, which only smelled slightly better than the flatulence.

"Breathe deeply. Cast aside thoughts of everything else. Keep your core tight and centered," a solemn, soft-spoken woman up front said.

I tried to listen. To relax. To make the most of the class.

But then Bill and Katarina walked in. I tried not to stare.

Bill gave me the look—the one that said, "What in the world are you doing here?"

This was where Bill and Katarina did yoga also? Suddenly, things were beginning to make sense.

As the instructor told us to grab our left foot, I attempted to do just that. Only I couldn't reach it.

I hated yoga. I hated it before, and I hated it more now.

Clarice, on the other hand, had grabbed her foot, and she was breathing calmly, deeply, and her face looked angelic it was so relaxed.

I hated Clarice too.

Okay, not really.

"I need everyone to focus." The instructor looked at me like I was personally responsible for disturbing the relaxed, positive Zen in the room.

I turned away from Clarice, Katarina, and Bill and reached for my foot again.

I was even more horrified when I glanced over and saw that Bill could touch his foot.

I had to get back on the get-in-shape bandwagon. For real.

"Now let's do the half lord of the fishes. This move will promote spinal health and digestive fire by detoxing the kidneys . . ." the instructor said.

Wait . . . half lord of the fishes? Jerry had mentioned Emma Jean talking about that. That's what she'd meant.

The rest of the class was painfully slow. I attempted to do some kind of downward dog that made my arms shake, a warrior pose where I literally fell on my side, and my favorite, the resting child—which would have been great if that was the only pose I had to do for the entire class.

Making matters worse was the fact that the instructor kept calling me out because I was doing the moves incorrectly. The last thing I wanted right now was any extra attention on me as my butt was in the air.

Did Emma Jean actually do yoga? That half lord of the fishes move seemed especially difficult.

It was the longest hour of my life.

Finally, the class ended. As soon as it did, Clarice wandered to get some water, and Bill charged toward me. All of his calm centering appeared to be gone. "What are you doing here?"

I draped a towel over my shoulders. "What are *you* doing here?"

"This is where I do yoga."

"Well, apparently this was a favorite haunt of Emma Jean's, so I thought I'd check it out."

He snorted. "Emma Jean never came here. Katarina would have told me. She's here every Tuesday, Wednesday, and Thursday."

"That's not what Emma Jean's best friend said. She apparently *loved* yoga. Especially that parable move with the loaf and fishes."

"What?"

"Half loaf of the fishes?"

"Half lord of the fish—never mind." Bill snorted again as he chewed on some kind of thought. "Emma Jean didn't have any friends."

"You might be surprised." I wasn't sure why I wanted to defend the woman. But everyone deserved a friend. Except maybe Charles Manson.

He paused. "I don't get it. Why would she come here?"

"I have no idea. Why would you eat at The Crispy Biscuit when she worked there?"

He scowled, but his expression instantly converted back to pleasant as Katarina approached. She eyeballed me with a sneer. "Nice moves."

I knew she was being sarcastic and capitalizing on my humiliating experience in exercising. Women like her were the reason I didn't come to classes like this.

Jerk.

"Come on, Bill." Katarina took his chunky arm into her thin, sculpted one. "All my peace evaporating quick."

I wanted to roll my eyes. Instead, I watched them leave. Clarice finally joined me.

"What was that about?" she asked, following my gaze.

"I'm not sure. But neither of them seemed to realize that Emma Jean came here."

"That's weird."

"Isn't it?" I pulled up her picture on my phone. "Let me see if anyone else has seen her."

I showed the picture to the receptionist. She shook her head. So did three other employees.

So Emma Jean said she was going to yoga, but she never actually came inside. Interesting. She'd really just been spying on Katarina.

"My maternal unit always told me to be careful who you love," I sang.

"What?"

As a hint, I did the moonwalk across the carpet, which earned me another dirty look from the receptionist.

Clarice snapped her fingers as her eyes lit with realization. "You're singing a Michael Jackson song?"

I applauded quietly. "Very good. My own version of it, however."

"'Billie Jean,' right?" She sang a few lines.

I shook my head and raised an imaginary microphone. "Oh no, I'm not singing about Billie Jean. I'm singing about someone just as infamous. Emma Jean."

Both were women that men should have stayed away from.

If only they'd listened to their mama's advice.

When I walked outside several minutes later, I noticed Bill's car was still there. He must have lost his little merry gang of paparazzi, because I didn't see any angry mobs out here with their "Kill Bill" signs.

Where had he gone, though?

My gaze perused the strip of shops.

There was only one place that made sense: a trendy little restaurant a few shops down. I could hear live music blaring from it every time someone opened the door.

"What are you thinking?" Clarice asked.

"I'm not sure. I'm still trying to figure out what role this yoga studio may have played in all of this." I glanced around one more time. "You want to take a walk?"

She shrugged. "Sure."

I followed the sidewalk, past all of the shops, trying to picture Emma Jean coming here. Had she remained in her car in the parking lot, just waiting for Bill and Katarina to come out of The Yoga Tree? She wouldn't have been able to see much from that vantage point. Plus, staring in the front window would have been suspicious.

So where would she go to get the best, unobstructed view?

I stopped at the edge of the shopping center. Woods stretched behind the buildings, allowing privacy at the back of the shops.

I scanned the cars in the parking lot again.

My gaze stopped at one of the plates.

ISPYEJ

"What?" Clarice asked.

"I think that's Emma Jean's car!"

CHAPTER
TWENTY-FIVE

IT COULDN'T BE . . . I peered inside the old, rundown sedan. There on the dashboard was a picture of AJ.

This was definitely Emma Jean's car! I'd found it.

"Do you see anything?"

I squinted, trying to see through the glass. It was too dark and the flashlight app on my phone only created a glare. "No, not really. But maybe the police can find something."

"Good job, Gabby!" Clarice said. "What do we do now?"

"In a minute, I'll call the police. Right now, humor me as I talk this through."

"I'm reviewing Emma Jean's timeline. She was at work at The Crispy Biscuit on Tuesday morning. What if she came here after she got off on Tuesday night? Katarina apparently works out here on Tuesdays. That was also the night Emma Jean died."

"Sounds plausible, but how do we prove it?"

"I'm not sure. I want to look one more place to satisfy

my curiosity." I headed behind the buildings, to dumpster and delivery-entrance land. However because The Yoga Tree was located on the end, a fence blocked us from entering on that side. We had to walk all the way around the other end of the building to get there.

There were windows at the back of The Yoga Tree, I remembered. What if Emma Jean had parked and walked around the building for a better view? She could remain in the shadows back there.

Imaginary spiders danced across my spine as I walked deeper into the darkness and farther out of sight.

I turned on the flashlight app on my phone.

That familiar feeling of being watched tingled my senses.

I glanced around but saw no one.

"What's wrong?" Clarice asked.

"Probably nothing." I tried to brush off my jitters.

"The probably part isn't comforting." Clarice shivered.

Who might be watching me? Godfrey? Was Godfrey still following me? I told him he couldn't have a quote. But would that really deter him? Maybe he was looking for dirt on me so he could use that against Bill also.

"I don't really love it back here." Clarice shivered again. "Doesn't your brother do dumpster diving or something? He would like this."

At the mention of Tim, my heart thudded. Apparently Clarice hadn't heard yet that Tim might be responsible for the explosion. Maybe that was a good thing.

I pushed those thoughts aside for now.

Now that Clarice mentioned it, the stench of trash was heavy back here as we passed various dumpsters.

Finally, we reached the end, where The Yoga Tree was located.

"I still don't understand what you're looking for." Clarice wrinkled her nose with disgust.

"I don't know what I'm looking for. A clue as to what Emma Jean was doing here."

"Isn't it obvious she was sitting in her car and spying?"

I paused by the dumpster. "Not necessarily. She wasn't found dead in her car, for starters. That must mean she got out at some point. And somehow she got from this shopping center to the freezer of The Crispy Biscuit. What happened in the meantime?"

She glanced at the woods behind us. "I don't know. I'm not sure I want to know. I'm just glad her body has already been found. Otherwise, I might think that stench is a dead body."

"Dead bodies smell much worse. You know that."

"Thanks for reminding me." It was one of the perks to being a crime scene cleaner. You learned about various smells. Most of them weren't good, which really wasn't a perk at all.

"Well, I don't see anything. I guess we leave." Clarice twirled, ready to leave.

"Wait!" I shone my light along the back of the studio. One of the brown doors boasted a sign reading "The Yoga Tree." The area didn't appear to be well used. I couldn't imagine the yoga studio had very many deliveries here since they sold no merchandise.

I shined my beam around in one last desperate attempt to find answers.

That's when I hit the jackpot.

"Look at this, Clarice." I moved closer to my discovery.

She squinted, leaning forward to get a closer look. "What? I don't see anything except what looks like a can of soda that exploded."

I took a step closer, the answer clear in my mind. "That's not soda, Clarice. That's blood spatter. I think we found the crime scene."

CHAPTER
TWENTY-SIX

"HOW'D YOU DISCOVER THIS AGAIN?" Detective Adams asked as we stood behind the shopping center with mobile lights illuminating the area.

"It's a long story. I heard Emma Jean liked to come to The Yoga Tree. But she didn't do yoga, and no one in the studio recognized her. As we were leaving, I saw her car. Then I decided to come back here behind the businesses—"

"Just because?" He stared at me, looking slightly dumbfounded.

I nodded. What was so hard to understand about that? I was surprised they hadn't checked out this lead before tonight. "Yes, just because. I mean, it's good detective work. No offense. Anyway, we found this."

"Mm hm." He tapped his pen against his paper, and I couldn't tell if he was humored or annoyed. Maybe both.

"I already talked to the owner of The Yoga Tree. She said the only time they really come back here is in the evening—that's the only time they're open for business. Since it started getting dark earlier, that would mean that every time someone took the trash out, it was dark. The employees wouldn't have seen the blood spatter. The dumpster is on the other side of the doorway. Not even the garbage pick-up crew would have been able to see this since it was on the other side."

"If Emma Jean was spying on her ex-husband, why go to the back of the building?" Adams asked, casting a glance at the forensic team, who took photos and collected evidence.

"Standing out front would have been too obvious. Back here it was private—and there are windows. Plus, I believe this all fits with her time of death."

"How do you know when her time of death was?" the half-humored, half-annoyed expression returned again.

I shrugged, realizing I'd gotten ahead of myself, and brought my confidence down a notch. "I mean, I'm just basing it on what I know about her schedule. Did the medical examiner ever get back with you about her stomach contents?"

He nodded. "Her last meal was at The Crispy Biscuit. It was some kind of salad and soup. We confirmed that she ate it for dinner that evening before she left."

So she ate, left work, came here to spy, and somehow ended up dead. Why did the killer choose that exact moment? That exact way of killing her?

"Why would someone kill her here and then take her to the freezer at The Crispy Biscuit?" I wondered out loud.

"That's what we need to figure out."

"Boss, come see this," one of the crime scene techs said.

I tried not to leer when Adams paced over toward the CSI. They talked quietly, and then the CSI slid something into a paper bag. I strained to get a better look, but it did no good. I couldn't see a thing over the men's shoulders, which formed a wall of sorts as they huddled together.

I waited right where I was until Adams finished. I wasn't leaving without finding out what they'd just discovered.

Adams looked at me and sighed. "You don't have to wait, Gabby."

I offered my most pleasant smile. "I want to."

He twisted his lips in agitation and then tapped his foot. "You want to know what we found?"

I nodded like an over eager puppy waiting for a bone.

"We believe we found the murder weapon," he said.

My pulse spiked. "What was it?"

"A wrench. It fits the size, and there was blood on it."

"A wrench?" My thoughts raced.

"What?" He tilted his head.

"What kind of wrench?"

"Earl, what's the brand name of that wrench?" Adams called.

The CSI tech looked in the bag. "Williamson."

My heart sank as thoughts collided in my head. It couldn't be right . . . could it?

"What is it, Gabby?"

"That's the brand name that Jerry Lewis uses at his shop. He has advertisements for the company all over his house."

Thirty minutes later, Clarice and I started back to my car. Night had long since fallen and stars, along with a full moon, shone overhead. On this side of the building—the public side—no one had a clue what was happening just out of sight.

"You mind if I grab some water at that convenience store before we leave?" Clarice nodded at a mini-mart on the corner, within easy walking distance.

"Sure thing." I was a little thirsty also, now that she mentioned it. Must be all of that yoga I'd done.

Walking would help burn off some of my adrenaline. Because something was bothering me. Someone who was careful enough to move Emma Jean from this crime scene and plant her at The Crispy Biscuit would be smart enough to dispose of the murder weapon in the dumpster. That way, the trash crews would have taken it away to the dump and it would virtually be undiscoverable. But leaving it behind the dumpster made it much easier to find and identify as the murder weapon, especially if there was still blood on it.

And would Jerry really use one of the tools he sold at his shop? Certainly other people used that brand, but it wasn't extremely popular. It clearly was meant to point at Jerry.

I slowed my steps as I walked and rewound my thoughts for a minute. I needed to think about the flip side of the coin. I needed to consider the fact that maybe Jerry *had* been careless.

Maybe Jerry had followed Emma Jean here to confront her. He was probably upset because she wanted custody of their son. However, if that was true, then he'd come with malicious intent. That was the only reason he would have been carrying a wrench with him.

I could maybe—maybe—understand if the argument had turned ugly and she'd accidentally died. But Jerry planning on killing Emma Jean? I couldn't see it.

I had a lot of questions, a lot of thoughts to sort through. My brain was on overload, though.

I glanced across the parking lot. Bill's car was now gone. He'd missed all the excitement.

"How does Bill fit into all of this?" Clarice asked.

I glanced over at her. "What do you mean?"

"If your theory is right, then how is Bill involved in this? You said stuff has been happening to him also, right? Are the threats against him unrelated?"

I thought through everything I'd learned. I couldn't mention that information he knew about Munich, which may very well play into all of this. I'd wondered myself many times if there were two separate crimes going on.

"The threats against Bill are, most likely, because people jumped to conclusions and thought he had something to do with Emma Jean's death," I finally said. "They were looking for a legitimate reason to hate him other than his big mouth. They thought they'd found it and jumped on the band wagon."

"But didn't you say someone tried to abduct Katarina in the parking garage also?"

My moment of victory at finding the crime scene—and, consequentially, the murder weapon—was quickly fading. "That's right. It could have been random."

"That's a lot of random."

My sneakers thudded against the asphalt. "I agree. But stranger things have happened. Sometimes we fight the truth when, in fact, reality truly is stranger than fiction."

"There's something that bothers me even more," Clarice continued.

I waited for her moment of insight.

"How did Bill and Katarina end up together?"

I held my breath before letting it out in a gushing

chuckle. "Everyone has been wondering that. It's amazing what money and newfound fame will get you."

"Despite that, they're such an odd pair. Even if Katarina is money grubbing, she has to have standards. It's not like Bill is filthy rich and about to die so she'll get everything from him by default."

"Agreed." I looked over and saw another car pulling into the parking lot. It was going fast. Was it a police officer hurrying to the scene?

I kept watching the vehicle as Clarice talked about why Katarina and Bill didn't work as a couple. She muttered something about the rule of pretty and ugly and how she bet they were even voting for different candidates.

As the headlights got brighter and brighter, I realized one thing.

That car was headed right at us.

I grabbed her arm. "Clarice, run!"

CHAPTER
TWENTY-SEVEN

CLARICE and I darted away from the two-ton bullet headed our way. My muscles strained—they were already tight from yoga—as I looked for shelter of some sort.

I knew better than to duck between cars. If that vehicle charged into the row of cars, we'd be smashed between them like an accordion.

No, we had to make it to the convenience store. It was our best hope.

I glanced back once more. The car was close—too close. I quickly estimated that we had ten seconds to get to safety or we'd be toastier than The Crispy Biscuit.

We were almost to the building. Almost.

With one last burst of speed, we finally reached the entry to the convenience store. We were going so fast that we both slammed into the glass. We'd had no time to open the door. I kept my eyes closed, waiting for a crash. For pain. Agony.

Someone shouted in the distance. Tires squealed. I held my breath.

But there was nothing.

I dared to pull my eyes open and look around.

Only feet away, the vehicle swerved, narrowly missing hitting the building.

As it drove away, I spotted the dent in its bumper.

And no license plate.

This was the same person who'd tried to snatch Katarina and who had followed Riley and me, I realized.

What in the world was going on? I was getting closer to finding the right answers, I realized.

Then a worse thought occurred: Was Jerry driving that vehicle? He worked as a mechanic. He probably had access to all kinds of vehicles.

My heart pounded in my ears.

"He tried to kill us!" Clarice leaned against the building, bent over as she tried to catch her breath. "Why would someone do that?"

"That's the question."

I leaned against the wall also, trying to gather my wits.

A couple of people walked over to see if we were okay. We insisted we were.

"I'm not sure what good it would do to try to kill you now if the crime scene has already been discovered," Clarice said.

"I agree. Something weird is going on." I had to keep looking for answers. Until an arrest was made, I was on the case.

Until then . . .

"You call Adams this time," I muttered, handing Clarice my phone. "He's sick of me."

The next morning, I had a workshop in a town about an hour and a half north of here in the city of Seaford. Thankfully, I had enough supplies in the back of my car to make do—the rest had been destroyed in the fire. I'd left quite a few in my trunk for easy storage.

As I stepped out of our temporary hotel home, a familiar face caught my eye.

Godfrey.

I let out a sigh and paused on the sidewalk in the midst of vehicle and pedestrian rush hour. "What are you doing here?"

"Is that any way to greet an old friend?" He sneered and tugged his khaki beret lower.

"You're not an old friend. What do you want, and why are you following me?"

"Meow." He made little cat claws and scratched the air before snapping from his melodrama. "I just wanted to talk."

"I'm not giving you a quote about Bill in an effort to ruin his career and get Philip Munich elected." I hated politics more and more every day.

He had the nerve to look offended. "I get that. You think I'm here just for you?"

"Aren't you?"

He wiped at his shoulder as if brushing off my insult. "I'm headed to a fundraiser rally tomorrow. You did hear that Philip Munich was going to be in town, didn't you?"

"It seems like I did hear that somewhere. Where's that taking place again?"

"At the theater down the street from you."

Down the street from me . . . Frustration pinched at me. "You know where I live?"

"Where you *lived*," he corrected with a gleam in his eyes.

I scowled, the pinched frustration I felt turning into downright anger and my hands flying to my hips as I stared Godfrey down. "You've been following me? Do you drive a SUV with a dented bumper, by chance?"

"No way. I'm a sports car kind of guy." He shrugged. "Anyway, the event's being hosted by Walker Manning."

"The media mogul?" Walker owned more magazines than I could count. Why he'd chosen Virginia Beach as his hometown, I didn't know. But I'd heard rumor he owned a big oceanfront mansion.

"That's the one."

I moved out of the way as the dance troupe Riley and I had encountered last night left the hotel and headed across the street to The Scope. "You said it's tomorrow. So you're here early?"

"I'm trying to see what I can dig up. I don't have one of the most popular blogs in the country because I publish unsubstantiated fluff."

"What do you publish?" I was anxious to hear his answer, mostly so I could nail him when he blatantly lied.

"The truth." His eyes dared me to defy him.

I wanted to snort, but I didn't. "You know someone has been trying to hurt Bill. Are you behind it? Don't even try to justify your actions with excuses about the greater good."

"What? No. I would never encourage violence."

This guy seriously irritated me. I rolled my eyes instead of smacking him. "I've read your blog. I don't agree."

"My blog is passionate." He raised a fist in the air as if he deserved to be up there with the ranks of famous speechwriters of the past. Was this his "give me liberty or give me death" moment?

"Call it what you want. You called for protesters. You published Bill's address. Someone shot at him—when there was a baby nearby. That's irresponsible at best, reprehensible at worst."

"We were trying to send a message."

"A message to what?" This guy's logic was nowhere near on the same plane as mine.

"To stop spreading lies!" he exclaimed.

"Some would say that Bill is just passionate, as well." Maybe the problem was that people needed to tamp down their passions a little, especially when it boiled down to choosing passion over people.

He crossed his arms and raised his chin. "I suppose we each choose our sides."

"I suppose we do." I stared him down, silently letting him know I wouldn't be changing my mind. "Why are you here, Godfrey? It's not to have this conversation. And I'm going to be late if I don't leave soon."

"What's Bill planning?" His voice took on an intense edge, and he stepped closer.

I felt like a virtual target, caught in a sniper's crosshairs. I tried to keep a straight face and not give away that I knew anything. I was terrible when it came to having a poker face. "What do you mean 'What's Bill planning'?"

"I know he has some big announcement he's going to make. What is it? Stop acting like you don't know."

"You really think that I would tell you—if I knew, that is. I'm not admitting to anything except that you have flawed logic and an amazingly misplaced sense of innocence."

He twitched back a step. "I can do good things for you, Gabby. Really good things."

"What kind of good things are you implying I need done in my life?" I married the man of my dreams. I loved my job. I had great friends. This guy was off his rocker.

"I could profile you. Give you national attention. I know all about you and your crime-solving ways. You're really quite fascinating. My readers would love to read about you. It could do great things for your career. Take you to the next level."

"I don't need you to help me. I like to fight my way to the top."

He guffawed. "Think about it. Just think about it."

He gave me one more smoldering glance before he walked away.

CHAPTER TWENTY-EIGHT

WHEN I STEPPED out of the police station in Seaford that afternoon, the familiar sensation of being watched returned. I glanced around but saw no one. Despite that, I still couldn't shake the feeling that danger was trailing me.

Godfrey? Was he the person who'd tried to run me down? Had he followed me from the hotel?

Or was it Jerry? Was he behind this the whole time and determined to keep me quiet?

I mulled things over as I drove back home, but still had no answers. This whole investigation made me want to scream.

Finally, thirty minutes from home, I called Detective Adams. I was surprised he answered. I figured he'd avoid me like a brain-eating amoeba at this point.

"Any updates?" I started, feeling hopeful that I might get some information from him.

"As I'm sure you've put together, we're looking at Jerry Lewis. We don't have enough evidence to charge him."

"How about a murder weapon and motive?"

He paused, and I was certain he wasn't going to tell me.

"His fingerprints were on the wrench, but he has an alibi for Tuesday evening," he finally said.

I recalled my earlier conversation with Jerry. "That's right—he said he was working late."

"But he actually wasn't. He was with his girlfriend."

Girlfriend? Love could bring out the best and worst in people. "His girlfriend? Do you have a name?"

"I can't share that."

"Are you sure?" I pressed, slowing so I didn't miss my exit.

"I'm sure, Gabby. Sorry I don't have anything else I can say. If you can't tell, the answers aren't coming very quickly in this investigation."

I thanked him and hung up. Just as I was about to pull into to the hotel's parking garage, I saw someone familiar pulling out.

Katarina.

She didn't see me. Spontaneously, I turned around and followed her. I wanted to see exactly what she was up to. I couldn't forget my original thought that there was something suspicious about her. Remember that whole mafia theory? Maybe I really should explore that. If only it didn't seem so outlandish.

I stayed a safe, unnoticeable distance behind her—courtesy of some online tips I'd picked up about tailing people without being caught—as she traveled to Virginia Beach. She wove in and out of traffic like a crazy woman. Maybe because she was a crazy woman.

Finally, she stopped at a restaurant near the oceanfront. I pulled in behind her, waited until she went inside, and then I slunk into the swanky restaurant, quickly realizing I was entirely under-dressed.

Which could present a problem.

"Can I help you?" The young, pretty hostess at the front door eyeballed my casual business attire with confusion that clearly stated I wasn't their normal customer.

I had to think quickly. I looked into the dimly lit dining area and stopped at an idea.

"I'm here to inspect the saltwater aquarium."

Her gaze zeroed in on my Grayson Tech shirt. I saw her wheels turning as she probably wondered if that was the name of their normal company. I waited, keeping my expression neutral. She squinted as if uncertain.

"Are you the normal company we use?" She stared at me with large, brown eyes that matched her bobbed brown hair.

I shook my head. "You didn't hear? We took over at the end of last month."

"Really? I don't remember hearing about that." She tapped a manicured finger against her red lip.

What I'd first interpreted as snotty was actually insecurity, I realized.

That's when I launched into Plan B. "Look, I have one more aquarium to check before I call it a night, so do you mind? I'm running behind and I'd really like to get home in time to see my husband." I waved my hand, emphasizing my ring finger. "We just got married."

I'd noticed her engagement ring and hoped she would understand my plight.

Her eyes widened and brightened. "I'm getting married next month." She glanced behind her. "Okay, go right on ahead. You won't be disturbing any of our patrons, though, right? Because that makes my manager really, really mad."

"Of course not. They'll never even know I'm here."

"No supplies?" She glanced on the floor as if she expected to see more equipment with me.

"Everything I need is right in here." I held up my purse, hoping I didn't ruin this ruse. I knew nothing about aquariums except that they housed little creatures with fins.

She nodded. "Oh . . . okay then. Right."

I let out my breath and walked toward the fish tank. I had no idea how to take care of a saltwater aquarium. Did I use a chlorine test strip? The problem was I didn't even have one of those. Maybe I could at least find a filter to check.

I quickly ducked behind the wall-sized enclosure. From where I stood, I had a decent view of Katarina. She was seated at a table with . . . an older man with white hair. Something about him screamed "distinguished" and "rich."

Katarina leaned toward him and giggled. Her hand touched his across the table.

Was Katarina cheating on Bill with this man?

I fiddled with a drawer at the back of the aquarium stand, trying to get a better look. I definitely didn't recognize the man, but I'd guess, based on the way he carried himself, that he had money.

"So how is it?"

I nearly jumped out of my skin. I turned and saw the hostess standing beside me.

That's right. The aquarium. Awesome.

I stepped back and smoothed my hair. "Oh, yeah. I was

just looking at the fish and making sure they all looked healthy. That's always the first thing I check."

"That makes sense. I always worry about this." She pointed to a little blue and yellow one. "What kind is it again? I always forget."

I stared at the flat blue and yellow fish. "They're . . . dories. That's right. Dories. One of my favorites."

"Mine too. I didn't realize they'd taken the actual name of the fish and used it to name the character in the movie. That's so cool. Anyway, I was thinking about getting an aquarium like this for my home. But smaller, of course. What do you think? Is it a good choice for a first timer?"

Oh great. Of all the hostesses I could have encountered, she was actually interested in this stuff.

I stared at the gurgling water, the serene fish, the colorful decorations.

"Oh, yeah. These kinds of aquariums are great. Super easy. I'd totally recommend one."

Her eyebrows shoved together. "Really? I heard salt-water was hard."

I cringed. "Well, it just depends on how you look at it. The hard work is really worth the pay off."

She nodded, her shoulders relaxing. "I see."

I glanced back at Katarina. She looked my way. I almost ducked until I remembered that the aquarium mostly concealed my face.

"Well, I should get back to checking this out." I pointed to the tank.

"Oh, totally. Go right ahead."

She didn't move. I reached for the area where I thought the filter was located. She stayed beside me.

This wasn't going to work.

"I actually prefer to have some space when I do this. I'm sorry."

Her eyes widened, and she stepped back. "Of course. I was just curious about how hard it was. I'm sorry."

"I'll come back another time and give you some pointers." Note to self: Bring the girl an aquarium how-to guide.

Just then, Katarina and the man stood and began walking toward the exit. I couldn't let them get away!

"Oh, would you?" She clasped her hands in front of her. "That would be so fantastic."

My gaze strained to see what was going on through the glass. Where had they gone? Were they holding hands?

"Of course." I nodded toward the tank. "Now, if you don't mind."

She mumbled a few more things before scurrying back to her station. But, by the time she disappeared, Katarina and her mystery man were gone.

I scrambled along the edge of the restaurant, trying to get to the exit. When I emerged on the other side, a gigantic lobby greeted me. People walked every which way. Elevators dinged. An outside exit yawned open across from me.

Katarina could be anywhere.

It didn't appear I would be finding out who the mystery man was tonight.

Now I needed to figure out whether or not I should mention this to Bill.

Sierra called me on my way home, and we decided to meet at Riley's gym tonight. I'd been promising him that I'd come and watch him train, but I also wanted to talk to my bestie. I figured I could kill two birds with one stone. Plus, talking with Sierra would be a nice distraction from my confusion over this case.

She slipped inside a moment later, pushing Reef in his stroller. I rushed to help her, pausing for only long enough to babble talk with Reef. Sierra limped forward in a knee brace.

"No Rhonda tonight?" I asked, walking slowly beside her.

"No, I think she needed a break. And I'm desperate to feel normal, even if I'm not." She glanced around. "This place is nice."

I followed her gaze. The gym was large and located in an old warehouse. Everywhere around us were various obstacles and trampolines that had been set up for challenges. Everyone participating was having a timed trial tonight, and various supporters had come out to watch. Thankfully, this place didn't smell like the yoga studio. Instead, it reeked of sweat and testosterone, which was still preferred over the paper-mill stench.

We found seats along the edge of the room, and Reef stared at us from his stroller. I had to remind myself to stop making baby faces at him and to watch Riley.

And Riley was a sight to behold as he climbed walls, swung across bars, and ran up curvy rampy thingies.

"How's the house?" I asked Sierra.

"I don't want to move out. It's wonderful. Spacious. There's even a room above the garage just for my cats."

"Sounds amazing." I was about to launch into my apology when Riley jogged over and gave me a sweaty kiss.

"You're here," he said. "Thanks for coming. Finally."

"You're amazing out there," I told him. "I'm trying to

think of some kind of rad name to give you. Like the Leaping Lizard or something."

"The Leaping Lizard? No thanks." His hands went to his hips as his chest rose and fell.

"Gabby's Sugar Glider?"

Sierra snorted before bursting into laughter.

"Really?" Riley asked.

"I'll keep thinking. I'm going to be your biggest fan club this weekend, though. I promise you that."

"You alone will be my biggest fan club?" Riley's eyes twinkled.

"You know it, baby." I winked, feeling like I should get an A+ for being a supportive wife.

"Oh, you two are so cute," Sierra said. "You know what it's time for . . . a baby of your own!"

My mental music ground to a halt, and I handed Reef back to her. "A baby? We just got married! I love Reef, but no thank you. Not yet."

Had she forgotten that my brother just blew up our apartment? I had some issues to work through. To say the least.

"All right then." Riley took a step back, as if glad to have an excuse to leave this conversation. "I've got to get back out there."

"You do that, my big strong flying salmon."

He squinted, as if that description was physically painful. "Keep working on that one."

Silence stretched as he went back to the course for a moment.

"I'm so glad none of you were home," I finally said. Tears rushed to my eyes at the thought of it. I wouldn't forgive myself if my friends had been hurt.

She gave me a quick hug—and my friend wasn't a

hugger, so that meant a lot. "I know, Gabby. No one blames you."

"I feel like it's my fault, though. I should have kept better tabs on Tim. I thought he might be on drugs, but I had no idea that he was actually manufacturing drugs. In my apartment. I mean, he never buys anything."

"He may not have bought those supplies. Knowing Tim, he got them for free somehow."

I shook my head. "I still can't believe any of this. I mean, doesn't he know that Dad—"

"Actually, he doesn't, Gabby. He wasn't there to see that."

I nodded soberly at her reminder. "You're right. He wasn't."

"He told me once that the couple that kidnapped him weren't in their right minds. He never outright admitted that he did drugs in high school, but that was my impression. He tried to numb the pain."

"He told you that?" My heartbeat echoed in my ears.

She nodded, her gaze fixated on the obstacle course in front of us. "I don't think he wanted you to know. He knew it would be too hard for you to hear. But I told you because maybe it will help you understand what he's been through. It's not an excuse. It's just a window into his past."

"Thanks, Sierra." Her words had been insightful—just what I needed to hear. I'd been so blinded by my anger that I'd forgotten about everything my brother had been through.

"Enough about that," Sierra said. "What's going on with the case?"

I gave her an update.

"This obviously goes back to the election somehow," she said when I finished.

She took Reef from his stroller and he faced us in her arms, cooing and drooling. As the crowd beside us began cheering for another participant, Reef jerked his head toward him, eyes widened with adorable alarm that made me want to forget everything else.

Except I couldn't.

"You think?" I asked, bringing my thoughts back to our conversation.

She shrugged. "That's what makes the most sense to me."

"I'm hoping this will all fall in place. And soon."

"I hope it does too, Gabby."

———

The next morning, after Riley went to work, I went out to my car, climbed inside, and sat for a minute. I wasn't sure where I was going, but I was going to go somewhere. I couldn't stay in that hotel room all day—not unless I wanted to lose my mind.

I started the ignition and began driving. I didn't stop until I reached my apartment complex.

I stopped on the street outside and put my car in park. Then I stared at the structure. It truly was almost all ashes now. A few of the building's main supports still stood, charred and black. Most of the brick foundation remained.

But it was mostly gone. All of it.

I still couldn't believe it. No more impromptu talks with my neighbors. No more watching the crazy antics of the eclectic community around me. No more reminders of where it had all started for Riley and me. I held back my tears.

Someone knocked on my window. I jerked my head toward the sound and saw Sharon. The owner of The Grounds had a personality as colorful as the community around us. She had more piercings than I could count, and constantly changed her hairstyle and color. Right now it was short and dark with purple highlights.

As I rolled down my window, she slipped a cup of coffee inside. "I thought you might need this. It's your favorite—a vanilla latte. Lattes always make everything better."

"Thanks . . . a latte."

"At least you still have your sense of humor."

"At least." I allowed the drink to warm my hands. "How are you doing?"

I glanced at The Grounds. Wood covered the windows. Someone had spray painted graffiti on one of the boards. A few pieces of broken glass glimmered on the sidewalk.

"I have a crew inside working to restore everything," Sharon said. "I hope to open again by the beginning of next week."

"That's good." Did she know that Tim might be responsible? I wasn't going to ask. Not yet, at least.

"How are you?"

I shrugged. "I thought I was doing okay. But seeing this place now just makes reality kick in again."

"That's understandable. It will take time. Can I do anything for you?"

I thought about it a moment before shaking my head. "No, I don't think so. Only if you can turn back time."

I almost launched into Cher's song by the same name, but I stopped myself.

"Well, you know where I am if you need me." She tapped the car roof as she stood.

"Thanks, Sharon."

Where would I ever find another place to live that was in walking distance of my favorite coffeehouse?

I had to stop feeling sorry for myself, though. Enough was enough. There was a time to mourn and a time to move on.

With that thought in mind, I put my car in drive and took off again. This time I headed toward Jerry Lewis's place.

I pulled up just as someone bounced out of a car in the driveway. I stopped a safe distance away, hoping Jerry's guest wouldn't see me. Then I watched carefully.

My eyes widened when I recognized the person getting out.

Sarah Babble.

Sarah Babble? Was she stopping by to offer her condolences? Or would she confront the man because she heard he may have killed her best friend?

I held my breath, waiting to see what would play out.

To my surprise, Jerry stepped outside, strode across the sidewalk, and the two threw their arms around each other. Then they. . . kissed?

I blinked.

Was Jerry's secret girlfriend Sarah Babble?

Just when I thought I'd seen it all . . .

CHAPTER
TWENTY-NINE

I ALMOST CHARGED out of the car to confront the two lovebirds when my phone rang. I glanced down and saw that it was Garrett Mercer calling.

I frowned, glanced back at the happy couple, and I knew I had to answer. Garrett was one of the few phone calls I knew without a doubt I had to take.

"Gabby St. Claire, I saw you left a message for me. For what do I owe this honor?"

I bit down as I remembered the main reason I'd called. How would I break the news to him? "I have bad news, Garrett."

"I know about the apartment building."

I sat in stunned silence. "You do?"

"Yes, the fire department called me."

I swallowed hard as my thoughts flopped from one thing to another. "Did they tell you what happened?"

"As far as I know, they still haven't determined a cause. Did you hear differently?"

My throat tightened. "No, that's what I heard also.

They only have theories at this point. How are you dealing with it?"

I watched as Sarah and Jerry held hands. They walked over to his motorcycle and climbed on.

I frowned, contemplating my options. Should I follow them? No, that wouldn't give me any answers. I already figured they were dating. Following them would do no good and only waste my time.

Garrett let out a chuckle. "Sweetie, don't worry about me. I'll be fine. I was worried about you. How are you dealing with this?"

Relief swept through me at his compassion and understanding. "I'm doing as well as can be expected. I'm sad, but I'm also grateful to be alive."

"I'm grateful you're alive also. That's the important thing. Buildings can be replaced. People cannot."

"You're a good person, Garrett Mercer."

"Well, thank you. I take that as a compliment, especially coming from you."

I swallowed hard, fearing I might sound like I was taking advantage of him. That was the last thing I wanted. "Can I ask you another question?"

"Of course. Anything. Unless it's about that conversation I want to have with you."

That was right. He wanted to meet with me about something. Hopefully, it wasn't about us.

"I promise," I said. "We'll talk. I just need a little time to get myself together. I've been a little busy."

"Becoming an Internet sensation?" Humor laced his voice.

I really hoped no one else had posted videos of me. I couldn't handle anymore. "That was only once . . . right?"

He chuckled. "As far as I know it was only once. I try not to Internet stalk you, though."

Whew! "Okay, I haven't forgotten. I still want to talk. But I have another question in the meantime. I beg for forgiveness in advance if I'm overstepping my bounds. I do that frequently."

"Overstep away."

"I need to go to that fundraiser tomorrow night for Philip Munich."

"Munich, huh? I saw you as being more of a Stead supporter."

"I have not officially declared who I'm voting for, thank you. This is for . . ." How much did I tell him? I stared out the window in thought, noting that Jerry and Sarah were now long gone.

"An investigation," he finished.

"Yes, an investigation. You know me too well."

He clucked his tongue. "Do you know how much tickets are per plate?"

"I'm sure it's a lot." I should have never asked . . . except how could I not?

"You can say that again. But I might be able to get some for you. I have some connections." He didn't sound taken aback at all. Thank goodness!

"I'd be forever grateful. And I'll pay you back."

"Remember that payback when I ask you for my favor."

"Your favor?" He hadn't worded it that way at first. Now I really was curious.

"Yes, a favor. Next week. Next week we'll meet. I can't wait any longer."

"That sounds perfect." I hung up, more curious than ever.

As I walked down the hallway toward my hotel room, I spotted Katarina exiting her accommodations. I planted myself in front of her before she could pass.

"We need to talk," I said.

Her eyebrows flickered up in surprise, but she stopped and crossed her arms. "I busy."

"Where are you going? To the spa again?"

She pursed her lips ever-so-slightly, and I knew I'd hit the nail on the head.

"This can't wait," I continued. I realized I was using my mom voice, which was weird since I wasn't a mom. I'd been aiming for my kick-butt crime-solver tone. I need to work on that more.

"Fine. What you want?"

"Why are you dating Bill?" I started with the basic and most pressing question.

Her eyes widened as if I'd offended her. "Because I love him. Of course. What you saying?"

I probably wasn't going to get very far with that line of questioning, so I switched to the next most pressing question. "You weren't at the gala for the Harrison Group last week. Why did you lie?"

Her eyes went from wide to narrow. "Why you think that? Of course, I at charity gala."

I moved aside as a bellhop passed with a brass cart in tow. "I called. You weren't there. You've been lying, and I want to know why. I'm beginning to believe that you're the one behind all the incidents around Bill."

She gasped. "I almost abducted. You think I do that to self?"

"Maybe."

She gasped again, this time even bigger than last time. "Then you no smart."

"You knew one of the men who rescued you, didn't you? The tall blonde."

"I have no idea what you talk about." A family passed this time, but I barely budged. I feared if I gave Katarina too much room, she would run.

"Then where were you when Emma Jean was murdered? You weren't in Atlanta."

Katarina huffed. Looked away. Glanced at the floor.

I waited for her to deny it again.

"I here," she said instead.

I let that announcement settle over me. "What were you doing here, and why did you lie about it?"

"I try to revitalize my career. I lose contract with Harrison. I want more jobs."

"So you lied?" I clarified.

"You no understand how hard to get jobs at my age. I practically ancient."

"I thought Bill was paying your expenses?" Maybe I shouldn't have gone there. But I did.

"I like be my own woman."

Sadly, I believed her. She was a has-been catalog model having an identity crisis. Did that also mean she wasn't guilty of any of this?

I wasn't done with the conversation yet. "Who was that man you met with last night?"

She blinked, as if my question shocked her. "I answer enough questions. I done. No follow me anymore or I call police."

CHAPTER
THIRTY

I HAD to work the next morning, but, thankfully, my training workshop was close by in Newport News. Instead of eating with the officers as I normally did for lunch, I decided to take my food and eat in my car alone. I just needed a minute to think.

I took a deep breath as I sat there. The autumn sun hung low in the sky, casting an orange glow around me. My tuna salad sandwich didn't seem very appetizing, and I really hoped I had a breath mint for later.

My thoughts went to Tim. Detective Adams had called this morning and confirmed that the cause of an explosion was a meth lab in my apartment. Tim would be going to court soon, and my father hadn't gotten him out on bail.

Those thoughts only churned up my angst, though. I needed to think of something happier. Something like . . . this investigation.

All along, I'd been trying to deny the fact that this could have anything to do with the presidential election. It seemed too big, too out of the normal scope of the crimes I investigated. But what if all of this *did* somehow center around the election?

I sighed. Tonight was the fundraiser. Garrett had texted me earlier and said I had two tickets. Maybe I could discover something there. Maybe I could even decide for sure whom I was going to vote for. I thought my choice was clear, but lately I wasn't so certain.

My phone rang. I looked down and saw that it was Leona from church. Great. Had she somehow heard about yoga? I almost ignored the call, but I was too curious to do that.

"Hi, Leona," I started, keeping my voice upbeat.

"Gabby." Her voice sounded reserved. "I heard about your apartment. I'm sorry."

"Thank you."

"Our Bible study group would like to throw you and Riley a shower. We intended to do one anyway since you got married. But we're accelerating the process in light of what's happened."

Surprise ricocheted through me. "That's kind of you. Thank you."

A shower would help us rebuild. We still had nothing. No plates or silverware or towels even. I'd tried not to dwell on it too much because it felt overwhelming. I knew that one way or another it would all work out.

"And I'm sorry about what happened at church on Sunday. My emotions got the best of me."

She'd apologized? I hadn't expected that. "I appreciate the apology."

"But I still don't think you should vote for Munich."

I finished my tuna sandwich and washed it down with a sip of water. "I never said I was."

"Just in case."

I smiled as I hung up. Well, at least that had happened. If nothing else good came from this evening, I could remember that Leona had apologized. Maybe good always would win over the ugly. We just had to give it time.

That night, I showed up at the fundraiser dressed in my newly-purchased best. And I had the best-looking man in Virginia with me.

I stepped out of Riley's rental car and took his arm as we walked to the stairway of the parking garage. I paused by one vehicle, and my breath caught.

"What is it?"

"This is the vehicle driven by the person who tried to snatch Katarina at the mall, and the guy who followed us."

He stepped closer and peered inside. "I can't see anything. It's dark in here, but the insides look clean. I'm not sure how much you're going to discover looking here."

"That means that whoever tried to abduct Katarina must be here tonight."

I took his arm as we continued toward the rally. But I no longer felt relaxed and relishing this moment. Instead, I glanced around, half-expecting someone to jump out and hijack this moment.

We managed to get to the sidewalk outside without injury. It was already dark, and a strange fog had fallen over the street. Other guests were also exiting their vehicles and heading to the historic theater. It was normally a dinner theater, but tonight it would be transformed into a banquet hall.

Inside, we were shown to our table. I soaked in the strings of lights hanging above us, setting a romantic, cozy atmosphere. There was a stage up front, and I had no doubt that's where Munich would be seated. A stringed quartet played soothing music in the opposite corner.

I wasn't sure who everyone here was, but I'd guess they were wealthy business leaders, local politicians, and community movers and shakers. Several people stopped by our table and chatted with Riley. He knew more people in these circles than I did. I used the opportunity to let my gaze wander, looking for a sign of the person who'd been driving that dented SUV.

Finally, I spotted some familiar faces. Starting with Godfrey. He mixed and mingled and even seemed to have a fan club.

Go figure.

Bill was also here, which was surprising since he didn't like Munich. Katarina was at his side, like the trophy he wanted her to be. He also mixed and mingled.

There was a lot of that going on. I needed to get more comfortable at circulating in these situations, but everything in me rebelled against the whole networking thing. I wanted to build relationships with people because I cared about them, not because of what they could do for me.

My gaze caught on someone else in the distance: the older gentleman I'd seen Katarina with at the beach restaurant.

I nudged Riley. "Do you know who that is?"

His gaze followed mine. "That's Walker Manning."

My eyes widened as realization hit me. "The media mogul? Really?"

"Yeah, why?"

"I saw Katarina meeting with him."

My gaze shot across the room again. Was that . . . Sarah Babble? Why would she be here? She was a carhop at a drive-in restaurant. I knew how much tickets to this event cost—I'd looked it up earlier to satisfy my curiosity. How could she afford it? Was Jerry with her? I didn't see him.

My thoughts continued to churn, turning things over and over.

I was almost ready to try my hand at the whole being social thing, mostly so I could talk to Godfrey, Sarah, and Bill, when Garrett Mercer appeared at the table. Handsome, rich, and charming Garrett Mercer with the incredible British accent.

"Gabby, fancy seeing you here. You look lovely, as always." He winked before turning to Riley. "Riley, you too. Congratulations, you two, on your marriage. I can't think of two better people to end up together. Truly."

I released my breath. He knew! Thank goodness, he knew. That saved me having an awkward conversation with him later.

"Thank you," I murmured. I kept one eye on Garrett and the other on the rest of the room. I didn't want to miss anything.

Garrett leaned closer. "Look, I know we're supposed to meet next week about that favor I mentioned to you. But I'm just going to throw my proposal out there to you now. I'm putting together a cold case team, and I want you to lead it."

I flinched, certain I hadn't heard correctly. Of all the things I'd thought he might say, that wasn't one of them. For a moment, I forgot about all the suspects I was supposed to keep my eye on. "What?"

He nodded with a sly grin. "That's right. It meant so much to me to have closure after the murder of my family. I want to do the same and help others, so I'm personally funding a cold case team to review unsolved cases that I've chosen. I want you to head it up. What do you say?"

"I'm . . . I'm flattered." Truly, I was.

His intelligent gaze locked on mine. "I'm not trying to flatter you. I'm asking you because you're good at what you do. You put your heart into it, and that's what these families need: compassion and closure."

I glanced at Riley. He nodded with encouragement.

"I . . . um, I'll need to think about it." I didn't want to be too hasty.

"There's pay involved, and you get to pick your own team. Plus, you work on your timetable. You can continue to work your other job and do this on weekends or vacations."

"Wow. That sounds amazing." Like, *amazing* amazing. What an opportunity.

"So say yes." Garrett's eyes sparkled as he looked down at me.

"I'd be a fool to answer without sleeping on it. But I'm very interested."

He smiled. "I thought you might say that. So sleep on it. Let me know tomorrow, okay?"

I nodded. "I will. Thanks, Garrett."

"I'll catch up with you later." He offered a wave as he walked way.

Riley squeezed my hand as the candle on the table warmed his gaze with its flickering flame. "What an opportunity," Riley said. "You should go for it."

"Really? It wouldn't make you uncomfortable if I was working for Garrett?" That had been my main concern.

"I think he's a stand-up guy, and I trust you."

I planted a quick kiss on his lips. "Thanks, Riley. That means a lot to me."

"It really sounds right up your alley too. And you get to pick your own team? It's perfect for you."

Excitement buzzed through me at the possibility.

For now, I needed to focus. I slid my chair back.

"Will you excuse me a minute? I'm going to run to the restroom."

"Of course."

I slipped from my seat and found the ladies' room. When I stepped from the stall a few minutes later, I nearly collided with someone.

Sarah Babble stood there, waiting for me, with a deranged roller derby girl look in her eyes.

CHAPTER
THIRTY-ONE

DERANGED ROLLER DERBY GIRL? No, I decided. She looked like a rejected prom queen as she stood there in her bubble gum pink evening gown. I braced myself, wishing I'd brought my gun. But, since there was a metal detector when we entered, I knew I couldn't have brought it inside.

"Gabby," she started, cracking her knuckles. "I didn't realize you'd be here."

"What can I say? It's the place to be tonight." I swallowed hard, bracing myself for whatever was to come. I skirted out of the stall and hurried toward the sink "I wasn't expecting to see you here."

Her cheeks reddened. "Munich is actually my uncle."

"Is he? I had no idea." I hadn't seen that one coming.

"Yeah, I don't go around talking about it because people get so weird when it comes to politics. Plus, with my anger management problem, it could be bad press for him. I don't want that. He's a wonderful person who deserves good things."

I wondered exactly how much trouble her anger

management problem had gotten her into. I certainly didn't want to find out here in the granite-encased bathroom. At least granite was easy to clean. I'd had to get blood out of it before and—well, that wasn't important.

I turned the water on, careful to keep an eye on Sarah. "When did you and Jerry happen?"

She shrugged and rubbed her glossy lips together as she turned toward me. "A few months ago."

I cut the water. Why was there no one else in here? Women usually came in here by the herds at events like these. "Did Emma Jean know you were dating her ex?"

Sarah nibbled on her lip and frowned. "She found out, and she wasn't happy."

"So you're the one Emma Jean wanted to use as an excuse to get custody of AJ, is that right? She was going to say you were dating Jerry before the baby came, somehow proving that her estranged spouse was cheating?"

She fisted her hands. "But we weren't. We didn't start dating until Emma Jean was officially out of his life."

I dried my hands, balled up the paper towel, and tossed it into the trashcan.

"Jerry gave me your name. He told me you were friends with Emma Jean. Why would he do that when he knew I might put everything together?"

Someone knocked at the door.

Knocked at the door? Had Sarah locked us in here? That wasn't good.

Sarah didn't seem to notice as she continued, cracking her knuckles again. "Neither of us wanted to hide this, but with everything that had happened we knew we had to be careful. He told me that you might be in contact and asked me to keep quiet about our relationship for the time being. Communication is everything in a relationship."

"I suppose it is." I turned toward her, tension still stretching across my shoulders as I tried to anticipate what she would do next. "Why'd you find me in here?"

Something changed in her gaze. Actually, it ignited. "I wanted to explain everything. I knew you'd seen us and become suspicious. But we didn't have anything to do with Emma Jean's death. I promise. In fact, Jerry and I were together at the time of the murder. We were at a biker bar in Chesapeake. There are witnesses."

Was that right? Interesting. "Thanks for letting me know that. I'm sure Detective Adams has checked that out."

She stepped closer. "I really want to find Emma Jean's killer, Gabby. I promise I do. If you need any help, please let me know."

After a moment of contemplation, I nodded. I believed she was innocent. I hoped I didn't regret it, but I did believe her. "Okay, Sarah. Thank you."

When I arrived back into the dining area, Riley was talking with a group of people near our table, looking incredibly handsome and comfortable, so much so that I nearly pinched myself when I remembered he was mine.

Since he was occupied, I took a moment to stand back and watch the people around me.

Godfrey continued to mingle, acting like he was a superstar of sorts. Munich was also walking through the masses, shaking hands, and working the crowd. Servers walked around and offered hors d'oeuvres until dinner was ready.

The soothing music in the background offered a direct

contrast to the anxiety in my stomach. Was something going to happen here tonight? That was my best guess.

I kept my eyes open, waiting, watching, and expecting.

At that moment, a new face caught my eye. Was that . . . ?

It was! It was the Nordic god who'd saved Katarina in the parking garage.

He lingered against the wall across the room. No one was with him. And his eyes surveyed everyone in the room.

Interesting.

Confront him or watch him?

I volleyed the two ideas back and forth.

I had a feeling the man had some answers, answers I wanted.

For that reason, I decided to confront him.

I started to charge across the room but then changed tactics. It would be better if I came at him from the side so he didn't see me approach.

I skirted around the edges of the room, dodging people and never taking my eyes off the man.

He continued to scan the crowds, as if looking for someone.

Strange.

Finally, I reached him, ready to spring it on him that I knew he was here.

"Took you long enough to see me," he muttered.

I let out a mental sigh. "Really? You knew I was here and I was coming?"

"You're not that sneaky. Sorry."

I shoved my pride aside. "Who are you?"

"You really don't know yet?" He asked the question without any emotion or reaction.

"Would I be asking if I did?"

He glanced around and his jaw flexed. "Let's go in the hallway and talk."

"We should stay here." I crossed my arms.

"If we stay here, I'm not saying a word. Your choice."

The man was playing dirty, and I didn't like it. Yet I desperately wanted to know what he had to say.

I glanced back at Riley. He was still talking to a small audience. That meant that no one knew where I was going or whom I was with.

I hoped I didn't regret this.

CHAPTER
THIRTY-TWO

"MY NAME IS ROBERT HAWK, and I'm a PI," he started once we were in the hallway.

"A PI?" That wasn't what I'd expected to hear. "You were hired to follow Katarina?"

He shook his head. "I was hired to follow Emma Jean."

I shook my head. "I'm entirely confused."

"Of course you are." He smirked like the arrogant jerk I'd already determined he was.

I scowled, not appreciating his demeaning remarks. If I wasn't so curious, I would simply walk away from this conversation. But he knew I wouldn't do that.

"Please explain," I finally said with an exasperated sigh.

Satisfaction gleamed in his eyes. "I'm formerly Secret Service."

This was no time to ask him how I'd performed while acting like a Secret Service agent while protecting Bill. He'd really think I was a joke if I did.

"Impressive. Maybe," I said. Was he telling the truth? I didn't see any signs of deceit.

He let out a sardonic laugh. "Maybe . . . anyway. I was hired by my old friend from high school to follow Emma Jean."

"Greg Borski?" I guessed.

He nodded. "That's right. Emma Jean had been acting suspicious in the week or two before her death. He was afraid she was going to try to go public with the information on The Crispy Biscuit—their nonorganic food as well as their money troubles."

"Go on."

"So I started following her, trying to see what she was up to. That's when I discovered that Emma Jean was following Katarina."

"And somehow your case shifted from one woman to the other?"

He shrugged. "I'll get to that. Be patient. Emma Jean was not only following Katarina, she was taking pictures of her. And it wasn't always when she was with her new beau, Bill McCormick. So I started doing some research."

"What did you discover?"

"I know this sounds too big to be true, but I'm nearly certain she has ties with . . . the Russian mafia."

Wait . . . what? Sierra had been right this whole time? Next thing he'd be telling me that Katarina actually *was* a mail-order girlfriend. Maybe Sierra was more insightful while on painkillers than I'd given her credit for.

"Are you serious?"

He nodded. "Dead serious. I believe that's why she's been meeting with Walker Manning as well."

"But that would mean that Walker Manning has ties with—"

He put a finger over his lip and glanced around, as if to

make sure no one was listening. "Exactly. There has always been talk."

"Really?"

"They need someone to fund them. Why not one of the richest men on the East Coast?"

I felt like I'd just stepped inside a James Bond movie or something. Was this case really this big?

"Were you there the night Emma Jean was murdered?" I asked. "Were you following her then?"

He shook his head. "No, unfortunately, I wasn't. In fact, I was following Katarina that night. She had a meeting with Manning."

That's the person she'd been with! "So you have no idea who murdered Emma Jean either."

His jaw flexed. "No, I don't, though I suspect she stumbled into more than she ever imagined when she was spying on Katarina."

"So she was essentially killed by the Russian mafia?" I really couldn't get past that point.

"You've got to understand that there isn't a large network of them here. They only have a few operatives."

"And what's the goal of these operatives?" I couldn't believe I was asking that.

"That's what I'm not sure about."

None of this could be real. That was the point I couldn't get past. I kept thinking that at any minute, someone was going to burst from a hidden room with a camera and yell, "Gotcha!"

"So Borski then hired you to tail Katarina?" I clarified, trying to follow the logic here.

"No, I did that on my own, just to satisfy my curiosity."

"Did you discover anything else?"

His nose twitched. "Not yet. But I'm close to finding

the answers. I feel strongly that it has to do with this election."

Why did he look uncomfortable? Was he disappointed in himself for not having answers? "Did you report this to any of your former Secret Service colleagues? Maybe even the FBI?"

"Why would I do that? I need more proof."

I shrugged. "Just curious."

Curious and not entirely convinced.

With all of those new thoughts brewing in my mind, I sat back down at the table with Riley. Bill was beside him, chatting about politics—of course. I didn't see Katarina.

"Where were you?" Riley whispered.

"It's a long story," I said. But all I could think about was: Russian mafia? I was having trouble buying it. But I'd run into crazier crimes and motives before.

I pulled out my phone and found the picture I'd taken at Emma Jean's house. The one of Katarina with the mystery man. I enlarged the picture, removing Katarina entirely from the screen.

"Bill, do you recognize this man?" I asked.

"Yeah, that's Frederick Mason."

I sucked in a breath. "What? The frat boy who died?"

He nodded. "Yeah, where'd you get that picture?"

"From Emma Jean's house . . ."

"How—?"

I shook my head. "I have no idea."

Before I could launch into more questions, a server set my soup and salad in front of me. I looked up and did a double-take. "Julian?"

This was like a reunion of all the people I'd met over the past week. I'd known tonight's fundraiser was *the* place to be, but wow. Everyone else in town thought so too.

He also did a double-take. "Gassy?"

My cheeks reddened at the name. "I wasn't expecting to see you here."

"You didn't know? The Crispy Biscuit had already signed on to cater this event before everything hit the ceiling. We won a contest to cater this event."

"I see. Is Borski here also?"

He shook his head. "No, Greg is still having a temper tantrum over everything that happened. Selena and I are heading things up. We already had the menu down, and, let's face it, Greg wouldn't have done anything here tonight except lend his persnickety perspective on everything we're doing wrong."

I raised my spoon. "Well, I can't wait to try the food. I've heard your cuisine is delicious."

"I hope you'll enjoy it."

Since there was a slight chill in the room, I decided to start with the soup first. I'd heard so much about it, and I wanted to see if it was as good as people said it was.

I took the first bite, and my taste buds approved. If only I could truly enjoy it. Instead, my thoughts were churning, on the brink of realization.

"It's good," Riley said. "Savory and flavorful."

My phone began singing "What's Up" by 4 Non Blondes.

I excused myself when I saw the name of an old friend who worked with the medical examiner, Lela.

"Detective Adams gave me permission to share some

information with you," she started. "I just found out something interesting about Emma Jean Lewis."

I put my spoon down. "What's that?"

She let out a sigh. "Between you and me . . . you know the restraints we have on us working here in the coroner's office, right?"

"Sure." Why was she prefacing what she had to tell me with this? I wasn't sure, but I let her have her time.

"I mean, we're limited by our laboratories, by time, by taxpayer dollars."

I had no idea where she was going with this or why she almost sounded apologetic. "Right."

"Anyway, usually in a case like that of Emma Jean Lewis, we know the cause of death. I did the autopsy and determined she died from blunt-force trauma. It seemed pretty obvious from her wounds."

"Right."

"Something was bothering me, though. There were a few other symptoms that I wasn't sure were connected or not. The fact that she was frozen didn't help. On a whim, I did a tox screen. As you know, the average tox screen can identify only around three hundred toxins, only the most popular ones that are found in crimes."

My curiosity wound tighter and tighter. "Right."

"But we can use gas chromatography, which will still pick up on less than fifty percent of all the possible compounds people could die from."

If I didn't respect her so much, I would tell her to get on with it. "Right."

"This is what is boils down to: I found some evidence of oleander in her system," she finally said.

"Oleander? The plant? Really? I would have never expected that."

"Yes, I would have never realized it if I hadn't done this test. But I'm glad I did."

I leaned back in my chair, chewing on that revelation. "How did oleander get into her system?"

"I can only assume it was from something she ate."

What had been found in her stomach as her last meal? "You said you found evidence of a salad and soup in her stomach, right? That was the last meal that also helped to identify her time of death."

"That's correct. The soup seemed to be interesting. There was butternut squash, rutabaga, basil, maybe even some pumpkin."

I looked down at my harvest bisque and frowned. Oh. My. Goodness.

I glanced over at Riley and saw him raising his spoon to his mouth. I swatted it out of his hand, splashing soup on the person next to him. The man shot me a dirty look.

"Gabby . . . what?" Riley picked up his napkin and began wiping the liquid from his suit.

"Don't eat any more. Trust me."

I glanced around. Everyone else was eating the soup also.

Was Philip Munich also eating this soup? I had a better idea of what was going on here. But my conclusions were scary.

Panic fluttered through me.

This wasn't good. It wasn't good at all.

"Thanks, Lela. I've got to go. Tell Adams he needs to get out to the Munich fundraiser on Granby Street, though. Right away."

CHAPTER
THIRTY-THREE

I JUMPED TO MY FEET. "Don't eat the soup. I just found a . . . rat in mine!"

People would probably react more quickly to that reasoning than by me saying their food could have oleander in it. Besides, everyone's soup probably hadn't been poisoned, but I had to err on the side of caution.

I glanced at the stage area. There was Munich, about to eat this award-winning soup. I had to stop him. Somehow.

Without thinking it through, I rushed toward him.

If I wasn't careful, I could start mass chaos and panic in here. That wouldn't be good either.

Think, Gabby. Think.

I decided to utilize my acting skills. This plan was the best I could come up with off the cuff. I slowed my steps until I reached the table. I drew in a deep breath before "accidentally" tripping and landing on the table. As I hoped, everyone's soup flew out of their bowls.

The guests of honor rushed to their feet, gasping and saying not-so-nice things about me. Several people assisted Munich. Almost all of them gave me dirty looks.

"I'm so sorry," I muttered, placing my hand over my heart in what I hoped looked like distress. "I'm such a klutz."

Munich wiped his suit with a napkin and looked up at me. "Don't worry about it."

He actually sounded sincere.

"You need to watch where you're going," another man said with a growl to his voice.

At least Munich hadn't eaten that soup.

I glanced across the room and spotted Julian. Our eyes connected.

He knew that I knew, I realized.

He started toward the hallway. No way was I letting him get away. Not a chance.

I dashed across the room, dodging two men who looked like security for the event. Where was Riley? Robert Hawk? I needed both of them right now.

"Ma'am!" one of the guards yelled.

I ignored him and kept on going. I wasn't letting Julian out of my sight. Not if I could help it.

I managed to slink away from security. Julian cut into a back hallway, near the kitchen if I had to guess.

He darted in a room in the distance.

Just as I stepped into the space, screams sounded behind me. I glanced back in time to see flames burst to life.

Fire? What had happened? This wasn't good.

My lungs burned by the time I reached the door where Julian had disappeared. I threw the door open and stepped inside. It was dark.

Which should have been my first clue.

Before I realized what was happening, someone shoved me. The door slammed. The lights came on.

Katarina stood there in the middle of the supply closet, pointing a gun at me.

"You should have left well enough alone," she muttered, her English suddenly perfect. "But now we have to do this the hard way."

This wasn't good. I swallowed hard and stepped back, unable to pull my gaze away from the gun barrel. "There's no hard way necessary."

"You ruined our plan that we've been working on for weeks," Julian said. "Me getting a job at The Crispy Biscuit was no mistake."

We began doing the whole "circle while you walk with your hands raised in the air and a gun is pointed at you" thing.

"Was Emma Jean your test subject for poisoned food?" I asked.

Satisfaction gleamed in Julian's eyes. "As a matter of fact, yes. I wasn't sure exactly how much oleander I would need. Who better to test it out on than the ever-annoying Emma Jean?"

"I'm guessing that when you gave her that last dose, it didn't act fast enough. She suspected you were up to no good, but it was too late to add more poison to her soup. So you followed her that night. Saw her spying on Katarina behind The Yoga Tree. You're a smart man, and you wondered if it might ever come down to this. So you stole one of Jerry's tools when you took your car into the shop to have it fixed. You knew it would come in handy."

"Smart girl," Julian said.

At least one person thought so tonight.

"You killed her, left the wrench where it would be discovered, but then you went on to make things even more complicated. You hated Greg Borski, and you saw an opportunity to make his life miserable as well. You brought Emma Jean back to The Crispy Biscuit and put her in the freezer."

"He almost messed up everything," Katarina said, her gun still raised toward me. "With the restaurant being shut down, we could have lost this catering event."

"That would have ruined your whole plan."

"Thankfully, it didn't." Julian scowled at Katarina, who scowled back at him.

"So you two are Russian mafia?" I said, remembering Robert's words.

They both froze and stared at me.

"What? No. Why would you think that?" Julian looked at me like I'd said he was Mother Teresa reincarnated.

Why did they look so shocked? "Why else would you want to kill Philip Munich?"

"There are plenty of reasons. That's such a generalization. Insulting, really." Katarina raised her nose.

Where was Riley? Robert? Anyone?

The fire was stopping them, I realized. It had blocked the entrance to the hallway. It would stop me also if I wasn't careful. Who knew how far the flames had spread? My best guess was that no one could get to us right now. I was flying solo.

I licked my lips. "So who do you work for?"

"No one," Julian said. "Philip Munich killed our brother."

My jaw dropped. "Frederick Mason was your brother? The boy who died of asthma?"

Katarina scowled. "That's right. Munich left him there to die. He should be held responsible."

"How'd you find out? I thought it was a secret."

"I heard that Steve Patterson was shopping it around,"

Katarina started. "That news got back to me. I found out through the grapevine. That's no way to learn the truth about your brother's death. Then I heard that Bill McCormick was spineless enough to buy it."

I guess that explained why they were dating . . .

"But I thought you were a victim here," I continued. "Who tried to abduct you in the parking garage?"

Katarina shrugged as she stood in front of the door. "I had to set that up. Julian was driving. Of course. I had to make sure Bill thought I was a victim."

"So you tried to run me over in the parking lot?" I turned to Julian.

He shrugged. "Maybe."

"You knew that day when I was cleaning the freezer who I was?"

"Yeah, of course, *Gassy*." He chuckled.

"And you locked me in the freezer?"

"You made it easy. If only someone hadn't found out and rescued you."

While I was at it, I might as well ask this final question, "And did you shoot at us at my apartment?"

Julian shrugged. "Yeah, that was me. I was trying to discourage you from pursuing this anymore. It didn't work."

"None of this matters," Katarina continued. "What matters is this: Philip Munich must pay. His behaviors can't be rewarded by allowing him to win this election."

"Why not just go public with the information then?" I asked. "Why go through all this trouble instead?"

"Bill is the only one who has proof. If it's our word against his, then no one will believe us" Katarina said. "They'll think we were planted by the other political party to ruin him."

Julian raised his gun. "Okay, enough talking. You're also inconsequential."

My heart pounded faster. Would this be the time I didn't get out alive? I knew it was just a matter of time. "You don't have to do this."

"Of course, we do," Katarina muttered.

Just then, the door opened, slamming into Katarina. The gun fell from her hands. I grabbed it before Julian could.

Bill stood there, looking more confused than I'd ever seen him.

"Katarina, I was so worried about you. I barely managed to get through the doorway unscathed because of the fire—" He froze when he saw me. "Why are you holding a gun, Gabby?"

I sighed. Really? "Your girlfriend just tried to kill me."

"Katarina? She would never do that." Disbelief etched every word.

Bill had it bad. He'd been blinded by his love—or lust, whichever it was.

I kept the gun raised, just in case anyone tried to make any moves. Everyone seemed frozen.

"Oh, you're so not smart, Bill McCormick." Katarina crossed her arms and frowned, not looking quite so pretty with that expression. "You think I really loved you?"

His face went slack, and I felt sorry for him. Like, really, really sorry.

"What do you mean?" His voice made him sound like a wounded child.

She sneered. "I was only dating you to find out the information you had on Munich. I heard you'd purchased it, you disgusting excuse for a human."

"What?" His bottom lip dropped open. He was truly shocked, I realized.

"Do I look like your type?" Katarina continued, kicking the poor man while he was down.

"I'd say so," he said. Like any red-blooded man, he believed beautiful women were definitely his type. His chest puffed out even more.

At that moment, the cops rushed into the room.

I lowered the gun as Katarina and Julian were arrested. Riley followed behind law enforcement, dashing into the room and pulling me into his embrace.

"I was so worried," he said. "The doorway was totally blocked by the fire, and the emergency doors were locked."

"I'm just glad you're okay. I didn't know what was going on out there."

"The fire . . . it's out now. No one was hurt. Someone knocked a candle over and it set a curtain on fire. Munich was rushed somewhere safe."

Adams appeared a moment later with Robert at his side. The former Secret Service agent rubbed his head. When Robert saw me, he scowled.

"Look who I found locked in a closet," Adams muttered. "He said he knows you."

"I thought you might come and act as backup," I said to Robert. Then I remembered his incorrect assertion about the mafia. "And you were wrong, by the way."

He rubbed his head again. "You're right. I wasn't part of the Secret Service."

That hadn't been what I was talking about, but . . . "What were you?"

"I was an administrative assistant," he admitted. His entire face seemed to droop.

He was embarrassed, I realized. Good. After he'd put me down so many times earlier, he deserved a little humbling.

"Mrs. Thomas?" a suited man asked at the door. "We're going to need to talk to you."

Maybe he was the real Secret Service. I nodded and made sure Riley stuck with me this time, just in case.

CHAPTER
THIRTY-FOUR

SIERRA AND CHAD sat with me on the bleachers as we waited for Riley's turn to compete in the National Warrior Challenge qualifying competition. Bill had just shown up, and my dad and his fiancée, Teddi, were supposed to be here soon.

The competition was being held in a large festival park in downtown Norfolk. Lights, bright and glaring, were set up around the course. Excitement filled the air as everyone cheered for their competitor. Several cameras recorded the whole thing, and two commentators sat in a high-perched booth, offering commentary from their vantage point over the loudspeaker.

The weather this evening had also turned chilly, and I was glad I'd brought an oversized sweatshirt with me. I gripped the coffee in my hands and waited for Riley's turn to begin. I might have been more nervous than he was.

As I watched a woman mess up and flop into the water beneath the course, my mind drifted to everything that had happened over the past couple of weeks.

Katarina and Julian had been arrested. Their real names were Katarina and Julian Mason. Frederick was their brother. A case into what had happened to him was being opened. That meant that Philip Munich's role in that was also being examined. Limited portions as to what was going on had been leaked to the media. Bill McCormick had beat the mainstream press to the information, which had surged his ratings again. It seemed to quickly heal him of his broken heart.

Munich claimed he was innocent and that this was an election ploy. The public might not find out the real truth until after the election, which was unsettling, to say the least.

Last I'd heard, Borski had decided to close The Crispy Biscuit still, but he was talking about starting a new restaurant near D.C.

"There's something I've been meaning to ask you," Bill said.

"What's that?" I took a sip of my coffee.

"Why aren't you more fired up about this election? Everyone else is acting like life and death hinges on who wins. You seem pretty relaxed."

I quickly tried to think of the best way to explain it to him. "I guess I can sum it up with this: Some trust in chariots, but I trust in the name of the Lord my God."

Bill literally scratched his head. "Huh?"

I shook my head, realizing there were better ways to explain my faith to someone who didn't have any. "I'm just saying that my trust isn't in any politician. The next president of the United States isn't going to save the world. Even if he's a Christian, he's not going to convert everyone to Jesus. My trust is in a Higher Power, one who controls the wind and waves. Who holds tomorrow in His hands. Who's reigned through all the storms of life."

Bill nodded slowly. "I think that's a great perspective. I'm not sure I agree. But I like it and think it's admirable."

Silence fell for a minute.

"You doing okay, Bill?" I finally asked, sensing a heaviness about him.

He shrugged. "I guess. I have a lot to talk about on my show. That counts for a lot."

"And your ratings are through the roof."

"It's true."

I shifted, thinking about all the changes that had happened in such a short amount of time. "Have you looked for another place to stay?"

"I found an apartment I can use until I find something more permanent. I think it will be a good choice. As much as I'd like a big house, I'm not home enough to take care of the maintenance of it. I'll probably look for a condo eventually. You?"

"Riley and I are going to start looking for a place to rent next week. We need a little more time to save for our down payment before we can buy our own place, you know? We weren't ready to go here quite yet."

"Makes sense," Bill said.

"Chad and I are looking also," Sierra added, leaning over to join our conversation. "But I've got to get through this knee surgery. There's no way I can move with my knee like this. Thankfully, my friend is out of town for another few weeks and said I can keep using her place, so that will buy me some time. Plus, their house is really nice."

My heart sagged again. I didn't want to think about us all moving in different directions. But that was life, and I had to deal with it.

"How's Tim?" Sierra asked. "I've been meaning to ask."

My heart sagged even more. "He's going to be locked up for a while. I did go see him in jail. He's doing okay and is very apologetic now that he's sobered up. I hope the time behind bars will be good for him."

"No one blames you, you know," Bill said.

My heart ached again. "You should."

"You're the only one who blames you," Sierra said. "Your brother made his own choices."

"Thank you, guys. I appreciate how you've been there for me." I had the best friends. Really. Especially when they weren't dating a psychopathic ex-model with vengeance on her mind.

"Oh look. Here comes Riley." Sierra sat up straighter and raised her pom-poms.

It was good she didn't take that pain medication today. I would have had a hard time deciding what was more entertaining to watch: her or Riley.

I turned my attention to the obstacle course, another flutter of nerves rushing through my stomach.

The timer went off, and Riley rushed into action. He flew across the monkey bars, up the salmon ladder, over some oversized roller thingies, and swung on ropes like Tarzan as he headed toward the timer at the end.

It was truly impressive.

I stood and cheered. "Go, Gabby's Gibbon!"

"That's terrible," Bill muttered.

"Rollicking Riley to the end!" I said instead.

"Not any better," he continued.

"How about this: I love you, Riley Thomas!"

"Those are the words that any man would be happy to hear," Bill said. "Stick with that one."

. . .

~~~

Thank you so much for reading *Cunning Attractions*. If you enjoyed this book, please consider leaving a review!

Keep reading for a preview of *Clean Getaway*.

AVAILABLE NOW

CLEAN GETAWAY: CHAPTER ONE

"I have to admit that I expected my first case to take me out of town," I told Garrett Mercer as we sat across from each other in his office. "To new and exotic places." My voice dropped. "Or, at least, to just *new* places. I'd settle for the Deep South, though I was rooting for New England since I'd never been there before. Maybe not exotic, but it was different, at least."

"I know, Gabby." Garrett's British accent rolled through the air. "I did also, and I'm glad you're prepared for that because I don't intend for your work to be only local. But I felt strongly that this case was where you should begin this project."

Garrett had started a privately funded—also known as funded by him—Cold Case Squad and had asked me to head it up. I'd tried to think of a different, cooler name than Cold Case Squad.

The Dead-End Division.

The Baffled Inspectors Brigade.

The Difficult Case Club for Peculiar Investigators.

Dead Motives Society.

None of them had stuck.

I got to pick the team of my choice to take part in it. The only caveat was that Garrett got to pick the cases.

I'd solved his family's unsolved murders not terribly long ago, and that had apparently deemed me worthy of this task also. The two of us had become good friends in the process.

The philanthropist was one of my biggest fans.

"Tell me about this case." I took a sip of my coffee.

I'd put it in the contract that the team would get free coffee. It only seemed right since Garrett owned one of the largest organic companies on the East Coast. He was happy to oblige. So now I indulged in some new kind called *kopi luwak* that Garrett's assistant brought me. I had to admit—it was delicious and oh-so smooth.

He leaned back in his sleek wooden chair. The office around him perfectly matched his persona. There were pictures of Garrett in Africa, his face next to the faces of toothy children wearing dirty clothes and surrounded by a dusty landscape. An aquarium stretched against another wall, immaculately clean, filled with exotic fish. Awards for young businessman of the year and framed magazine articles hung behind his desk.

All those things fit Garrett. He was handsome, rich, and down-to-earth. Some girl was going to be very lucky one day. Once upon a time, I was that girl, but I was quite content with my Riley.

"As I mentioned to you earlier, Jessie Simmons works for me in the marketing department," he explained. "Her parents were both found dead ten years ago up on the Eastern Shore."

The Eastern Shore of Virginia was a peninsula squeezed between the Chesapeake Bay and the Atlantic Ocean. It was mostly farmland dotted with various small towns and historical sites. I found the area pleasant, like stepping back in time.

"I'm sorry to hear that," I muttered.

"Ron and Margie Simmons went out for a date night in Cape Charles," he continued. "Jessie, their daughter, was only thirteen at the time, and she'd gone to a friend's house for the evening. Her parents never came home. The next day, state troopers found her parents' bodies in the water. Their pickup was located off the highway, no signs of any foul play or anything to give an indication as to why they'd pulled over."

I imagined the impact of that moment on Jessie, and compassion squeezed at me. No one should go through that, especially not a thirteen-year-old. "Were her parents into any sort of trouble?"

"From what Jessie told me, absolutely not. She remembers them as a wonderful, loving couple. Her dad was an oyster farmer. Her mom was a homemaker. Both very blue-collar and simple. She was an only child."

In other words, she was alone after their deaths. In the blink of an eye, life had gone from full and secure to solitary and uncertain. "Where'd she go after they died?"

"She moved in with an aunt and uncle who lived in the area. She said she had a good life. But, of course, she's always wanted to know what happened to her parents."

"Of course."

"The rest of the information can be found in this file." Garrett slid a folder across his desk. "Jessie said she's available for anyone on your team to talk to at any time."

"Perfect."

"And here's the check for this case. Do with it as you please." He handed me the money.

I saw the amount, and my eyes widened. "This is . . . generous. Very generous."

"I want to use my money to do good in the world. Your time and skill set is valuable to me. I know you'll do every-thing within your power to find answers."

If only everyone had that much faith in me. "I'll read the specifics of the case and then develop a plan of action."

"Weekly updates?"

"I'll give you hourly ones, if that's what you want. I could do updates on my Twitter feed with hashtags and snarky memes. Maybe some Facebook Live. Whatever makes you feel like you're getting your money's worth."

"Unnecessary, but thanks for your willingness." He flashed a smile.

"I like to go above and beyond."

He sighed and leaned back in his chair, his long body stretched out and relaxed. His dark hair glistened with gel, and his eyes sparkled. "How do you like the kopi luwak?"

I raised my cup and took another sip. "It's really good. Impressively good, for that matter."

He smirked. "Your first time having it?"

"That would be a yes."

"I thought you might hesitate."

"Why would I hesitate?" I took another sip, liking it more and more with every swallow. It was so earthy and smooth.

He shrugged. "Some people take issue drinking coffee made from cat turds."

Coffee spewed from my mouth and across his desk. "What?"

Certainly, I hadn't heard him correctly.

He grabbed a tissue and began dabbing at the spray of coffee on his things, acting unfazed and like the consequences of my reaction were worth the cleanup. "That's what it is. I thought you knew."

"There are many things that I am. Cultured is not one of them." I grabbed an extra tissue and dabbed my mouth, just to make sure there was no cat turd coffee left on my chin. When I got home, I'd be sure to use some Listerine or maybe gargle some boiling water.

Garrett looked a little too amused for my tastes.

"I really did think you knew," he said, halfway apologetic.

I let out a skeptical *mm hmm*, not sure if I believed him or not. It was too bad that kopi luwak was what it was, because I'd really liked it . . . for a moment.

Garrett remained nonplussed as he took another sip of his drink. "How's the house hunt coming?"

That was just one more thing to appreciate about Garrett. Even though I knew he had a million more things to do, he acted as if he had all the time in the world.

"Riley and I are still looking." My brother had set up a meth lab in my old apartment, unbeknownst to me, and the whole building had gone up in flames. Thankfully, no one had been injured, but we were now homeless, so to speak.

"Anywhere in particular?"

"Norfolk still. It's central, and Riley and I both like it here. It's much more interesting than the suburbs."

"And your brother?"

My gut twisted as my brother's face flashed through my mind. "He's doing some time. I'm hoping it will be good for him. But it's complicated."

"Family usually is." He sat up and glanced at his watch. "As much as I'd love to chat more, I do have a meeting in ten minutes. Let me know if you need anything, Gabby."

I stood. "I appreciate that. And I will."

The next day, I wrapped up an early morning workshop in Newport News and headed back to Norfolk so I could meet with Jessie Simmons.

I'd arranged it so I would have a week off from my job with Grayson Technologies. I worked for them part-time, doing training seminars in my district and teaching law enforcement officials how to use equipment and technology developed by my company. Most of it involved forensics, the most popular being fingerprinting techniques.

Anyway, I'd arranged to do this week's workload and next week's workload all next week. That gave me the next seven days free to work on this case. In the meantime, I had a million things to do before I left.

Starting with meeting Jessie.

She'd agreed to come to The Grounds, my favorite coffeehouse. I didn't come here as much as I used to, not since my old apartment across the street had been destroyed.

I parked in the lot beside the coffee shop and stepped onto the sidewalk, which was bustling with college kids headed to class and businessmen and women grabbing an early lunch. I paused, my former apartment building snagging my attention.

Crews had already torn down the remains of my old home. I was sure the charred structure had been a public safety hazard. The lot had been cleared of everything but the cement steps that once led to the front door. Soon, another apartment building would go up. This one wouldn't be an old house converted into several living units. There was no way a new structure could ever match the character of the former building.

So many memories had been made there. It was where my best friend, Sierra, and I had bonded over our life's passions and figured out the future together. Where I'd met Riley in the parking lot while trying to catch a wayward parrot. Where we'd lived after we'd gotten married. Package bombs had been sent there. Killers had broken in. Suspects had hunted me down. You know, all the normal stuff. Such good times.

As I looked at the empty space, my heart lurched. I knew change was a part of life, but I just wished it hadn't ended as it did.

I shoved down my bittersweet feelings and stepped onto the wooden floors of The Grounds. Some indie artist sang an acoustic version of "Zip-a-Dee-Doo-Dah" on the overhead, and, at once, I felt at home.

Sharon, the coffee shop owner, waved me over, and I met my blue-haired friend at the counter. Some months her hair was pink. Other times it was rainbow-colored. This month she'd picked azure.

"Good to see you," she said, swirling some frothy whipped cream on top of an iced coffee. "Every time I look out the window, I think about you. How are you doing?"

"We're living at a place over on 21st Street." It was the simplest answer I could give her.

"I know. I heard it's a dump."

I shrugged. She must have been talking to Sierra.

"Yeah, it is. But it's only temporary." I leaned closer. "Say, have you ever heard of kopi luwak?"

"Cat poop coffee? Yeah, I've heard of it. It's too expensive for this venue. Please don't tell me you were going to request it."

I shook my head. "Oh, no. Definitely not. But I'm apparently the only one on this planet who hadn't heard of it."

"Well, one pound is like three hundred fifty dollars last time I checked."

My mouth dropped. "No way."

She nodded. "Way."

"I'll stick with my vanilla latte, but can I get it with coconut milk? I want to mix things up a little bit. I'm obviously stuck in a rut with my java choices."

"Your caffeinated wish is my command."

I sauntered over to a corner table to wait for Jessie.

As I sat in the chair, I shifted, hoping I'd chosen my attire wisely. It was always a hard choice: more casual usually equated to more approachable but less professional. And the opposite was true also. I could earn respect by dressing professionally, but that never seemed to put people at ease. Unless they were also professionals.

Choices, choices.

Normally, I'd wear one of my snarky T-shirts and flip-flops. But there were a couple of problems with that, starting with the fact that it was January and freezing cold outside and ending with most of them consumed by the fire. Instead, I'd donned some Converse sneakers decorated with an awesome Wonder Woman canvas. Sierra had gotten them for me.

I'd forgone the snarky T-shirt and made up for it by indulging in some snarky sayings on my key chain instead. Right now, a portion of it poked out of my purse, reminding me, "Sarcasm: Because Smacking People Isn't Kind."

It wasn't that I wanted to smack everyone—just those conniving people who preyed on others they viewed as weaker.

I noticed Jessie right away when she walked in.

I'd looked her up online, so I knew what she looked like. She had long hair that was a beautiful shade of auburn. It almost had a hint of mahogany. Freckles sprinkled across her cheeks and the bridge of her nose. A wholesome smile, skinny legs, and a full-figured top rounded out her look.

She also looked hesitant. Fearful. Like she might turn around and walk the other way. No, not walk. Dart away as if her life depended on it.

Digging up the past was never a fun thing. It was painful, for that matter. Exhausting. Dirty. Skeleton-uncovering. Nightmare-inducing. But, in the end, the plan was to bury the past permanently.

I stood and waved at her. A tense smile pulled across her lips as she started toward me.

"You must be Gabby," she said.

"And you're Jessie. Thanks for meeting with me."

She glanced around before sitting across from me. "I've never been here before."

"Well, their coffee isn't GCI—" That was Garrett's company—"but it's pretty good."

Her hesitant smile widened. "I heard Garrett let you try some cat poop coffee."

My eyes narrowed. "I guess this was a joke around the office?"

"I don't think he intended it that way, but you apparently spit it all over his desk? He got a kick out of that and even talked about utilizing that kind of reaction for an ad campaign. He thinks millennials would love it."

Glad I could be a source of entertainment. "Yeah, well I looked up a picture of said coffee last night on the internet. That stuff is some serious turd-age."

I thought it would look like rabbit droppings or something. Instead it looked like . . . well, I won't go there. Let's just say it was gross and leave it at that.

"Yes, it is. Don't tell Garrett I said this, but I'm not a fan."

"I knew I'd like you." My smile faded when I remembered the oncoming conversation. "Can I get you something to drink?"

"Some black coffee would be great. I've never been one to add a lot of fancy stuff to my drinks."

"A cup of black coffee it is then."

When I picked up my own latte, I grabbed Jessie's also —and paid for it, of course.

As I took a seat across from her, I tried to prepare myself to pry into her past and possibly open old wounds with what I hoped was minimal damage. It was like opening a can of sardines—which was bad enough in itself —only to discover they were rotten. There was nothing pleasant about this.

"I know this can't be easy for you," I started.

She frowned but only for a moment. "It's not. But it's been ten years. Don't be afraid to ask me whatever you need to ask me."

I leaned back and gripped the paper and pen in my hands. "Would you mind telling me about your parents?"

A far-off look drifted into her eyes. "They were great. Salt–of-the-earth type of people, you know? My mom was a nurse, but she gave that up when I was born, and she stayed home with me. My dad was in the navy for a few years. When he got out, he farmed oysters. He had his own company. It was a small one, but he made a decent living. We didn't have much or go on fancy vacations, but we were happy."

"No brothers or sisters?"

She shook her head, nervously rubbing the edge of her hand-thrown coffee mug. "I always had the impression my mom and dad wanted more but weren't able to conceive."

"What do you remember about the night they died?" I asked.

I knew we were getting to the hard stuff, and I hated that for her sake. But it couldn't be avoided. Each question had to feel like a sucker punch in her gut.

Jessie inhaled a shaky breath. "They were going out for a date. They hardly ever did that. We mostly did things as a family, you know? But it was their anniversary, and my dad wanted to do something special. He took Mom to this seafood restaurant in Cape Charles. It's not there anymore. Well, the building is. But it's no longer Saul's. It's Rock Fish Tavern or something."

I made a note of that.

"I was spending the night with one of my friends from school—Hope McClain. We didn't know anything was wrong until Hope's mom went to drop me off at home the next morning. My parents weren't there, and neither was their truck." Her voice caught, and she rubbed her throat.

My blood pressure elevated a bit as I anticipated what would happen next, as I imagined what she must have been feeling.

"I had no idea what to think," she continued, tension pulling across her expression, her gaze distant. "I suppose my first thought was that they'd had an accident. But then the police would have come to get me, right? Unless they couldn't find me because I was at my friend's house. Then I thought, what if Mom and Dad left? But I knew my parents would never do anything like that. They loved me. I had no doubt about that."

"What did you do next?" My throat tightened as I listened to her recount what had to be the worst day of her life. I couldn't even imagine.

She drew in a shaky breath, and her eyes looked a little duller. "Hope's mom tried to call my parents. They didn't answer. She could tell I was getting nervous, so she drove me to Cape Charles. Maybe they drank too much and got a room at the inn there, she told me. She was just trying to make me feel better. As we were driving down the road, I saw my parents' truck on the shoulder. They weren't inside. That's when we called the police."

"I see."

"A few hours later their bodies were found down the shore from our home." Her voice broke. "They'd both been shot."

"I'm so sorry." I wanted to reach forward and squeeze her hand, but we were seated too far apart and it would have been awkward. Jessie also seemed too withdrawn, as if she needed space to get through this.

She nodded quickly, her eyes haggard. "Thank you."

My own latte suddenly didn't seem that appealing. I moved it to the side. "You went to live with your aunt and uncle afterward?"

"That's right. Carol and Talmadge Banks. I didn't know them well because of an estranged family relationship. But they took me in anyway, and they were a huge blessing to me. I didn't want for anything."

"I'm glad that worked out for you." That sounded

awkward. I tried to think of what I should have said—
what would have been more couth—but nothing else came
to mind.

"They said they'd be more than happy to talk to you.
I'll give you their phone number."

"That sounds great. I also have your old address, and
I'd like to see your childhood home, if at all possible. Is
someone else living there now?"

She shook her head and absently played with her neck-
lace. At the end were two rings. Her mom's and dad's
wedding rings? I figured it was a pretty safe assumption.

"No, it's actually up for sale," she said. "My friend
Hope is a realtor, and she can help you take a look."

"Where are your parents' things?"

"I put most of them in an old garage owned by Uncle
Tal and Aunt Carol," she said. "They bought some property back in the woods when they first got married, hoping
to use it one day as rental income. Then the market tanked.
It's a good place to keep everything, though, because I
don't have to see the building every day and think about
what's inside. It's far off the beaten path, but accessible
enough that I could get to it if I wanted."

"I see."

She shrugged. "I didn't know what else to do with their
stuff. I still haven't had the heart to go through it all. I
know that sounds crazy."

"No, actually it doesn't sound that crazy. I'd probably
be the same way." I paused and shifted—a sure sign I was
about to say something hard or difficult. "Jessie, I've
looked at the police reports, so I know who the cops think
could have been behind it. But I'd like to hear your opin-
ion. You were young, but was there anyone you can
remember who had any kind of beef with your family?"

She remained quiet a moment, staring into her coffee as if the grounds would materialize and offer an answer.

"I've been over it many times in my mind," she started, her voice strained. "There's not much I remember. If my mom and dad had problems, they didn't tell me about them. But I do remember overhearing my dad arguing with one of his workers once."

"Do you have a name?"

"His employee was Ray Franklin. He died three years ago, unfortunately. My dad thought he was a bad worker . . . I think. Constantly late and kind of lazy. I think my dad wanted to fire him, but he knew that Ray had some financial issues and was trying to provide for his family."

"Your dad sounds like he was a good man."

She nodded, a wistful smile across her face. "He was. The best."

"Even though Ray is no longer with us, I'll check him out, just to be certain he didn't take secrets to the grave."

I was trying to choose my words carefully. I could tell that she was already fragile, so I wanted to take this slowly and be extra cautious—two things I wasn't always known for. But I was trying to do better.

"I'm also curious about this." I pushed a paper toward her. "The police report says that your mom withdrew ten thousand dollars from her account three days before she died. Do you know anything about that?"

Jessie shook her head. "No, only that my parents didn't have a lot of money. Their bank records should be in the information Garrett gave you."

I nodded. "They are."

"You'll see that they believed in paying for things with cash. We lived on a very tight budget."

"I know what that's like."

She offered a quick smile. "Hope—my best friend—still lives there. She said she'd be more than happy to answer any of your questions about the area, if you have any."

"I'd love her information then."

Jessie's eyes locked with mine. "You really think you can figure this out?"

I contemplated my response before nodding. "All I can say is that I'm going to do my best. I promise you that."

Because no one—I repeat, no one—should get away with murder.

Click here to continue reading.

ALSO BY CHRISTY BARRITT:

BOOKS IN THE SQUEAKY CLEAN UNIVERSE

On her way to completing a degree in forensic science, Gabby St. Claire drops out of school and starts her own crime-scene cleaning business. When a routine cleaning job uncovers a murder weapon the police overlooked, she realizes that the wrong person is in jail. She also realizes that crime scene cleaning might be the perfect career for utilizing her investigative skills.

ABOUT THE AUTHOR

USA Today has called Christy Barritt's books "scary, funny, passionate, and quirky."

Christy writes both mystery and romantic suspense novels that are clean with underlying messages of faith. Her books have sold more than three million copies and have won the Daphne du Maurier Award for Excellence in Suspense and Mystery, have been twice nominated for the Romantic Times Reviewers' Choice Award, and have finaled for both a Carol Award and Foreword Magazine's Book of the Year.

She is married to her Prince Charming, a man who thinks she's hilarious—but only when she's not trying to be. Christy is a self-proclaimed klutz, an avid music lover who's known for spontaneously bursting into song, and a road trip aficionado.

When she's not working or spending time with her family, she enjoys singing, playing the guitar, and exploring small, unsuspecting towns where people have no idea how accident-prone she is.

Find Christy online at:
www.christybarritt.com

www.facebook.com/christybarritt

www.twitter.com/cbarritt

Sign up for Christy's newsletter to get information on all of her latest releases here: **www.christybarritt.com/news letter-sign-up/**

facebook.com / AuthorChristyBarritt

x.com / christybarritt

instagram.com / cebarritt